GREEN GODDESS

JON PEPPER

"My salad days, when I was green in judgment…"
—*Cleopatra, regretting her dalliances with Caesar*

From William Shakespeare's *Antony and Cleopatra*

PART ONE

Green Power to the People!

1.　REVOLTING BEHAVIOR

A blistering summer sun baked the limestone canyons of New York's Financial District, drawing beads of perspiration on Missy Mayburn Crowe's brow as she trudged up Liberty Street. What further proof of the climate emergency did the nation's corporate evildoers need to cease and desist? Climate change was rendering Mother Earth uninhabitable and making this protest march unacceptably moist and sweaty.

Missy and the disheveled squadron of Planetistas crested the hill in front of the Capital Grille and maneuvered around a series of metal barricades that protect the historic nerve center of capitalist America from nutjobs in explosive vehicles. Anarchists once blew up a wagon outside a JP Morgan bank at Wall Street and Broad, killing thirty people, but no such disaster was possible today. The most potent weapons wielded by this contingent of grad students, teachers, artists, freelancers, and freeloaders were vials of fake blood and a few baggies of killer weed.

Blair Upton grasped her sorority sister Missy by the upper arm to steady herself on the pitted cobblestones as they descended the slope toward Wall Street, chanting their outrage against corporations that were fascist, greedy, or something else. Blair, distracted by other issues, wasn't quite sure. She leaned close and spoke in Missy's ear. "These people smell," she whispered.

Missy admonished her with a look. "They're real people, Blair."

"Well, they really stink," Blair said. "Pee-*yew*."

Missy sighed and marched on. "See? There it is: just one more problem caused by climate change. No deodorant could stand up to this heat."

"Mine has," Blair said, before giving her armpit a quick sniff. "...I think."

"You do know they have vegan deodorant sticks now," Missy offered.

"I don't plan to eat it, Missy."

"I know. It's just better for the environment... somehow."

"Is that what you use?"

"Of course."

Blair scrunched her nose. "Uh-huh."

They continued their march. "You know what really stinks?" Missy asked. "The fact that my name has become, like, such a total embarrassment. I can't stand even telling people I'm a Crowe. Everyone—*everyone*—knows my mother is Lindsey Harper Crowe, and that she runs the Crowe Power Company. And they know the company is completely irresponsible. All of those people at that company are like pushers, feeding our addiction to oil and gas." She shook her head sadly. "If my mother won't do something about climate change, then I will. I have to. My family practically invented this problem."

Blair shrugged. "They seemed to do okay with it. I mean, seriously. You've lived a pretty good life with the money they've made."

Missy raised her chin. "Blood money, Blair. How can I possibly keep it?"

"I don't know. Put it in a bank, maybe? Under the mattress? Whatever. You've got a pile. And it's yours to keep."

"I want to give it all away."

"Now there's an idea," Blair said, rolling her eyes. "You can find me on Venmo. Just transfer it over and I'll take care of it. You won't have to worry about it one more minute."

"No, no, *no*. I'm not giving it to you," Missy said. "I want to give it to these incredible people out here, fighting for environmental justice. Like Ernesto, our leader." She nodded toward the front of the pack. "You know he has to work at a coffee shop to make ends meet? I hear he actually sleeps on a cot in the back. With a little support from someone like me, he could be out fighting for justice twenty-four seven. Most of these people live on nothing but student loans and unemployment checks. They come from practically *nothing*." She lowered her voice to a near-whisper. "Don't look now, but the people behind us? I saw them coming out of Burger King a little while ago. *Burger King!* Can you *imagine?* Their lives are so bleak."

Blair shrugged. "Maybe they're meat monarchists and they're supporting the crown."

"Oh stop. Can't you be serious?"

"All I'm saying is if there's a BK nearby, I'm there. I'd love some of those little mozzarella sticks right about now."

"Blair! *Gag* me! That is so dismal."

"You obviously haven't tried those cheesy little treats."

"*Ewww!* Grrr-oss!"

A roar went up from the crowd as it passed a smattering of New York City police officers casually watching from the fenced-off entrance to the New York Stock Exchange, a columned Greek Revival edifice that practically shouted, "Capitalism HQ."

Scraggly-bearded Ernesto, the charismatic comandante of the group, safely buffered from the cops by his mob, tossed a series of F-bombs in their direction: "*Fuck off, you fucking pig fucks! And then…*" He paused. What else was there to say? "*Fuck off some more!*" Dressed in jungle fatigues and a black beret with a red star on the front, Ernesto looked every bit the part of either South American revolutionary or Manhattan coffee shop barista, which was his day job. Through a bullhorn, he started a new chant, "*System change, not climate change! System change, not climate change!*"

A harried man with a briefcase trying to push through the thicket yelled back, "Ah, go change your underwear." His gripe did not diminish the marchers' revolutionary fervor. They raised their clenched fists in the air to show they were deadly serious, maybe even menacing.

Bored and weary police, fatigued from months of daily protests and political assaults on their authority, appeared completely nonplussed as the group passed. Missy noticed their casual indifference and broke from the pack, approaching a burly officer whose badge said MORGAN. Wearing a helmet and a plastic shield pushed up over his head, he remained as still and impassive as a guard at Buckingham Palace.

Missy squared herself to Morgan and stepped close, peering up at his inscrutable expression. "How do you live with yourself, Morgan? All you cops do is protect these greedy corporations destroying our planet."

Morgan looked down at her with hooded eyes. "We do other things."

Missy mockingly rolled her head from side to side. "Oh yeah? Like what?"

"We protect your right to act like an asshole."

Why… why… *the impudence!* "I pay your salary!"

"Great. Then how about a fuckin' raise, alright?"

"You've got some nerve!"

Morgan said, "They don't pay me enough to babysit a bunch of spoiled children."

Missy flushed with rage. "How *dare* you!"

"Get a job, sweetheart. Then come back and tell me about mine."

Missy, frustrated, turned away to rejoin Blair and the group.

Blair pulled her close. "Oh my goodness! You were so *brave!* What did he say?"

Missy shrugged, grimly. "Oh… I don't know. Nothing. He doesn't get it at all. Totally brainwashed by the ruling elite. He's being exploited and he doesn't even—" She opened the leather bag that hung over her shoulder. "I'll show that blue bastard. I'm going to make a real statement—like, literally."

Blair peered inside to see two cans of red spray paint and recoiled in dismay. "Really, Missy?"

"One's for you."

"Oh no, no, no," Blair said, shaking her head. "You've got me all wrong. I'm no Banksy. I'm just your support dog. I don't want anything out of this but the afterglow."

"There's no afterglow, Blair."

"Then maybe I'll make one of my own. Your friend Ernesto's kind of cute. I kinda dig all that agitated energy he's got. You think it translates to, you know… other things? I mean, if you don't go for it, I was thinking maybe he and I could start a little revolution south of the border, if you know what I mean."

"You do what you like," Missy said. "For me, this ends at the police station."

"Seriously?"

"I bought this top specially for the mug shot. You like it?"

Blair apprised her fashion statement: a vintage grunge denim jacket, circa 1985. "It's kinda cute. I could see you getting arrested in that."

"Good—because I intend to," Missy said. "To me, getting handcuffed should be the new rite of passage for women of our generation. Forget about having a debut with some bougie ball and an orchestra and punchbowls. That is, like, so 1950s. We need to make our entrance in *jail,* getting booked and standing in solidarity with the oppressed peoples of the world. We can rouse the lumpen proletariat."

"The lumpy *what*?"

"Blair, please," Missy said, impatiently. "Don't you know anything about Marxist philosophy?"

"I know a bit," Blair protested. "I'm just trying to understand that last part. You said these people were *lumpy*?"

"No. Lumpen. Lum-*pen*."

"What does that mean?"

Missy mused. "Now that you mention it… I have no idea. They just kinda… just sit there and act like lumps, maybe?"

They both shook their heads, baffled. "Well, whatever. It's not like I care," Blair said. "But I'm going to get ready for my own close-up, just in case they rope me in with the troublemakers like you." Blair pulled out her lipstick and applied it. "I wonder what your mother is going to think about you marching on her company."

"She won't like it a bit, but you know what? *Good!* We're actually helping her."

"How?"

"To drive needed change. Someday, she'll appreciate that." Missy grasped Blair's upper arm as they walked. "I understand you're not as into this as I am. But… don't you think it's exciting that we can change the world? Given what our families have done to destroy this planet, you and I have an extra obligation to do more than the ordinary schmoes out here."

"I'm fine with that," Blair said. "As long as we're back in New Haven in time to watch *The Bachelorette*."

Missy pulled Blair along with the group as it continued to shuffle past the diminutive bronze statue of the Fearless Girl, who had her hands on her hips and stared defiantly at the New York Stock Exchange, admonishing its members for their evil ways. They passed an Hermès store, whose bright display windows glowed with the pastel colors of scarves and shoes, which appealed more to Blair than this marching with the lumps.

"If you're going to give all your money away, why don't we make a quick stop at Hermes?" she sighed. "If there's a fight, I wouldn't mind swinging a new Kelly handbag."

Missy shook her head and pushed on toward their ultimate destination: the towering white terra-cotta headquarters of the Crowe Power Company, a global energy goliath started by Missy's great-great-great grandfather Homer Crowe more than a hundred years earlier. Now chaired by her mother, Crowe Power remained the primary source of Missy's deeply embarrassing wealth. These greedy capitalists needed to be shown exactly how their power plants and refineries and pipelines were destroying the planet and foreclosing the future for people and penguins alike. Crowe spent millions creating a glossy public image suggesting they were all about producing and distributing energy needed to power homes, offices, and businesses, making the world a better place. But this propaganda was just one more of capitalist America's Big Lies. They were driving higher temperatures, generating rising seas, and causing the imminent death of rare species. How many more polar bears had to roast in their little white fur coats on melting ice floes before terrible companies like Crowe Power took this threat seriously?

As the revolutionary debutantes approached a line of white police vans, a ring of cops in riot gear blocked the Crowe Power lobby entrance. A smattering of reporters stood by as Ernesto called for the group to halt its march and begin its demonstration. A dozen of his comrades selflessly laid down on the filthy cobblestones, running with rivulets of dog pee and smeared with scraped up poo, and poured vials of fake blood on their clothes in the hope that acting as if they were dying would shame the leaders of Crowe Power into rethinking their toxic scheme. If not, perhaps they could at least elicit applause from the *New York Times*, which was on the lookout for events to support its narrative that the earth was catastrophically changing and drastic action was required to stop it. Protesters who weren't rolling over and playing dead or dressed like Grim Reapers and skeletons erected cardboard tombstones on the street, with epitaphs reading, "COULDN'T TAKE THE HEAT," and "DROWNED IN RISING SEAS." One sign depicted Missy's mother, Lindsey Harper Crowe, behind bars as Planetistas chanted: *"Prison time for climate crime! Prison time for climate crime!"*

Missy winced at the depiction of her mother but told herself: *Wait. This is justified.* Crowe Power was feeding the world's oil and gas addiction and it had to stop. Her father had tried to stem the destruction but failed to move the company toward his amorphously grand green vision, and the Crowe family kicked him to the curb. Now it was left to her, as the last brave dissenter in the family, to bring it all down. She watched the demonstration with her adrenaline surging and heart pounding. *At last!* She was in the trenches, taking meaningful action! Not just talk! Not just words! *Action!* No one could blame her for complacency. She looked over to the entrance of the Crowe Power headquarters and saw its head of security, Tom Michaels, standing with a couple of cops. Had he seen her? Would he report her to Mother? Oh, she hoped so! With no path to breach the Crowe Power building, Missy would need to find another target to express her rage with spray paint. Breaking away from the demonstration, Missy stealthily walked behind her comrades, scanning adjacent buildings for other corporate transgressors. There, at 30 Broad Street, was a brass plaque near the door that read:

LARRABEE INDUSTRIES

Since 1954

Aha! She turned to Blair, who was tagging along behind her. "Check it out, Blair. This is Larrabee's headquarters."

Blair smiled. "Oh my god! That is so *cool!*"

"What do they do?"

"Wasn't it, like, plastics or something? I remember Bog— "

Missy cut her off. "Plastics!? Oh my god! You're right! They're made from petroleum! And they brag they've been doing it for seventy-seven years? What assholes! They're killing *dolphins* with that crap!" she said. She reached into her handbag and walked quickly toward the plaque, as Blair called after her.

"Oh, no, Missy. Don't do that. I don't think you understand."

Missy was on a mission and would not be denied. She removed a can of red spray paint and shook it vigorously as she approached, rattling the pea inside. Glancing over her shoulder, she saw police fixated on the demonstration in front of Crowe Power. She aimed the can at the limestone facing next to the plaque and scrawled in red as rapidly as she could:

FUCK LARRABEE!
CORRUPT CORPORATE CRIMINAL$$$

As she finished drawing a line through the last dollar sign, she was roughly grabbed from behind and pushed against the wall, her face smushed into the limestone. Two cops pulled her arms together and zip-tied her wrists, then turned her around to face them as photographers and videographers hurried over to record the moment. Officer Morgan eyed her contemptuously as he announced she was under arrest and advised her of her rights.

"You have the right to remain silent," he said, "and I wish you would…"

Blair picked up Missy's handbag and stood next to the officers. She was mortified but Missy was elated. Arrested fighting for the great cause! This was *glorious!* To hell with these companies. She was letting the world know where she stood. Maybe she'd even make the news as a martyr to the struggle! And now, to top it all off, here came corporate security drone Tom Michaels to witness her self-sacrifice and see for himself what true character was all about. She almost pitied poor Tom, such a hopeless corporate drone in his little suit and tie. He would never step out of line as courageously as this.

"You know Larrabee Industries is fake, right?" Tom said.

Missy was confused. "What do you mean?"

"The landlord of this building put it up as kind of a joke."

"What are you talking about? It says right there—"

Blair sighed. "I tried to tell you, sweetie. It's an homage to an old movie. You know, *Sabrina*? With Humphrey Bogart and Audrey Hepburn? We watched it the other night, but you fell asleep. Larrabee Industries is where Bogart worked. I think this was his office or something."

Missy looked stricken. "Oh, come on."

Tom said, "She's right."

Missy: "Seriously?"

Blair said, "You might have been a little stoned."

"Oh," Missy said quietly.

Tom sighed. "Yeah. *Oh.*"

"Well," Missy said, defiantly, "I think I made my point."

Yes, Tom thought. *An idiotic one.* "I'll let your mother know," he said.

2. FOUNDERING

Eager to meet her best friend upstairs for lunch, Lindsey Harper Crowe walked briskly through what was known as the Crowe Power Company's "Hall of Fam," a wood-paneled gallery of oil-painted portraits of its august leaders from the past century, all of whom were in the family. The bloodline began outside Lindsey's office door with a painting of illustrious founder Homer Crowe, a notoriously cranky old coot who invented an innovative power plant in the early 1900s and built a fortune, and it ended near the lobby with Lindsey's predecessor, her ex-husband Robbie Crowe, who proved in his five years as chairman that the last strains of genius in the gene pool had been drained before he arrived.

Had she more time, Lindsey wouldn't mind stopping and addressing each man in the portraits, one by one, and asking: *What in God's name were you thinking?* She had spent weeks studying the tangle of enterprises that comprised the Crowe Power Company and decided that none of it made sense, all smooshed together into one big messy conglomerate. She could see a certain logic in joining a few of the major business lines—those engaged in related aspects of energy, such as transporting natural gas and generating electricity. But why did Crowe Power have a division that makes dolls? (Word was that it was created as a gift for Homer's mistress and her daughter.) And why did Crowe Power own a winery in California? (Apparently, drinking was the only activity that could rouse Les Crowe out of bed in the morning.) And why did Crowe Power still own a fleet of jets, a hotel in Palm Beach, and a condo complex in Las Vegas? (It's complicated.) No doubt, the coming reckoning for the Crowe Power Company would require pawning a few family baubles.

As the muffled roar of yet another protest raged outside her building, Lindsey reminded herself there was a time when most of these men were considered upstanding, respectable citizens, leading an important enterprise that provided the fuel for economic growth and high standards of living around the world. Such public esteem was now in the distant past. Under the climate sensibilities of the age, executives at Crowe Power and other traditional energy companies were considered at best dim-witted troglodytes who were choking the planet with carbon emissions, and at worst, greedy, sociopathic profiteers. Someday in the distant future, she mused, this hallway might be examined by paleontologists studying the lives of corporate dinosaurs.

Beyond the gallery, Lindsey passed her own outsized portrait in the executive lobby, which showed her seated on the edge of her desk with the Statue of Liberty glimmering faintly in the distance. It made her wince to see the humongous artwork, more appropriate for a dictator in Caracas or Havana. She privately considered it her Saddam Hussein poster, but she had reluctantly relented to the demands of family members who insisted that the first woman to lead the firm in its hundred-and-eight-year existence needed recognition just as much—if not more—than the men. Painfully aware of her looming presence, she nodded almost apologetically to executives sauntering through the lobby, as well as to their hustling support staffers, who nervously edged closer to the wall out of deference to the Queen of Crowe as she passed. Lindsey smiled and slipped past the uniformed guards at the reception desk, who popped up from their seats as if they were on springs, and stepped up the sweeping spiral staircase to the 25th floor, where the Board Room, fitness center, and other executive amenities were located. There, she headed to the Founders Room, unofficially known as the Crowes' Nest, an elegant dining room reserved exclusively for Lindsey, Uncle Chuck, and other members of the founding family to host private luncheons and coffees away from the prying eyes and ears of the hired help in the Executive Dining Room down the hall.

"There you are," Lindsey said brightly as she greeted her former sister-in-law, Bits Pierrepont, with air kisses.

"Oh, Linz! How *are* you?" Bits asked, as if the entire world breathlessly awaited word.

"Surviving," Lindsey said.

Bits looked disappointed. "That rhymes with 'thriving.' But it's not quite the same, is it?"

"No," Lindsey said. "Not even close."

The ancient, white-gloved waiter, Horace, held a Chippendale chair first for Lindsey, then again for Bits, and the ladies sat. Bits placed a monogrammed napkin on her lap, cupped her face in her hand, and stared intently at Lindsey, gazing at her like a favorite photo. "God, I've missed you! Bergdorf Goodman misses you. The Chanel store misses you. Ralph Lauren and all the other shops uptown send their fondest regards." She shook her head and sighed. "The Upper East Side is just not the same without you."

Lindsey smiled and patted Bits' hand as Horace delivered an unsweetened iced tea for her and poured a second glass of Puligny-Montrachet for Bits. "Thanks for seeing me. You have no idea how often I've missed *you*, and our lunches together, and our afternoons hanging out in the shops on Madison Avenue and at the museums and spas... I daydream about all that sometimes, especially when I'm staring up at my mountain of crises. They seem to stack up higher by the hour. Any more days like today, and I'll be back there with you, prowling through miles of aisles and heading to the Met for tea."

"Let's," Bits said. "Let's do it today."

Lindsey regarded Bits skeptically. "You're not serious."

"I am—a bit," she said. "Day drinking isn't nearly as much fun alone," she said, swirling her wine in the glass, "even though I give it my best shot." She took a sip and patted her lip with her napkin. "But I'm also worried about you. I mean, is this really worth it? Everyone in the whole wide world seems to hate our company."

Lindsey sighed. "Oh, I know. Pardon my French, but it's a constant shitstorm."

Bits shook her head from side to side. "I didn't know that was French, but okay."

"I'm under siege from all sides," Lindsey said. "The government, the media, investors, protesters... The attacks on our company, and on me personally, are relentless. Every day's a crawl through the wickets, getting spanked on the bottom."

"Hmm," Bits mused, sniffing the aroma of her wine. "I thought you said it wasn't fun."

"I'm not talking love pats from Digby."

Bits scoffed. "Who said anything about him?"

The conversation shifted to more innocuous topics as Horace slowly brought the entrees. As they dined on Salade Nicoise, Lindsey told her friend that Bits' husband, Digby, was a tremendous source of comfort and strength in his role as General Counsel. She lamented that her daughter, Missy, had become a persistent pain in the ass, due to her sudden affinity for ideological fashions, but that her son, Chase, a recent graduate, seemed interested in a career with the company and was easing into a senior management role by working, sort of, at the power plant in Tahiti.

As Bits dug into her salad, Lindsey sliced into her critics. "These people are out for blood. They'll do and say anything to get companies like ours to mend our ways or go out of business. God help us if they succeed in shutting us down. There'll be no end to the blackouts and brownouts and requests from the governor to turn down your air conditioning just when you need it most. Did you see what's going on out front today?"

"No. My driver brought me around the back."

Lindsey said, "I understand there are protesters outside right now demanding that I be put in *jail*. Can you imagine?"

"Oh, honey, that's horrible." She paused, thinking. "Where would they put you? Rikers?"

"I'd prefer an island like St. Bart's," Lindsey said. "But I don't think that's in the cards."

"Well, don't worry," Bit said. "I'll visit you in the slammer. Maybe I'll bake you a cake."

"With a nail file in it?" Lindsey asked.

"Whatever it takes to bust you out of the joint," Bits said.

"Honey," Lindsey said, deadpan, "I'll just need something to do my nails."

Bits laughed to herself as she fiddled with a fork. "Oh, Linz. I'm sorry you're going through all this. It can't be easy taking all this abuse, but I suppose marriage to Robbie for twenty-five years was pretty good practice."

Lindsey looked around to see if any waitstaff were in the room, then said, "He was even worse as a chairman than he was as a husband. You have no idea how bad it was when I took over. Crowe Power didn't have two nickels to rub together. We could barely cover coffee in the break rooms. The truth is, I wouldn't have taken the job had I had known how dire it was. You look at the mess we were in, and you'd wonder: what in God's name was that man doing all day?"

"Well, obviously, he was chasing women around the conference table."

"Doubtful. He never went to meetings." Lindsey kept her voice low, so as not to be heard beyond her lunch companion. "I'm not a business wizard, Bits. You know that. I majored in Fine Arts at the University of Chicago, for goodness' sake, studying periods of history when the energy industry was centered around candles and whale oil. There are times when our CEO comes in to explain a technical issue we have with a refinery or power plant and I worry she'll notice my eyes twirling. I have no idea what she's talking about."

Bits rocked back in her seat. "Yikes. Do I have to sell my stock?"

"Absolutely not. I need your vote."

"Well, you're not exactly boosting my confidence, Linz. Digby and I have an awful lot of our net worth tied up in this joint."

Lindsey patted the back of her friend's hand. "I'm going to straighten it out."

"Can it be done?"

"I think so," Lindsey said. "First, we have to unwind a lot of the structural damage that occurred over the years. I've spent a ton of time studying the company's history, and I finally understand how we got into this mess. It wasn't just Robbie who screwed up. It was a long line of Crowes who got overly comfortable with all the money this place generated. They went on shopping sprees, buying businesses and cobbling them all together until we ended up with an unwieldy behemoth that can't get out of its own way. I want to get rid of the junk—so we can focus on the parts of our business that create value for our shareholders."

"I hope you can raise our dividend," Bits said. "That would help reduce some of the noise."

Lindsey dropped her fork. "What noise?"

"Oh, you know…" Bits said. "Some people in the family are getting a bit restive without that steady stream of income. A few of them are even thinking of getting jobs."

"The horror," Lindsey said, flatly.

"Well, you know they're not suited for it," Bits said. "I think that's why I've heard some complaining—especially from the younger generation. They all have their knickers in a twist about Crowe Power's lack of green energy."

"Oh, I know," Lindsey said. "But it's not like we're not trying."

"So tell me. What are you doing? I could use some ammo with my little wokesters."

Lindsey sighed and sat back in her seat. "If I could wave a magic wand, I'd go all in on nuclear energy. But you know how that scares the bejabbers out of people. All they can think about are disasters like Chernobyl and Three Mile Island and mushroom clouds. Renewables can provide some energy, but I doubt they're the answer; there's too much resistance to that now, too. So, we keep scratching around for something we think can make a real difference without all the tradeoffs. Believe me, I understand the family's concern. If we don't make more progress in identifying a green pathway, these activists will put us out of business before Walker Hope gets around to it. Washington's already threatening to kill the plan to replace our oil pipeline from Canada to the Gulf."

"Why would they do that? Wouldn't gasoline prices go through the roof?"

"That's the least of their concerns," Lindsey said. "It's all about climate in D.C.—and nothing else. Our application is allegedly under environmental review, but we know it will be a political call. The president's donors want to make fossil fuels uncompetitive with their own renewable products, so they're deliberately pushing up our costs." She looked at her watch, then up at the ceiling and sighed. "I have a call with Jessica Holtgren this afternoon. You know who she is?"

Bits chewed the tip of a nail. "The Secretary of Energy?"

"That's her. She has no background in our industry and no understanding of it whatsoever. But that doesn't matter. She looks good on TV, and she can knit together a few coherent sentences on MSNBC. So, she's in charge. I'm dreading what she's going to say."

The dishes were cleared, and Horace shakily set down rattling cups of coffee as they gazed for a moment out toward New York Harbor, the Verrazzano-Narrows Bridge, and the sparkling bay beyond. Bits looked at her watch. "Am I holding you up?"

"Yes," Lindsey said, reaching over and patting her arm. "And I can't thank you enough."

Bits smiled, sympathetically. "I'd love to have you back full time."

Lindsey sighed. "I can't. You know that, right?"

Bits nodded. "I know you well enough to know you don't quit."

"At some point, I'll have to quit. But not until the job's done. I want to get this company on the right footing again. I want to make it something we're all proud of again. I want the Crowe name to stand for something good again. That's why I need your help with something."

"Name it."

"Can you manage your baby brother?" Lindsey said.

"Name something else."

Lindsey's shoulders sagged. "Robbie keeps telling people I stole his job."

Bits sighed. "Well, you kinda did."

"For good reason! He was a disaster." Lindsey reached out a hand. "Everyone knows it, but he still can't let things go. He spends half his day calling people here and asking what we're up to. I think he fancies himself the once and future king of Crowe. Some days, I'd love to toss him the keys. But if Walker Hope moves on us, I worry Robbie will get involved somehow and screw up our defense."

"Okay, Bits said, putting her napkin on the table. "If I have to, I'll kick his butt. I've done it before. I can do it again."

Lindsey smiled and squeezed Bits' arm. "I'd pay to see it."

"You won't have to," Bits said. "This one's on me."

Horace approached the table and leaned close to Lindsey's ear. "Mrs. Crowe, Tom Michaels would like a word with you right away."

"Oh, no. Where is he?"

"In the corridor, just outside."

Lindsey stood up and addressed Bits. "He never interrupts a meeting with good news."

Bits sat up with a start. "Do I need to go?"

Lindsey shook her head. "Don't move. I'll see what he wants first."

Lindsey stepped out into the hallway where Tom stood, ramrod straight like the former cop that he was. "Sorry to disturb you, Mrs. Crowe. But I wanted to let you know your daughter Missy was arrested today."

Lindsey sagged. "You are kidding." She took a deep breath. "Where?"

"In the protest outside our building."

Lindsey's jaw dropped. "She was with the people who want to put me in jail?" She pondered the absurdity: a young woman whose life of enormous wealth and privilege had been financed by the proceeds from this company, demonstrating against it—and her own mother. "I hope this is a case of mistaken identity."

"Sorry, ma'am. I saw her myself."

"Where is she now?"

"They're holding her at the First Precinct pending charges."

"What kind of charges?"

"Hard to say exactly." He explained Missy's vandalism of a mythical corporation's building.

Lindsey muttered, "Serenity now."

"I know the guys at the First Precinct," Tom said. "I can take care of it."

Lindsey waved away that idea. "You'll do no such thing," she said. "She found her way into jail. She can find her way out. You focus on the security of our company. We need it more than ever right now. Make sure none of these protesters breach our building. Power to the people..." She shook her head. "What the hell do they think we're giving them?"

"Would you like me to drive you over to the First Precinct?"

"Oh, hell no," Lindsey said. "I'm going to finish my lunch."

"Yes, ma'am."

Lindsey returned to the Founders Room and sat down as Bits looked at her, expectantly.

"As I said, Bits," she said, with a clenched smile, "I'm getting it from all sides."

Bits, alarmed, said, "Oh no."

"Oh yes," Lindsey said. "Now it's my idiot daughter."

"You're kidding."

"I wish," Lindsey said.

"What are you going to do?"

Lindsey smoothed the napkin on her lap. "I'm going to forget about it for a moment and have dessert."

Bits signaled Horace to pour her more wine, then turned back to Lindsey. "Someday, you and I need to go get ourselves a proper drinky-poo."

"That day may be coming sooner than you think."

3.   IDENTITY CRISIS

The deposed king of the Crowe Power Company was entirely out of sorts, his muscles twitching, his skin ill-fitting, his mind unsettled. Robbie Crowe's new office, with its sleek post-modern design, didn't fit him at all. There were no dogeared stacks of folders on his desk with important papers he needed to think about reading at some point. No phones ringing incessantly in the outer office from callers desperately seeking an audience he would invariably decline with a snarl that said: *I don't have time for that shit!* No visitors he could keep waiting in his outer office for hours just to show them he was an extremely important person. He was only a mile from his former office, yet it felt like he was oceans away, marooned on a distant, desolate island, far from the global empire he once ruled. Where was his court? Where were his jesters? And where, oh where were the lovely maidens auditioning for the role of queen and consort?

He idly gazed out the window, across the Hudson River to New Jersey. *Huh. Look at that. What's over there anyway?* He leaned back in his chair and cocked his head. *Let's see…* there's Teterboro airport, of course, where he used to board his corporate jet, Crowe Bird I, back in the day. The New York Giants football team played somewhere over there, too, but God knows where exactly. All he knew was that he would be dropped off at the gate and picked up in the same spot. Was the stadium north of here? South? Who knew, with all those freaking turnpike exits that sounded like neck sizes for a shirt. 16E, 15W… whatever. Someday, he'd have to explore Jersey and really learn what it's all about. Boris, his driver, lived there. Maybe Boris could give him a tour and explain what was what and tell the whole story about his family's immigration from Belarus, which would probably bore the shit out of him and… ah, *forget it*. Who cares? *That's a stupid idea.*

"Mr. Crowe, your two o'clock is here," a voice said through the intercom.

As the door to his outer office opened electronically, Robbie yawned, stretched, and creakily rose from his chair to greet Digby Pierrepont, his lanky former aide-de-camp, professorial ex-brother-in-law, and the enduring General Counsel at Crowe Power. Digby looked around, appraising the setting, and offered a sturdy handshake.

"So… The Crowe Institute for the Greater Good," he said. "Is that what this is called?"

Robbie waited for a skeptical judgment. "You have a crack about that?"

"Not at all," Digby said. "It looks… *good.*"

Robbie scowled. "I hate it."

Digby walked to the windows overlooking the sparkling North Cove marina, with a smattering of yachts and smaller sailboats, the busy Hudson River clotted with ferries and freighters, and the glassy skyline of Jersey City, which had suddenly sprouted as many skyscrapers soaring over five-hundred feet as either Minneapolis or Pittsburgh. "You have quite a panorama." He leaned forward. "Ellis Island. Statue of Liberty. Jet skis and tour boats. Perfect for someone who likes to stare out the window all day."

"Like that's me?" Robbie spat. "Don't be a jerk."

Digby folded himself into a chair across from Robbie's elevated desk and appraised his unhappy visage. "So, you're adjusting well to this new life, I see."

Robbie sagged. "This is just… it's just a different world. I'm out here in the middle of nowhere." He gestured blandly toward the world beyond his windows. "I don't even know what neighborhood I'm in. FiDi? Battery Park City? Elba? Somebody said it's Triberia, which sounds about right."

"Goldman Sachs headquarters is across the street. They're not a small outfit," Digby said. "The HQ for American Express is right next door. It's not exactly the wilderness."

Robbie shook his head. "It may as well be. Nobody knows me. A year ago, I was… you know. Kind of a big deal, if I do say so. Now I'm some… I don't know. *Foundation geek.* I may as well grow my hair long and wear a yellow bow tie." He glanced up at Digby and noticed that's what he was wearing. "No offense."

Digby rolled his eyes. "None taken, as usual."

Robbie stood up and paced. "Every day, Boris drops me off out there on Vesey Street. I stop for a latte at the Starbucks on the second floor and I have to tell the same idiot barista my name—*again!* And he always asks me the same fucking question. *Is that Robbie with an 'r'?* I mean, how the fuck do you *think* it's spelled, dickhead? With a *'w'*? You think I'm *Wobbie?* Jesus! The thought of it makes me want to go down there right now and kick his ass." He shook his head, sadly. "No one remembers me from one day to the next. I can barely remember myself."

"Okay, okay," Digby said, raising his palms to indicate Robbie should settle down. "I get it now. You used to be somebody. Now you're nobody. Is that what's troubling you, Bunky?"

Robbie stopped pacing and glared at him. "Did you come over to heckle me?"

Digby said hotly, "I came over because you insisted." He felt a vibration in his pocket and pulled out his phone to see an urgent message from his admin that Lindsey needed to see him right away. "I've got to get back. What do you want anyway?"

Robbie flopped onto the sofa near the bookshelves. "Digs… bro… *buddy*. I need help."

"Yes, you do," Digby said, wryly.

"I want you to run this thing."

"No, you don't."

"Why not?"

"I'm not qualified."

Robbie huffed. "What? You think I am? I don't know shit about foundations. At least you look the part."

"As you've noted," Digby said. He leaned forward, his elbows on his knees. "Let's be honest, Robbie. You didn't know a thing about energy companies, either. Over time, you learned… at least a little. Why can't you do that here?"

"Because I don't even know what we're supposed to *do!* The Greater Good? What the hell is that supposed to mean?"

"You named it."

"*Noooo,*" he spat. "A consultant did. I blew fifty K to have some asshole come up with a brand. This is the crap I get. Some airy-fairy name that doesn't mean anything to anybody."

"I thought the idea is to solve the world's problems."

Robbie looked incredulous. *"What* problems? Don't you *see?* All the good ones are taken. Gates already has poverty and disease. Hughes has medical research. Mellon has education and the arts. There's, like… nothing left."

Digby, exasperated, said, "Right. Everything's pretty much fixed."

Robbie waved a hand in the air. "Anything I do is just piling on."

Digby looked at his watch, then back to Robbie. He sighed. "Right. Well… Tough luck." Digby stood to leave. "Doesn't sound like there's a role for me."

"But there is." Robbie pointed over his shoulder to the door. "I've got a staff of ten or fifteen people out there that need direction. I certainly can't spend all my time managing them. You should come over here and run the team. Be my Chief Operating Officer. Then I can focus on what I do best."

"Which is?"

"You know… The big picture."

"Ah, right. That old vision thing."

"Yes!"

"Oh brother… in-law," Digby muttered. "I'm still dealing with your last vision, Robbie. I've spent the better part of a year shutting down almost all those green technology companies you bought when you acquired Greeneron. Methane capture from cow guts. Algae-fired electricity. Mini windmills. None of this stuff has worked. We could have created more energy if you bought Beany-Copter turbines."

Robbie sneered, "You mean to tell me you couldn't find one good technology out of everything I bought? That's just gross incompetence."

Digby tilted his head back and forth, thinking. "There might be one."

"Which one?"

Digby shrugged. "It's too early to talk about."

"Why?"

"Because I don't know if it will pan out."

"Oh, come on!"

"I doubt we have the money to develop it anyway," Digby said, sharply. "Any discretionary budget we have is going to defending ourselves in court, lobbying to stop regulations aimed at putting us out of business, and beefing up security around all our properties. We're under siege and I don't see it letting up."

Robbie walked over and took the chair next to Digby. "Digs, listen to me, because I'm serious about this," he said. "If you can't help me with this foundation, then the least you can do is help me with something else."

"Which is?"

Robbie took a deep breath. "Get me my job back."

Digby folded his arms across his chest and shook his head. "Why did I suspect all along this is what you really wanted?"

Robbie jabbed a finger in Digby's arm. "Because you *know* I'm right. That's why. That job was *stolen* from me. Lindsey is totally unqualified to take my place. And you know we need to rectify that situation if our family is going to have any hope of hanging on to Crowe Power. The company's a mess. And I'm the only one who can fix it."

Digby yawned and stretched. "Look, Robbie. I know you're bored. I know you don't like this foundation gig. And I know the chairmanship of the Crowe Power Company is not your job now. But it's also not going to be your job anytime in the future. It's not some entitlement you get as the first-born male child in the family. The job is Lindsey's."

"She's not even blood!"

"Her name is Crowe."

"*Hello!* Because she was married to me! She has no Crowe genes."

"Her children—*your* children—certainly do."

"She's an interloper."

"Then that makes me one, too."

Robbie waved him off. "Nah. That's different. You're not running the whole show. I'm a direct descendant of the founder. That means I've got that... that..." He struggled for the right term. "That *special sauce.*"

Digby laughed. "Right. You have some sort of magic goo mixed in with all that blue blood."

"Exactly."

Digby sighed. "I'm sure you'll find this impossible to believe, but, for what it's worth, Lindsey's proving you don't need some remnants of founder jizz coursing through your veins to run Crowe Power. She's doing an admirable job, with or without the eleven herbs and spices that make the Crowe blood so special," he said. "She's organized. She's decisive. She's working her butt off—getting in by eight o'clock every day. And the fact is, I am not going to abandon her at a critical juncture. It wouldn't be helpful to her, the company, the Crowe family, or, for that matter, the dividends that help finance all this—" He paused, looking around. "Goodness."

Robbie folded his arms. "So you're okay abandoning me? Leaving me out here in the wild to fend for myself?" He shook his head, sadly. "After all I've done for you… "

Digby laughed derisively. "All you've done—" He pushed his hair off his forehead and fixed a glare on Robbie. "Alright. Let's cut the bullshit, Robbie." He stood to leave. "I've had enough of these pity parties for one lifetime. I've heard it all before, and I don't need to hear it again. You made this bed. Lie in it. That's at least something you know how to do. But keep your pants on this time and maybe you won't get in so much trouble."

Robbie shook his head at the impudence. "As if I haven't paid enough of a price already. I lost the job that rightfully belongs to me. I lost my marriage. I have no standing in the community. What more do you want, Digby?" He gasped for breath.

Digby waved him off. "I don't want anything from you, Robbie. I'm done as your enabler. Done as your defender. Done as your bag man. It's over." He shook his head. "But I will give you one thing to consider, a radical concept. What if you—call me crazy—thought of others for a change?"

"As if I don't?"

"Did you hear your daughter was arrested today?"

"*What?*"

"She was protesting out in front of our headquarters with the Planetistas."

Robbie clapped his hands together in glee. "Really? That's *great!*"

"They were chanting that Lindsey should go to jail!"

Robbie belly laughed. "Oh my God! That's fan-fucking-tastic! Tell her to let me know in advance and I'll join her next time."

Digby shook his head and muttered, "You're hopeless." He left Robbie on the sofa staring at the ceiling, watching the imaginary storm clouds gathered overhead begin to part. Maybe with Missy on his side, he could start to build a bloc to remove Lindsey and put him back in office. Maybe now was the time to reclaim his inheritance, get back in the game, and develop whatever clean technology was left over from Greeneron. Why should Lindsey get the credit for his vision of a grand and glorious future? What a tragedy it would be if Lindsey got the accolades for the green dream that he envisioned, the dream that centered around… whatever that stuff was. With a bit of hard work, he could rightly take his place in the world. Nobody would call him Wobbie ever again. He'd be L. Robertson Crowe III once more! Energy savant! Green revolutionary! The barbarian inside his own gates!

He shook his head at the thought of Digby's reckless jabs. The nerve of that preppy dweeb to imply that he didn't work as hard as Lindsey. *How did Digby think he had climbed the corporate ladder?* Or that he wasn't decisive? *He made tough calls when he had to, like…well, there was definitely a time or two!* Or that he didn't put in the time his job demanded*—as if it were the hours put in sitting behind a desk or stuck at a conference table that mattered rather than the quality of the thinking—most of which was best done outside the office.* You can't put creativity on the clock. It needed space. It needed oxygen. It needed *room.*

He walked to the windows considering his next move. Outside were legions of walkers and runners and strollers on the promenade, jumping onto sailboats, buying ice cream, and drinking at the various bars dotting the marina. What the hell were all those people doing outside in the middle of the day, enjoying the weather while he was stuck inside, working his ass off? He checked his watch. Two thirty. *Shit!* He'd been stuck inside for almost an hour! Enough was enough!

He pivoted back to his desk, reached into a drawer for a tube of sunscreen and dabbed a bit on his forehead. Then he dashed out of his office, heading for the promenade along the water, where he could think creatively while checking out the talent jogging by.

4.   A PALER SHADE OF WHITE

The widely celebrated Chief Executive Officer of the Staminum Energy Company ran his middle finger along a line of print in the draft of a press release, moving his lips as he read, occasionally emitting a whispered word, looking up and rolling it around in his mouth to see how he liked the sound. Sometimes, Walker B. Hope nodded his approval and returned to the draft, squinting his eyes, stopping his finger, then shrugging his shoulders before moving on again.

Marty McGarry, the company's communications leader, found that having his writing reviewed by Walker was an ordeal akin to a witch trial. Would this press release float? Or would it sink, proving his incompetence? Marty distracted himself from the torture by gazing behind Walker to his carefully curated hero wall—a traveling tribute to himself that followed him from job to job, success to success. At the center was a framed front page from the Wall Street Journal with a lead story about Walker's hiring at Staminum a year ago.

Crowe Power Ousts CEO Hope, Who Takes Reins at Staminum
Showdown Coming Between Longtime Rivals?

Marty marveled at the scale of Walker's tribute to the Wonders of Walker, which seemed to be mutating and spreading like spores. Was there no recognition he had received that didn't deserve a place up there? There were, of course, the compulsory photos of Walker with presidents, Walker with professional golfers, and Walker with NFL quarterbacks—all intended to validate that Walker was himself a genuine celebrity, scaling the heights with the highfalutin'. Marty scanned the extensive collection of photos of his wife, children, and dogs at their summer home at the foot of the Sleeping Bear sand dunes in northern Michigan. There were plaques for his contributions to human progress, honorary doctorates from his alma mater in Kentucky and a Podunk college in Ohio, and citations of outstanding citizenship from his adopted hometown of Detroit. Marty scoffed. He had everything up there but the certificate from Publishers Clearing House saying he, too, might be a winner. And, wait… what did his eye spy down in the corner? *Are you fucking kidding?* Walker's idiot admin, always eager to please the boss, must have framed and displayed a bogus award that Marty made up late one night on his computer in a fit of inebriated creativity and mailed to Walker after he had chewed Marty's ass for failing to get him enough credit for something or other. It named Walker B. Hope the recipient of the "Righteous Dude" award from the F. Bueller Society of Chicago. Marty shrugged. *I'm sure as hell not going to tell him now…*

Marty shifted forward in his chair, trying to refocus on the task at hand. He couldn't see what Walker was reading, due to the low angle and vast expanse of Walker's massive desk. All he could see was his boss's extended middle finger. Was that on purpose? A subliminal shot? Maybe he wasn't such a righteous dude after all.

At last, the fickle finger stopped, and Walker frowned. "Oh, I don't know about this," he said.

"What is it?" Marty asked.

Walker read aloud, "It says here, 'These layoffs are difficult but necessary,' said Walker B. Hope, Chief Executive Officer. Uh-huh. I'm glad you recognize that, Marty. They're *very* difficult." Walker put the paper down and leaned back in his chair, clasping his hands behind his head. "Maybe we should add that to the quote. Somethin' like, 'Painful as these cuts may be to certain individuals, nobody hurts more than me?'"

Marty girded himself for artful negotiation. He had to disagree without directly contradicting his famously flinty boss, who regarded the slightest pushback as an assault on his dignity, intelligence, and, possibly, his sainted mother. "No doubt, laying off fifteen thousand people was an extremely difficult decision for you," Marty said. "I mean, I'm sure you know some of these folks personally."

Walker nodded. "I would think so," he said. Then, upon reflection, "I must have met a few, right?"

Marty continued, "Right. But see, they're all losing their livelihoods. It's been a rough time for so many people in the last few years, with the pandemic and all. Now, suddenly, it gets a whole lot worse—they're out of a job in a difficult market, especially for professionals in our shrinking industry, which makes finding a new job like musical chairs—they keep taking those seats away. My guess is that some of these people may be suffering a bit more than even you are, if that's possible."

Was it? Walker shrugged. "They get severance, don't they?"

Marty said, "Well, yeah. Anywhere from a couple weeks to a couple of months. Still…"

Walker nodded thoughtfully, then smacked the print-out with the back of his hand. "You might have a point there, Marty. And you know what?"

"What?"

"I'm gonna hold off on buyin' that boat," Walker said.

"Whoa."

"We all have to sacrifice. Don't ya think?"

"That's the word," Marty agreed, solemnly. "Sacrifice."

"It's all about the team, Marty. The team. The team. The *team*."

"You've nailed it yet again, sir."

Was Marty bein' a wise ass? Or was he truly absorbing yet another lesson in leadership? Oh well. In either event, it wouldn't matter much longer. Walker returned to the paper and read some more. "You say, 'This reduction in force will help us realize an annual savings of more than two hundred million dollars.' Then you got here, 'Combined with our previously announced plant closings, Staminum will save more than three billion dollars a year, with ten percent of our savings devoted to clean technologies.' To my mind, Marty, that's lean and mean. I don't understand why we don't say that."

"Oh, I think it's strongly implied, Walker."

"We should say it explicitly."

"Say what?"

"Lean and *mean*, man."

"Lean, I get. But… do you really want to say *mean*?"

Walker looked at Marty blankly. "Am I hard to hear?"

Marty quickly backpedaled. "No, no. It's just that saying we're mean seems redundant. A lot of folks might think that's pretty obvious. And you just said a little while ago that people are the source of our strength—"

"I did?" Walker looked puzzled.

"Yeah."

"I don't 'member that. What people were we talkin' about?"

Marty shrugged. "You know—our people. Staminum people."

Walker was getting dangerously agitated. "What about 'em?"

"Well, we're talking about their lives here. You have to remember, we've already announced pay reductions for all salaried employees, a freeze on vacation time, and a new health plan with a deductible that's forty percent higher than the last plan. How much meaner do you want to be when it comes to what we called,"—he looked through some papers on his lap—"our most 'treasured resource?'"

"I said that? Or you wrote that and *said* I said that?" Walker's eyes narrowed into a feral stare. "Get this straight, Marty. I want for Wall Street to understand somethin': I'm buildin' a cash hoard for a reason. I want them to think I'm gonna expand our company's footprint and provide for future growth. If you had any understandin' of business at all"—*a-tall*—"you'd know the success of Staminum Energy is the greatest employment security any of these people can have."

"Right—for those who weren't fired."

Lord, he was tired of this irritating man! "Marty. I don't want to argue. We're just trimmin' our sails, that's all, on our way to a horizon of limitless profitability." He shot his hand across some imaginary body of water—maybe the Cape of Good Walker Hope. "That's the whole point of these cuts. Wall Street *likes* mean. They *pay* money for mean. You need to understand that and get it in the dang release."

Marty sighed. Resistance was futile. "I'll add in a quote and see how you like it." *Because once you see it in print,* Marty thought, *you might realize you sound like a dick.*

"Fine," Walker said in a way that meant it wasn't "fine" at all. In fact, it was anything but fine. He was pissed, as usual, at this hopeless, hapless fella, who never could figure out when to shut up. *What a dumb bunny…*

Walker returned to the release, running his finger to the bottom of the page, then put it down. He removed his reading glasses and chewed on one of the temple tips. "There's one other part here that doesn't work for me."

Marty braced himself. "What's that?"

"See, where it says here down at the bottom, 'Media Contact: Marty McGarry,' along with your phone number."

"Would you rather they emailed me?"

"No," Walker said, sucking in his breath. "I'd rather they called Shanelle Pruitt."

The hair rose on the back of Marty's neck. Shanelle? His deputy? Why would he want the press to call one of his direct reports? *Unless…* "That's not our process, Walker. I typically handle all the top releases for the company."

"Well, yes," Walker said. "You *have.*"

Past tense? Marty blanched and his heart rattled around his rib cage like a pinball. Where was this going? Should he even ask? "And… going forward? What are you thinking?"

Walker pushed himself up from the desk and sighed. He stood and walked slowly toward the windows overlooking Midtown, Long Island, and the shimmering Atlantic Ocean in the distance. Then he turned back.

"You know, Marty, you've been a huge help to me, both here at Staminum and back when we were workin' together at Crowe Power," Walker said. "I can't" —*caint*— "tell you how much I appreciate it. But things have changed here lately, and you know we're all about diversity, equity, and inclusion now. Remember that ad we did in the Wall Street Journal? Couple hundred CEOs signin' on to DE&I? Well now, obviously, our chairman expects me to walk that talk, and, frankly, we've been kinda stumblin' out of the gate. I mean, look at my leadership team. It's all people of pallor. That's got to change. And you know what they say about change…"

Marty's pale face suddenly burned bright red. "No," he barked. *"What?"*

"If there is to be meaningful change, it must start with me."

Marty gritted his teeth. "So it starts with you?"

"No," Walker said, slowly, "it starts with *me,* meanin' *you.*"

"But you said, 'me.'"

"Well, clearly, I meant *you.*"

"But, I..."

"Gol-*dang*-it, Marty!" Walker exploded. "Are you *dense?* The change starts with you! Marty McGarry! Plain and simple! We're changin', man! Like right *now.*"

Marty saw his financial obligations flash before his eyes. His kids' college. His new apartment near Lincoln Center. His car that he never drove but paid a fortune to park. His health club membership that he had used only once in six months. All the things he signed up for when he joined Staminum Energy at a big raise that should have set him up for at least a few years. "Why me?", he asked, quietly.

Walker grabbed the chair next to Marty. "Goodness, Marty. Can't you see? Our diversity consultants say we've got a privileged white culture around here. And you're about as white as they come. What are you? Hundred percent Irish?"

"There's some Scottish in there. Maybe a little bit of German."

Walker laughed. "Well, c'mon, man! That's *nobody's* idea of diversity. Shanelle, on the other hand, checks just about every dang box under the sun, startin' with the fact that she's a *woman.*" Walker starts ticking off his fingers. "You got your African. You got your Puerto Rican. I think there's even some Vietnamese in there somewhere. And get this?" He leaned forward, conspiratorially. "Word is she's a *lesbian,* too! I mean, triple bonus points, brother!" Walker clapped his hands together in glee. "Can't wait to report *that* to the Compensation Committee. *Hoo boy!*"

Marty sighed. "She's very bright, I'll grant you. Does she really want the job? I got the sense she was pretty happy with what she was doing."

"It took a bit of convincing, but I think she wants to step up to the next level," Walker said. "I've been mentorin' her almost every day. And I gotta tell you: she's got all kinds of potential, 'specially for a job like yours. Let's face it, Marty. These staff roles? Like communications? They're totally interchangeable. How hard is it to tell the world that we're doin' a phenomenal job? I mean, it is *self-evident!* All you gotta do is look at the scorecard. Profits! Share price! Market cap! The numbers don't lie."

"I know that..."

"Then you should also know that in today's corporate world, the messenger is the message. What kind of message is it for me to have a guy as white as the

Michelin Man roll out there to represent our company durin' all these diversity initiatives? I may as well use Poppin' Fresh."

"Poppin'… *Who?*"

"You know… the Pillsbury Doughboy. That's his real name." Walker laughed. "Bet you didn't know that! It was a question the other day on *Jeopardy* and—"

Marty cut him off. "Okay, fine, Walker. Poppin' Fresh. Michelin Man. Whatever. I have no idea why this is even in the conversation. But if all this is as important as you say it is, then I suppose your job should be filled by a diversity candidate, too."

"Absolutely! And it will be! Someday… after I'm long gone," Walker said with a laugh. "But in the meantime, who the heck do you think is gonna do all this diversifyin' and equitizin' and includin' around here?"

"You, I guess."

"Dang right! I'm all about inclusion now, Marty." Walker looked sympathetic, almost. "I'm just not includin' you."

Marty waved him away. "Alright. Enough, already. I get it."

Walker stood up and regarded Marty kindly. "You know what I've always admired about you, Marty? You've been a team player. Which is why I'm sorry you seem upset about this. I would think you'd be glad—no, *honored*—to take one for the team. Not everyone gets to do that in their career. People think they'd do it. They say they'd do it. But it never happens. Now look at you! You have that opportunity to take the hit. It's wonderful, in a way."

All Marty wanted now was some air. Walker was suffocating him with his good ol' boy schtick. He stood up. "Oh yeah, it's the honor of a lifetime," he said flatly. "I'm getting goosebumps."

Walker nodded vigorously. "That's so good to hear, Marty. I'm so proud of you. Really appreciate your team spirit. And you know what? I trust you so much I'm not even gonna ask Security to escort you out."

"Wow. I'm… touched," Marty said. "You think I could maybe—I don't know—get an extra cardboard box?"

Walker clapped Marty on the shoulder. "It's the least I can do."

Marty nodded. "It certainly is."

5. PIPE DREAM

igby and Lucy Rutherford, Crowe's no-nonsense Chief Executive Officer, followed Lindsey into her private conference room, their arms laden with folders, exhibits, and any other documentation they might need to plead their case to the Secretary of Energy. Almost a year earlier, they had applied for a permit to replace the aged Alberta Clipper pipeline that ran from oil fields in Canada to refineries on the Gulf of Mexico, and had spent millions of dollars to lobby for its approval against stiff resistance from environmental activists. The pipeline had long been a vital source of oil for Gulf refineries and a dependable profit generator for Crowe Power, but it was facing extinction without a government okay.

Lindsey, carrying nothing more to the meeting than a cup of coffee, took her place at the head of the table and looked to Digby. "What do you think of our chances?" she asked.

Digby looked grave. "I'm not thinking a happy dance is in our immediate future."

Lindsey's executive assistant, Winnie, appeared in the doorway. "Mrs. Crowe, your call with the Secretary is coming through now."

"Thank you," she said. As the assistant left, Lindsey turned to Digby. "You know the secretary, right?"

Digby fidgeted in his chair. "We go back a ways."

Lindsey studied Digby's odd response. "Ways you'd rather forget?"

He grimaced. "Ways I'd rather *she* forgot."

"Sounds like a story there."

"Someday by the fire," Digby said.

The console buzzed and Lindsey punched a button for the speaker phone. "Hello?"

"Lindsey? It's Jessica Holtgren," she said, grandly. "How *are* you?"

Lindsey grimaced. "I'm fine, Madame Secretary. And how are you?" Lindsey glanced over at the credenza, which featured a White House photographer's shot of her with Jessica's boss: President Dewey Fenwick, a longtime political operative who had risen to high office as a compromise candidate between his party's warring factions. His most significant achievement during several decades in Congress was accumulating a vast personal fortune through his uncanny knack for precisely timing his stock trades to new laws, regulations, and subsidies.

"Great! Just great!" cackled the secretary, a recent appointee from Maryland, where she had been governor for two years. "Look, I wanted to give you the news first as a courtesy, since you and your family have been a very good friend to the president over the years. But I'm afraid we're going to deny your application to replace the Alberta Clipper pipeline."

Lindsey looked to Digby, blinked hard, and shook her head. This was a blow they had expected, but it still hit hard. "I'm deeply sorry to hear that, Madame Secretary. On what grounds?"

"Well, the environmental impact statement raised troubling issues we just couldn't get around. The president, as you know, has signed a pact with China to immediately reduce our carbon emissions in hopes that they will someday reduce theirs. He needs to demonstrate his good faith, and, well, killing your project shows his strong commitment to do our part. Bad timing for you, I suppose."

Lindsey took a deep breath. "You do realize that the current pipeline feeds a dozen refineries on the Gulf of Mexico and its permit expires next year. If we don't get a replacement for it soon, those refineries will have to get their oil shipped in by truck or rail, which means even higher emissions—or else they may have to shut down, too. Did you consider what this might do to the price of gasoline in the United States?"

The secretary burst into laughter. "What does that have to do with anything?" the secretary said. "You want to put a price on healing our planet? We know very well that the price is already getting up there. What did I hear? It's over—can this be true?—two dollars a gallon now?"

"It's over three dollars, actually. In some places, four."

"That's still cheaper than the bottle of Fuji water I have here. So what's the big deal?"

"Our pipeline capacity is critical for supply, which, as you know, impacts price, especially when demand is rising," Lindsey said.

"Of course," Jessica replied. "I understand your pipeline carries something like eight hundred thousand gallons of crude oil per day? We know that's an awful lot."

Lindsey slapped her forehead. Did the secretary do any homework on this issue before making her decision? "It's actually a great deal more than that. We carry eight hundred thousand *barrels* of oil a day. So to figure gallons, you have to multiply eight hundred thousand by fifty-five." Lindsey punched the numbers into the calculator on her phone. "That makes it forty-four million gallons."

The secretary laughed. "Well, you know, math has never been my strong suit," she said. "But that's hardly the issue. The bigger problem is that we have a climate emergency on our hands here and we all must pull together to save the planet. This is possibly our last chance before we all burn up or drown. In either case, I'm sure you know that if the Earth is destroyed, marginalized people will be impacted most, and the president is deeply pledged to equity."

Lindsey replied, "Maybe there's a way to ensure we all die at the same time."

"Huh? I don't quite get that."

"Nothing," Lindsey said. "I was just going to say…"

"Sorry for interrupting," the secretary said, "but I've got to apprise you of another issue before I get to another meeting. We are announcing later today that the president has directed the FBI to investigate all of our country's largest fossil fuel companies for price gouging. Somebody needs to take responsibility for these rising prices you're talking about, and, naturally, the president suspects the problem lies with Big Fossil."

"Big… *Fossil?*" Lindsey said.

"Oh yes. We've identified a lot of our nation's inflation problems are coming from greedy cartels. Big Meat. Big Cheese. Big Maple Syrup. Whatever it is. We're not pointing any fingers at your company in particular, but my staff suspects collusion in the industry. So get ready to start forking over documents. We're coming for 'em."

Lindsey bit her lip to control a rising temper. "Respectfully, Madame Secretary, your staff is wrong. Price increases can be traced to government policy aimed at shutting down oil and gas production in the United States."

"Of course you think that. But that's not the way we see it."

"If we don't produce and refine these products in this country, you realize we'll still have to get them from elsewhere—like Saudi Arabia, or Russia."

Jessica said, brightly, "Of course! But, hey, better them than us, right? Let the Planetistas march in Moscow. See where that gets 'em!"

"Don't you worry about how this impacts jobs?"

"Not in the least!" Jessica exclaimed. "All those people in your industry are going to get green new jobs… somewhere. They'll be making windmills and solar panels and hamster wheels—whatever. You just need to have a little faith that it will all work out in the end. Look, Lindsey, it's been lovely chatting with you, but I've got to run. I do hope you come see me some time in Washington, especially when you want to talk about your overdue transition to green energy. That's something we could help you with. Bye now."

Lindsey was dumbfounded as she hung up the phone. "What next?" she asked Digby. "Locusts? Plague? Protesters say we're not green enough. The Secretary of Energy says we're too brown. And now we're supposedly corrupt, too? We're damned if we do… anything."

Digby shook his head. "I feel like General Custer in a box canyon."

"What did he do?"

"He died, which pleased his adversaries."

"Sounds like her plan for us, too." She sighed. "Are we doomed?"

Digby winced. "The trend lines are not promising."

6. TAKE THIS JOB

Marty stopped by Human Resources to get the details of his severance package, which turned out to be a surprisingly substantial haul. In return for agreeing not to sue the company for discrimination, Marty would receive a year's pay, an immediate vesting of his stock and pension, and a release from his non-compete agreement. He could hang around Staminum for three more weeks, as welcome as yesterday's fish skins, or he could walk out today a free man and leave it all behind. As Marty gleefully bounded up the stairway two steps at a time, he thought this was the easiest decision he'd face all year. He was *outta here, baby!* And he was rich, relatively speaking. Getting fired was turning this into one of the best days of his life! What a feeling to have this sense of financial security going into his Tinder date tonight. His fortune was turning for the better!

He entered his office to find Staminum's new Chief Communications Officer sitting in a chair opposite his desk. A box with Shanelle's belongings was on the floor next to her, topped off by a copy of the No. 1 National Bestseller, *Stupid-Ass White Men,* an instructional manual Human Resources had distributed to every employee as part of their diversity re-education camps. She peered up at Marty through her horn-rimmed glasses as he walked past and shook her perfectly coiffed head of lustrous black hair.

"I am really sorry about your job, Marty," she said, in a low, smokey voice.

Marty shrugged. "You might be sorrier when it's yours." He looked at his watch. "And based on my agreement with HR, that looks like about an hour from now. Walker said he wants you to finish up the press release." He handed her his copy, with his notes on it.

She glumly snatched it from his hand and looked at it indifferently. "'Lean and mean?' What kind of shit is that?"

"Not my idea."

Shanelle sighed. "When does he want this?"

"An hour ago."

She shook her head. "For the record: I didn't want your damn job," she said. "You know that, right? I've *never* wanted your damn job. I like having somebody between me and the funhouse upstairs. But the man threw a big ol' bag of bills at me. And when I said, 'no,' he threw me another one, which was even bigger. What was I supposed to do?"

Marty shrugged. "Take the money and run. I would. In fact… I just did."

"Well, I ain't runnin'—not for him or for nobody," she said. "I wouldn't have taken the job if he didn't say he was firing you anyway."

"Huh," Marty grunted, as he pulled a few personal items from his desk drawer. "Did he say why he was firing me?"

Shanelle laughed. "Same damn reason you always get fired, Marty."

"What's that? I never get a straight answer."

"Oh, come on. You don't know?"

He shook his head. "Honestly. I don't."

"You suck at kissin' ass."

"How can that be? I'm on my knees every day, smooching away."

"Maybe you are. But you also roll your eyes when the boss says something stupid, which, in this company, is a lot. I've seen you do it."

Marty scoffed. "You're even worse at concealing what you really think. You have that withering stare."

"Fine. But I'm not kissin' his ass, Marty. He's kissin' mine." She slapped her hip. "And given how many L-B's I put on during the damn pandemic, he better pucker up. That could take all day."

"He thinks you're a lesbian."

Shanelle roared with laughter. "Whatever it takes, baby! I mean, what do I care what that man thinks? I think that was worth another twenty thousand dollars. All he's worried about is checkin' off the boxes on his identity chart. I can play this game just as well as he can—probably better."

Marty said, "Well just remember this, because it might come in handy someday: They pay you a whole lot of money to stay at this company—and a whole lot more to leave."

"I look forward to it," she said, pushing herself up from the chair with a heavy sigh. "I'll be back to say goodbye, Marty."

Shanelle departed in a cloud of Forever Red perfume. Marty turned on his computer and checked out LinkedIn, the business networking website he ignored unless he had to look for a job, and found five-hundred and eighty-two notifications. He scanned through the first fifty or so and noted that many of his connections were conveniently adding (He/him), (She/her), or (They/them) next to their names. Maybe, Marty thought, he should add something, too. He tapped on the icon of a pencil to edit his profile and added his own parenthetical interpretation.

Marty McGarry (Who/he)

That was a rather cheeky introduction to a biography, wasn't it? Ah, hell. Why not? Maybe some people would find it funny; it certainly captured his hardening *I-don't-give-a-rat's-ass* attitude. But… he didn't need the social media police crawling up his ass. He decided to cancel his edit before he himself was cancelled and looked at the rest of his description, containing the sort of bland boilerplate language that everyone on LinkedIn included to burnish their profile. He was a trusted advisor, an esteemed counselor, bold strategist, careful listener, leader, storyteller, curator of corporate character, blah, blah, blah, and rooty-toot-toot. He looked away and shook his head. Should he even bother to update this self-promoting blather? Why would he even want another job like this, stroking the wieners of more Walkers and Robbies? His separation agreement gave him a comfortable glide path out of Staminum. He could do nothing for a while. Or he could travel the world. Maybe he'd even get in shape. He looked down at his lumpy midsection. *Probably no chance of losing ten pounds before the Tinder date this evening.*

He shut his computer and gathered his tools of the trade—laptop, iPad, smartphone, and power cords as well as a couple of framed photos of his two kids—and shoved them into his well-worn leather satchel. The framed magazine covers with Walker's puss on the front could stay on the walls for Shanelle's continuing inspiration, adoration and, ultimately, he was certain, stupefaction. Walker probably didn't qualify as a genuine Stupid-Ass White Man just yet. But surely there would come a time when Shanelle would have her fill and let him have it.

At two minutes to five, Shanelle returned with a print-out in her hand. "You want a look at the revised press release?"

Marty shook his head. "Not a chance."

"C'mon, Marty. You still got a couple minutes. I could use another pair of eyes."

"I've crossed my last T and dotted my last I for this place. Time for you to earn that big raise."

Deflated, she let her hand fall to her side. "You're abandoning me in my time of need, Marty."

Marty came around the desk and offered a farewell hug. "Sorry."

"Yeah, well," Shanelle sighed. "Time's up."

7.   HACKSAW HARRY CUTS IN

A wraparound terrace at the top of the building known colloquially as the Tower of Crowe Power, featuring ornate copper buttresses, gargoyles, and three-hundred-and-sixty-degree views of the city, surrounded a suite that was built in 1927 for Homer Crowe to entertain his many illicit romantic liaisons. Now the entire floor belonged to Lindsey, who had turned it into a yoga studio for her and other executives to unwind as needed. It was there that Digby appeared at the threshold, looking more Digby-ish than ever: sallow, sagging, grim. He waited until Lindsey completed her spinal twist before tapping on the doorframe. "Knock-knock," he said, flatly.

Lindsey, flushed pink from her yoga practice, looked around. "Want to join me in a downward dog?" she asked.

"No," he said, his face twisted into a scowl. "We already have a problem with fleas."

"What are you talking about?"

"We were just served notice," he said.

"By whom?" she asked.

Digby held up a manila folder. "Harold Crenshaw."

"Oh no," she said, slumping on her mat. "Hacksaw Harry? The hedge fund guy?"

"Unfortunately, yes."

Lindsey rose from the mat and draped a towel around her neck. "What does he want?"

Digby shook his head. "He wants us to get clean and green—or die."

"Oh dear." Lindsey snatched the folder and sat down on a sofa in a conversation area off to the side, a gargoyle peering in through the window over her shoulder. She began reading, her eyes widening as she looked down the first page. "Hacksaw Harry is… a *shareholder?*"

"His company, Carrion Investments, owns four percent of our common shares."

She dropped the letter. "Shit, man!" she exclaimed. "How did we not know that?"

"Apparently, there was no way of telling. Investor Relations says he's been quietly accumulating shares under a variety of names for months."

Lindsey took a deep breath, picked up the letter, and read aloud. "'Dear Ms. Crowe. As an investor in the Crowe Power Company, I want to express my deep disappointment in your failure to make any significant progress toward a decarbonized future. Your dilatory approach betrays a lack of commitment…'" She looked up, flushed with anger. "Dilatory approach? The *nerve* of this guy."

"It gets worse," Digby said.

Lindsey returned to the letter, shaking the page, and blinking her eyes hard. "'…and a lack of commitment to join the global fight to address our ongoing climate emergency and heal our planet.' Our *planet?* Seriously? *Hacksaw Harry?* I thought he was a money-grubbing whore." She laughed. "When did he get religion?"

Digby shook his head in dismay. "You know and I know it's B.S. He's just doing what some of these other preening people on Wall Street are doing. They're raiding companies under the cover of climate. And they do it in a way that can't be criticized by the media or the politicians because this time, it isn't greed that drives them. It's *green.*"

Lindsey smacked the letter. "You're saying it's a cover story."

Digby nodded. "An effective one. I'm sure you've noticed big corporations waving the white flag when activist investors make demands. Last thing they want is to be perceived as resisting a virtuous cause. So they hand over board seats, change strategies, and, if they're very unlucky, lose control—and maybe the company, too."

Lindsey flipped to page two. "He says he wants 'aggressive carbon targets… an unequivocal demonstration of our climate commitment… hard timetables… improved governance…' I guess that means improvement over me." She glanced further down the page. "Looks like the standard list of 'reforms.' Then…" She flipped over another page. "He wants to nominate his own slate of directors. Says ours are old and decrepit.'"

Digby rolled his shoulders. "You have to admit: he has a point there. What's our average age? Ninety-two?"

"They may be ancient but they're loyal—at least when they can remember who I am. Can't tell you how many times Willard Clark has called me 'Myrtle.'" Lindsey looked down at the herringbone wooden floor and shook her head. Finally, she looked up. "Damn it all. I knew this was coming. Our stock price has left us exposed to exactly this kind of shakedown." She handed the letter back to Digby. "This is going to be bad, isn't it?"

Digby took a deep breath. "Very. Harold Crenshaw's taken down at least a dozen other companies and sold them off or broken them in pieces."

"Is this the end of Crowe Power?" she asked.

"Possibly."

"That can't happen on my watch," Lindsey declared. "First woman to run the company and she loses it in a year? I don't think so." She sagged under the possibility of it happening. "How much damage can he do with just four percent of our shares?"

Digby leaned forward, resting his forearms on his legs. "More than you might think. Once he goes public with his stake in our company, which he must do if he hits five percent, that puts us in play."

"At least we have the family, right?" she said, almost pleadingly. "Isn't that our last line of defense?"

Digby sighed and fell back in his chair. "The family agreement expires in September and it's not a lock we'll continue. There's a lot of noise out there right now, especially among the next generation."

Lindsey sighed. "I know. You heard about Missy, right?"

He nodded grimly. "I did."

"It's not just her," Lindsey said. "That whole generation is restless. They're getting the same grief about killing the planet that I am, and I worry they'll vote to break up the bloc and divest before I have a chance to make my case."

"That's one threat," Digby acknowledged. "We have another."

"I know," Lindsey said with a shudder. "We can't count on Uncle Chuck and Aunt Lizzie forever, given their ages. I mean, if either one of them dies, that would be enough to tip the balance of power—especially with Robbie out there as a wild card."

"More like a joker, I'm afraid." Digby rubbed his chin and they both looked out the window a moment. At last, Digby asked, "How do you want to proceed?"

Lindsey stood up. "Well, we're just going to have to fight our way out, quickly." She walked over to a windowsill to retrieve her phone and punched a button. "Winnie? Get me Bentley Edwards, will you?"

"Right away."

Lindsey walked back to the sofa but remained standing. "Bentley knows Crenshaw," she said to Digby. "I think they play squash or something. I want to get his thinking."

Bentley, of the uptown firm of Glickman, Edwards & Stein, had served as counsel to the Harper family and their Chicago-based business empire for decades, from Lindsey's great-grandfather to her dad. Bentley had also been instrumental in providing guidance to Lindsey as she considered divorcing Robbie, and in strategizing her drive to replace him as Crowe Power chair. A prodigious fee-generator for his firm, Bentley lived an expensive and extravagant lifestyle and was renowned for his extensive network of wealthy people in New York City, and for his skill at social triangulation.

The phone buzzed. Winnie said, "I have Mr. Edwards for you."

When Lindsey heard a click, she said, "Bentley, dear. How are you?"

"Better now that I'm hearing your voice," Bentley cooed.

Lindsey looked at Digby and rolled her eyes. "Bentley, I need your advice on something."

"Of course."

Lindsey told Bentley about the letter and its implicit threats. "How do I find out what he's after?"

"Why don't you ask him?"

"Seriously?"

"Absolutely. You could suggest a meeting," Bentley suggested. "That would give you a chance to feel him out a bit."

"That's a disgusting thought," Lindsey replied.

"Mentally, I mean," Bentley said.

"That might be worse."

"Come now," Bentley said. "Harold's not a bad sort, really, once you get to know him. He can actually be quite a pleasant fellow."

"Is he a client of yours?"

"No," Bentley said. "But I do know him a bit. How about if I arrange a lunch somewhere? It can be just the three of us. Something casual, relaxed. We'll go to a neutral spot away from the office and talk things over. A place where friends might go."

Lindsey sucked in her breath through clenched teeth. "I don't believe I need friends like this."

Bentley said, "Maybe you do. If you can't stop him, you might be able to at least neutralize him. Turn on that patented Lindsey charm that I love so well. It's worth a shot."

Lindsey agreed to the meeting, thanked him for his assistance, and hung up.

Digby asked, "Do you trust Bentley?"

"I'm not really sure if he's a good friend or just a good actor," she said. "I can't be sure until I see for myself. This lunch he suggests should tell me everything I need to know about Harry, and maybe Bentley, too."

Digby leaned forward. "What can I do to help?"

"Pull together our leadership team first thing in the morning," she said. "I want a report on our climate initiatives so we can respond to Hacksaw Harry."

8.   TINDER IS THE NIGHT

arty arranged to meet his Tinder date, Gwynne, at Nougatine, a busy, buzzy café adjacent to the famed restaurateur Jean-Georges' eponymous dining room on the ground floor of the Trump International Hotel at the southwest corner of Central Park. Gwynne looked a bit different from her profile picture—who didn't? —but there she was, right at the end of the bar, as he suggested. Feeling newly energized by his liberation from wage servitude, he swooped in with more ease and confidence than he'd felt in months.

"Hello there," he said, sliding onto the bar stool. "Is this seat taken?"

"It is now," she said with an inviting smile.

The bartender, Freddie, delivered Marty his usual, a dry Hendrick's martini with a slice of cucumber, and nodded approval of his companion, a fit, stylish woman with a dramatic sweep of lustrous brown hair and a look of wealth about her. Maybe, for once, he'd lucked out on one of these blind dates. Was it possible this one would even extend past seven o'clock? Marty was feeling lucky…

"I'm Marty," he said, offering a hand.

She raised her Aperol Spritz and they clinked glasses. "I certainly hope so. I've been eager to meet you."

Marty loved her enthusiasm. With money in his pocket, and no reason to get up in the morning, he tossed aside any sense of caution. Nothing could stop him tonight. "Let's just say it's nice to meet someone who actually looks like their Tinder photo."

Puzzled, she asked, "My Tinder photo?" It suddenly occurred to her that Marty thought he was meeting his date. Best, she thought, to play along. "You think so?" She turned her head slightly to give him a fuller look.

Marty studied her features and thought: *No. Not really, but damn—she was stunningly attractive.* "Even better," he said.

As Marty sipped his martini, she said, "I must say, you're exactly what I expected."

"Sorry about that," he said.

"Don't be hard on yourself." She patted his hand. "I wouldn't be here if I didn't want to see you."

Marty smiled shyly. Since his divorce from Jill, who had thrown him over for their young Salvadoran gardener, he had waded into the dating waters cautiously, carefully trying to find his footing without stumbling into depths well over his head. Online meetings were still awkward for him, and very different from the days he courted Jill, when romances were kindled through chance meetings at bars, parties, and clubs. He cleared his throat. "Have you been here before?"

"No," she said, nodding toward his drink, "but you obviously have."

"Enough to claim the bartender as a dependent on my taxes."

"I know how that works. I could claim an entire nail salon on Chambers Street."

He looked at her immaculate nails, apparently coated in some sort of titanium finish. "Well worth it," he said. "So tell me, Gwynne. Who are you? And what were you before? What did you do and what did you think?"

"Seriously?" she muttered. "Do you try that on every Tinder date?"

"No, but I thought I better try new material."

"Well, I've seen *Casablanca* a million times, so I kinda know the line."

"Then you now know that I only steal from the best."

"And what is it you do?" she asked. "Are you a thief?"

"I defend companies," he said.

"So… you're in security."

"I defend them from their critics."

"You're a lawyer."

"Critics in the media," he said.

"Ah. You're a flack."

"I prefer a more dignified term—like public relations professional—but yeah," Marty acknowledged. "You get the concept."

"So, who are you defending now?"

"Well," he said, looking at his watch, "up until about an hour ago, I was working for Staminum Energy."

She looked surprised. "You quit?"

"Let's just say I left to pursue other opportunities."

"Like what?"

"Maybe I'll spend more time with my family… if I can find them and they'll let me hang around."

"Then you were fired."

"Well, I suppose if you want to get technical about it, yeah."

"Goodness. You really do beat around the bush. No wonder you're a flack. You're perfect for it." She pulled a credit card from her purse, summoned Freddie over, and handed it to him. "These drinks are on me."

Marty blushed. "Thank you. But that's not necessary. I've got a good year to go before I'm destitute."

"Oh."

"I may have to sell my car, stop paying for my kids' college, and live on the A train platform, but I'll be okay."

She turned back to Marty. "So you're divorced, unemployed and possibly homeless. You're quite a catch, Marty."

"I'm vaccinated. Does that count for something?"

She shrugged. "Not much."

"Well, enough of my bragging," he said. "What about you? What do you do for a living?"

"Oddly enough, I'm a writer."

"Really? I know a few of those. What do you write?"

"I'm working on a piece for a website about the rise and fall of great family dynasties."

"Interesting coincidence. I just happen to know a couple."

"You don't say. Which ones?"

"I just left Staminum Energy, run by the Stamper family. And I worked for years at Crowe Power, and I'm sure you know who they are."

She nodded. "Who doesn't? Quite a story there. I've noticed their stock has been tumbling under Lindsey Harper Crowe. I hear a lot of grousing from investors about family control—like that's holding them back somehow. What do you think is going on? Is she in over her head?"

"Honestly, I don't know," Marty said. "I haven't paid much attention since I left."

"What about when you were there?"

Marty sipped his cold martini while he warmed to the topic. He explained his tenure, which began when Robbie Crowe was awarded the chairmanship by a captive board of directors and recruited Walker Hope to run the business as CEO. Walker was hugely successful, leading the company to one record quarter after another, but Robbie couldn't stand watching his employee get all the credit. So, after a fawning cover story in Fortune Magazine touting Walker as the best CEO in America, Robbie ousted him in a fit of jealousy and watched the company suffer under his replacement, blowing through cash, attacking shareholders, and, ultimately, cutting the dividend, which hit the Crowe family heirs right where it hurt. In revolt, Lindsey Harper Crowe pushed Robbie out of both their East 67th Street home and out of the Broad Street company offices. "I don't know what kind of chairperson Lindsey is, because I hardly know her. But it's hard to imagine she can find her way out of this mess. She had almost no experience when she took the job. From what I heard her main expertise was brunch. The family, I think, just wanted someone to watch out for their interests. It was a desperate move, in my view. She was their last hope."

She pulled a notebook and a pen from her purse. "Do you mind if I use your name with that quote?"

"Quote?"

"For my story."

"There's no story here…"

"Yes, there is," she said. "I'm doing a piece on Lindsey Harper Crowe for *Buzzniss*."

"I thought we were on a date."

"Did you?"

He looked at her incredulously. "You didn't?"

"I told you I was working on a story, Marty," she said. She hit a button on her phone, which was sitting on the bar between them.

"You <u>recorded</u> this?"

She shrugged. "I couldn't have been more plain, Marty. This is research for my piece. And, by the way, my name's not Gwynne. It's Veronica Sawyer. I heard you were a regular here on Thursday nights, which is why I'm here. I hoped to catch you." She smiled and made a motion of reeling in a fish. "And I did."

Marty looked over at Freddie, who had his ear cocked in his direction. Freddie shrugged and mouthed, *"she said she was meeting you…"* Marty, slack-jawed, turned back to Veronica. "I hope to God you're kidding me."

"Look. If it's any consolation, Marty, I really appreciate your insights. They're very helpful, and not just to me. If I were a shareholder in Crowe Power, I'd want to know this. I'll be sure to mention you in the piece."

"Please, Veronica: don't!" Marty was shell-shocked. "I was just here to meet my date at the corner of the bar. I thought that was you."

Veronica shrugged. "Sorry. I guess she didn't show."

Sensing Marty's mistake, Freddie nodded his head toward the other end of the bar, where a woman was standing up and pulling her purse over her shoulder. "What do they say when you get fired? Good luck in your future endeavors?" Veronica left as the other woman approached.

"You must be Marty," she said.

"I think at this moment," he replied, "I'd prefer to be somebody else."

"I'm Gwynne," she said. "Too bad we didn't get a chance to meet earlier."

"I am so sorry—in ways you couldn't possibly fathom."

Sharply, she said, "I was at the corner of the bar, like you suggested."

Marty took a deep breath. "I don't know what to say. I really hate to waste your time like that."

"You didn't," Gwynne said. "I was able to watch you from afar and get a sense of how you operate." She chuckled. "You know, a guy who can't figure out that he's on the wrong date probably isn't a good fit for me."

"But… you do look *a lot* alike. I mean, same color eyes, hair…"

"If you'd read the description on my profile, you'd know my hair was Espresso Brown. She was clearly a French Roast."

Marty was completely baffled. "There's a difference?"

"Not to you, apparently."

"I don't know what to say. Can I buy you a drink? Something other than coffee?"

She looked at her watch. "Sorry," she said. "Time's up."

Time's up *again?* Twice in one day? Gwynne headed for the door to grab a cab on Central Park West, leaving Marty alone with his drink. He caught the eye of the bartender, Freddie. "What the hell, man?"

"I thought you knew her," Freddie said, shaking up a cocktail for another customer. "You want another drink?"

Marty nodded. "I'll take one for each hand."

9.   MOM GENES' BAD FIT

Lindsey found Missy slumped sullenly in an oversized easy chair, clicking through messages on her phone, in the elegant second-floor living room of her townhouse on East 67th Street. Simmering in a broth of rage and indignation, Missy had not only expected to be in jail at this moment, but she *wanted* to be there, to experience first-hand the injustices suffered every day by oppressed peoples held captive for crimes against corrupt systems all over the world. Outside of Cuba and Venezuela, were there any other islands of enlightenment left in this world? Places where the people ruled, and the planet was undisturbed by profit-driven commerce?

"There you are," Lindsey said, sweetly, as she sat down on the ottoman across from Missy and patted her knee. "Lovely to see you, my dear. Did you have a nice day in the city?"

Missy seethed. *Was Mother being sarcastic?* "You should *not* have bailed me out."

"I didn't, darling."

"So… who did?"

"Why, I believe it was our New York State legislature and the governor."

"Oh really," she snapped. "How do you figure that?"

"If you read the news, darling, you'd know they let out everybody. You picked an excellent time to vandalize a building," Lindsey said. "You can pretty much get away with anything in our city these days, whether you're poor or rich."

"That's not fair at all!"

Lindsey was genuinely confused. "Well. Sometimes, life *isn't* fair."

Missy sprang from her chair, shaking her head from side to side. "I can understand why they would release people who don't have the wherewithal to pay bail. But I have the means."

"Not at the rate you're spending," Lindsey said.

Missy glared at her mother. Was she intentionally not comprehending? Or had her life of extreme privilege blinded her to the brutality of the system that insulated her in her comfortable little bubble? "As I've explained to you, Mother," Missy said with an exasperated sigh, "I'm giving my money away."

Lindsey shrugged dismissively. "Oh, really. And then what?"

"What do you mean?"

Lindsey stood and followed Missy around the spacious room, filled with antiques and heirlooms and priceless artworks by Van Gogh, Gauguin, and Monet. "What will you have accomplished, other than unburdening yourself of a fortune that took your family a century to provide? Will you still be as popular with this crowd you're running with once the money's gone, and you have nothing more to give them? What then?"

Missy crossed her arms, defiant. "Then I'll be just like them. I'll know the true meaning of the struggle against a rigged system. And I won't be complicit in crimes against the planet, like your company is."

"*My* company?"

"Well, I sure don't have anything to do with it."

Lindsey seethed. "Other than cashing our checks?"

"Oh, Mother. That is *low*. I have nothing to do with your relentless plundering of the earth."

Lindsey leaned against a credenza and regarded her daughter with dismay. "If that's what you believe, then you absolutely are complicit, too. Because you are doing *nothing* to help."

"Check your privilege, Mother!" Missy said, heatedly. "I'm the one who's out there pressing for change."

"Exactly!" Lindsey said, waving her arm toward the street behind her. "You're *out there*—on the fringe. Another melodramatic actor in a pointless street theater. Maybe it makes you feel good to demonstrate your idea of virtue. But if you want to truly change things, then I suggest you get real. Come to Crowe

Power. Get involved. Find out what the real challenges are and make yourself part of the solution."

Missy rolled her eyes. "You cannot be serious."

"Sitting on the sidelines heckling the rest of us does nothing to advance the cause," Lindsey said. "You think people are going to give up on the energy they need every day because of a protest they watched for twenty seconds on the news? In case you haven't noticed, nobody's turning off their lights. Nobody's deciding not to charge their phones. Nobody's avoiding planes, trains, and automobiles. All these things demand energy that we provide for them."

"Then get the right kind of energy."

Through a clenched jaw, Lindsey said, "I'm doing what I can, dear."

"You're not doing enough."

"And you're not doing one damn thing!" Lindsey couldn't help thinking, *my God. Missy's a nut.* How had this happened? Was she always like this? So smug and assured of her moral superiority? She had nothing but the best growing up, her elite education at Dalton, extensive travels abroad with summers in Europe, and no need to generate any kind of income for herself, even for casual spending money. Maybe that was the problem. Lindsey had to concede that she barely knew her own daughter growing up, entrusting much of her care to networks of nannies and housekeepers and tutors and teachers and professors she really didn't know. Now the results were in—and they were alarming.

"Alright, Missy, let's dispense with the bullcrap, alright?" Lindsey said. "First of all, you are *not* giving away your money."

Missy stepped toward her mother. "The hell I'm not!"

"The hell you are!"

"It's hardly your call," Missy said, haughtily. "It's *my* trust fund."

Lindsey smiled thinly. "As you said to me a moment ago: you may want to check your privilege. I mean that literally."

Missy looked as if Lindsey had connected with a roundhouse right hand and delivered a devastating punch to Missy's Tiffany glass jaw. "What are you talking about?"

"It's a *revocable* trust fund," Lindsey informed her. "Do you know what that means?"

"You can take it back?"

"Exactly."

"Why, I, I—I don't believe that. I'd always assumed…"

"Apparently, you've assumed a great many things—some of which I'd put in the category of fantastical nonsense." Lindsey rapped the table next to her with a knuckle. *"Read the fine print,* Missy. It's all right there."

Missy walked slowly to the sofa and sat down, her head falling back on the cushioned seat in surrender. Softly, she asked, "What do you want from me, Mother?"

Lindsey sat with her and addressed her calmly, directly, unequivocally. "The party's over, dear. You want your money? You'll have to earn it back—at Crowe Power."

Missy rolled her head back and forth in agony. How could she prevent this nightmare from happening? Could her father rescue her? "I still have school," she said, weakly.

"You'll work part-time at Crowe until you graduate next June. Then you're at it full-time on Broad Street—inside, rather than out. If you show that you're serious, I'll consider putting you on our strategy team to plan the future of our company. But you'll have to work for it and win not just my trust but that of your teammates."

Missy sighed. "I can't believe this is happening."

Lindsey persisted. "Believe it."

"What kind of job would I have?"

Lindsey said, "You can be an advisor to start."

"An advisor?" Missy huffed. "What kind of shitty job is that?"

"What do you expect?"

"Senior advisor, at least."

"Senior? You're twenty," Lindsey pointed out.

"Chase got vice president right out of school. Is that 'cause he's a boy?"

"You know what? Fine. If that's what it takes," Lindsey said, rubbing her temple. *"Senior* advisor. Do we have a deal?"

Missy rubbed her eyes with the palms of hands, then slapped the sofa. "I have to think about it," she bleated.

"Thinking is a very good idea." Lindsey patted Missy's knee and stood to leave.

Missy stopped her in her tracks. "I want you to know something," Missy said. "I'm dropping my last name."

"And changing it to *what?*"

Missy raised her chin. "I'm going with my middle name. Mayburn."

Lindsey burst out laughing. "Your great grandfather Winthrop Mayburn ran slaughterhouses and tanneries in Chicago."

"So?"

"He killed animals for a living! You and your friends good with that?"

"I… hadn't thought about it."

"Pick your poison, Missy. Like we all do."

10. CHIP OFF THE OLD BLOCKHEAD

Harold Crenshaw had earned his Hacksaw moniker for good reason: he had relentlessly and ruthlessly chopped up more companies at a higher profit margin than any hedge fund manager in history. Like a hungry wolf culling a herd, he kept an eye out for the fattest sheep with a little limp in their step and a hint of fear in their eyes. If they happened to be hemmed into a corral they could not escape, all the better.

Crowe Power made a pleasingly plump target, through no particular fault of their own. The firm was profitable and well run but stuck in an unfashionable industry and suffering from the disinvestment of politically pressured funds. As Harold saw it, the market value of the Crowe Power Company was worth less than the sum of its parts, which he could cleave away and trundle off at a tidy profit. In some ways, he told himself, he was doing the Crowe family a favor.

Still, the story he was watching on CNN as he trudged along on the treadmill in his Fifth Avenue apartment was a gift he hadn't seen coming: Missy Mayburn Crowe, a descendant of company founder Homer Crowe, was arrested at a protest staged by the Planetistas outside company headquarters. So at least one person in the Crowe family agreed with him? And he didn't even have to ask? They were making his job too easy. This had to be some kind of joke.

Harold shifted into a slower speed as Siri announced a call from his partner, Nelson Steckel. Harold pulled the towel from his neck to mop his forehead and told Siri to answer.

"Did you see this story about Missy Crowe?" Nelson asked.

Harold chuckled. "Un-fucking-believable! I just caught it on TV. Can this be true?"

"Apparently. It's all over the papers, too. The *Times* calls her a hero, as you'd expect, for renouncing her family's ways. A different take in the *New York Post*, as you might expect. You've got to check it out."

Harold stepped off the treadmill to retrieve the *Post* from the credenza and flopped onto a couch. The cover featured a photo of an anguished Missy with her hands zip tied behind her back, with a blaring headline:

MISSY FIT
- **Crowe Heiress's Arrested Development**
- **The Debutante's Bail: $0**
- **She writes fake news on fake biz**

Harold's chuckle rumbled into a belly laugh as he considered the ridiculing headlines and his good fortune. "What the hell did she do?" he asked. "I only caught the tail-end of the piece on TV. She was out there marching around with the Planetistas?"

"That's what they say."

"Our Planetistas, right? The group we just paid to put more pressure on Crowe Power?"

"One and the same," Nelson replied.

"And she *volunteered* to join them?"

"Looks that way."

Just to be certain, Harold asked, "We didn't push her?"

"No."

"Alright," Harold said. "So she's obviously got some higher calling than her trust fund." He scratched his head, thinking. "Is it possible she's as dumb as her dad?"

"Hard to imagine, but she might be even dumber. Get this. She sprayed graffiti on a building that she thought was the headquarters for Larrabee Industries. A company that doesn't even exist!"

"Oh my God." Harold laughed until he coughed. When he cleared his throat, he said, "I was counting on some useful idiots from the environmental fringe to help us get control of this thing. But I never thought we'd get help from the Crowe family. Dumbfuckery must be in the genes."

"I know, right?" Nelson said. "It's almost too good to be true."

Harold walked to the windows, looking out at Central Park's green expanse. "Bentley Edwards is arranging a meeting with Lindsey Harper Crowe next week. Do you think she has any idea of all the ways we're boxing her in?"

Nelson replied, "My sense is no. You'd think she'd connect the dots at some point, but I doubt she has a clue. I mean, these Crowes seem kind of stupid."

Harold scratched his chin. "Maybe we're better at this than I thought. Or the opposition is worse." He sighed. "I almost feel a bit of guilt over this one."

"Seriously?" Nelson said.

Harold paused, thinking. "Nah."

"Well. It was a thought anyway," Nelson said. "You get points for having a conscience,"

"I don't know," Harold said. "It worries me a bit. It feels too easy. Taking these naïve people to the cleaners like this? It's like stealing some kid's lunch money on the playground. An activity I used to enjoy, by the way."

"I bet you were pretty good at it."

"The best," Harold said. He shook his head. "You know, people pay me to see around corners, to expect the unexpected. I hate to think we're being sandbagged. Any chance we're walking into a trap?"

"I know what you're saying," Nelson said. "It feels weird there's no resistance. It's like Reagan invading Grenada, or the Germans waltzing into Paris. Maybe when we turn up the heat, she'll pack up all her artwork and head for the south of France."

"Maybe," Harold said, pacing along the windows. "I'm not putting it in the 'win' column just yet." He sat down on the windowsill and looked at the traffic jam on Fifth Avenue. "Let's do some research on our Miss Missy and try to figure out how far she's willing to take this. If she's truly serious—and not just showing off for her friends—maybe she can help stage a revolt inside the family."

"Against her own mother?"

"She marched against her."

"She did."

"And if she's willing, maybe we could enlist her old man, too. Everything I've heard around town tells me that the divorce was very bitter—especially from Robbie Crowe's side. What's he doing these days anyway? He seems to have disappeared."

"Far as I know, he's running some kind of foundation downtown."

"Check that out, too, will ya? If we get the Crowe family to crack, it's game, set, and match. The company will belong to us, and the pieces to our client."

PART TWO

Electrifying Idea

11. CON FUSION REIGNS

In a darkened conference room on the top floor of the Crowe Power Company, Lindsey and the firm's top executives looked grimly at a screen displaying the sad face of a desert tortoise.

Chief Executive Officer Lucy Rutherford, her stern face partly illuminated with a ghostly glow from her PowerPoint presentation, stood next to the screen with a clicker. "Say hello to Tommy," she said. "As you can see, this little fella's a desert tortoise. He lives under a rock in Nevada. But Tommy has come out of his shell to exercise more clout than you can imagine. He and his fellow tortoise buddies are the reason our solar power project can't get built." Lucy explained that the project was blocked by objections from environmentalists concerned about the critters' shrinking habitat. "Desert tortoises, like fossil fuel companies, are a threatened species. They've lived in the Mojave Desert for eons. Now the very same activists who demand more solar energy from Crowe Power complain that plastering the desert with a million solar panels might cramp the tortoises' style."

"They may have a point," Lindsey allowed.

Lucy clicked to the next slide, bringing up a shot of a pelican. "We call this chick Polly," she said, "Polly's a migratory bird endangered by wind turbines built along the East Coast." Lucy noted that while a half-million migratory birds are sliced and diced by the blades of wind turbines each year, a thousand times more birds are killed flying into windows. "Our critics who live in glass houses along the beach in the Hamptons are throwing stones at the offshore wind farm we're trying to develop in a joint venture with BlowCo. They claim it's because of the birds. More likely, we suspect, it's because of the view."

Lindsey sighed. "I know my neighbors. And, of course, you're right. Everybody loves the idea of renewable energy—as long as it's not generated in their backyard."

Lucy pointed the clicker and pressed again, bringing up a photo of a fish. "The last member of our zoological parade is an Atlantic sturgeon. Let's call him or her or zher 'Stevie.' Our activist critics insist Stevie's species will be endangered if we are allowed to build a natural gas pipeline through New York Harbor. Never mind that the gas in this pipeline would displace coal at our power plant and cut our carbon emissions in half. That's not enough for the Planetistas. They want to shut down our plant completely in favor of... well, they don't know, actually. Something else."

"You mean, like wind power and solar power that they also won't let us provide?" Lindsey asked.

"Pretty much," Lucy said.

Digby shook his head in dismay. "Heaven forbid that people still need electricity in New York City in a few years. Maybe we should invest in candles."

Lindsey sighed and tossed a pen onto the conference table. "What in the world are we supposed to do?" she asked. "We're trying our damndest to reduce CO_2, but we keep getting blocked."

Lucy took her seat. "The good news, if you want to call it that, is that the government's efforts to kill fossil fuels are limiting production of oil and gas and driving up prices. The trend we're on is for a profitable second quarter, even if our green projects are dead in the water—some of them, literally."

Armani Jones, Crowe's Chief Financial Officer, unfolded a spreadsheet from a three-ring binder and ran a bright orange fingernail down a row of numbers. "The question we have to ask ourselves," she said, looking up, "is whether we can afford to continue with these kinds of projects, especially with the coming shutdown of the Alberta Clipper pipeline. These green projects are cash sinkholes."

Lindsey acknowledged the dilemma, but sat forward, pressing her fingers together. "The harsh reality, Armani, is we can't afford not to continue. Our pledge of allegiance to the climate agenda is essential right now, more than ever." She turned to a control booth behind her. "Show the photo of Harold Crenshaw, please." Up flashed a photo of the notoriously aggressive hedge fund manager, dressed in a dark suit as he spoke at an investment conference. "Turtles, birds and fish are the least of our problems." Lindsey said. "We have a predator in our waters."

Armani was on full alert. "What's going on?"

Lindsey said, "Hacksaw Harry has acquired four percent of our common shares."

A murmur arose as people sat up in their chairs.

"Oh no." Armani said.

"Oh yes," Lindsey said. "And he's using our failure to make headway on these green initiatives as a pretext to launch an assault on our company." Lindsey stood up and walked toward the screen. "As I said some time ago, people: We're exposed. Every other company in our industry is running for green cover. Some is legit. A good deal is not. But that's hardly the point. A failure to make a go of it— or a show of it—leaves us vulnerable to people like Hacksaw Harry. He spotted our weakness, and he has pounced."

"Dear God," gasped Lucy. "Any idea of his end game?"

Lindsey turned to her General Counsel. "Digby?"

Digby stood up. "We can't be sure at this point what his true motivations are. But we all should recognize this for what it is: an existential threat. Harold Crenshaw has wormed his way into bigger companies than ours and broken them up under flimsier pretexts. We know he's preparing to nominate his own hand-picked slate of directors to our board. Should he succeed, you should be aware that they will impose his agenda on our company. At that point, anything can happen—none of it good."

Lucy said, "Perhaps I'm overstepping my bounds here, Lindsey. But couldn't your family block his nominees?"

Digby interceded. "Under normal circumstances, yes. Given, uh… current family dynamics, that's far from a sure thing. We have our own dissidents. And, based on his previous attacks on companies like ours, Harold Crenshaw will recruit other institutional investors to vote with him. They're all under the same extreme pressures that we are."

A pall fell over the room as the house lights came on. Lindsey looked around at the assembled executives, leading all aspects of the business, including Operations, Human Resources, Marketing, Government Affairs, and Legal.

"Unless we're willing to see an end to the hundred-and-eight-year run of this company and all its jobs—including ours—we need to come up with a better plan. Excuses won't cut it, not in this environment." Heads bobbed and weaved around her as the executives avoided eye contact. "Is there nothing left in our Greeneron portfolio that we can lean on? Robbie spent five billion dollars on it. Please tell me there's *something* in there."

Armani sighed. "We've written off ninety-two percent of Greeneron. I hate to put it so bluntly, but Robbie bought a lot of junk."

Lindsey shook her head. "What about that fusion company we had in there? That sounded promising. Don't tell me that's gone, too."

"Consolidated Fusion is the only company we have left," Lucy said. "But we're planning to pull the plug next month."

Lindsey, alarmed, asked, "Why on earth would you do that?"

Armani rolled her eyes. "They call it 'Con Fusion' for a reason," she muttered. "There's no clarity on when or if it will ever work. You know what they say, Lindsey: 'Fusion is thirty years away—and it always will be.' We're throwing good money after bad. Our financial team looked at it and said, 'enough's enough.' We have an offer from a real estate developer who wants to build a battery factory on the property in Jersey City where our lab sits. We think we should take it."

A hand rose in the back of the room. Sergei Baranov, the company's Chief Technology Officer cleared his throat. In heavily accented Russian, he asked, "Could I offer a dissenting point of view?"

Lindsey nodded to him. "Please."

Sergei directed his remarks at Lindsey. "As I have said to others in this room, Consolidated Fusion has been making incredible progress. We think its business model is not only unique, it's potentially very, very profitable."

Lucy scoffed. "Sergei, please. We've been over this. Con Fusion is *not* a business. It's a science project—and a very expensive one at that."

Sergei flushed red. "As you just showed, Lucy, Crowe Power has spent far more on solar and wind projects that have fizzled than it has on fusion. And fusion is the one area where we're not an also-ran; we have a distinct competitive advantage. I'm afraid that if we shut it down, we will squander our significant lead and lose our opportunity forever."

"The sooner the better," Lucy sniffed. "I need money to operate refineries."

"If that's where we're going to put all our money, we'll regret it," Sergei said. "There are many other companies out there who would like to take our place when it comes to fusion. They're just waiting for the opportunity. I'd hate to give it to them."

Lindsey said, "Can we slow down here, people? I'd like someone to explain fusion so that everyone here can understand." She looked around sheepishly. "That includes me, by the way. I have no idea how it works."

Sergei rebuked Lucy with a look, then trained his gaze back on Lindsey as he walked to the front of the room. An intense, wiry man with a goatee and an uncanny resemblance to the Bolshevik revolutionary, Vladimir Lenin, he radiated a few kilowatts of electricity himself. "Fusion is what powers the sun and the stars. It's called 'the holy grail of energy' for good reason. There are no carbon emissions. There's very little waste. And there is no danger of explosions or meltdowns. A bathtub full of seawater could provide as much energy as a hundred train cars full of coal. And it just so happens that Crowe Power owns several of the most promising technologies to make it happen. If fusion works—granted, that's a very big 'if'—we would revolutionize the energy industry."

Lindsey was intrigued, but wary. "How is fusion different from nuclear power?"

Sergei said, "Without getting too technical, let me sum it up in a few words. Today's nuclear plants use a process called fission. That splits heavy atoms like uranium and plutonium to create energy. In fusion, we do the opposite. We superheat isotopes of super-light hydrogen atoms to more than a hundred million degrees Celsius so that they fuse together and release energy. Many technological challenges remain, but we have seen enough progress in recent years that I am confident we will eventually harness this power to provide safe, clean electricity. It's just a matter of time."

"And money," Lucy interjected.

"That Crowe Power doesn't have," Armani added, "especially with our pipeline going down."

Lucy bore in on Sergei. "Here's a science question: How much cash you can burn at a hundred million degrees?"

Lindsey glared at her two top executives. "I understand your skepticism, but we may not have a choice in the matter. If we don't have a credible green strategy, we're in deep, deep trouble. Would you rather leave these decisions to Hacksaw Harry and his proxies? Or should we manage this ourselves?" She turned back to Sergei. "Why do you say that Crowe Power has an advantage in fusion?"

"We're one of a dozen companies in the world jockeying for position—so far," Sergei said. "There is no dominant player yet, nor an agreed-upon pathway to commercial viability, but all of them are raising capital from some very big names and someone is going to emerge from the pack to lead this industry. The one advantage we have over everyone else is that we have first-rate intellectual property. We hold more licenses for enabling technologies than anyone else. And our scientists are widely regarded as the best minds anywhere."

Sergei explained that the industry was attracting money from countries around the world, which was proof of fusion's growing strategic importance. Thirty-five nations—including China, Russia, and the U.S.—were collectively spending tens of billions of dollars to build an elaborate fusion research project in France called ITER—the International Thermonuclear Experimental Reactor. In addition, private companies were raising money from extremely wealthy individuals to further their research and apply the project's findings to their own fusion plans. "We can finally see the point in the future when fusion is not just one of many green options for generating electricity, but the best one. The stakes are huge."

Lindsey stood up and walked slowly to join Sergei at the front of the room. "Okay. Let's think this through, people. And let's ask ourselves: What if?"

Lucy did not like the direction this seemed to be going. "What if *what*, Lindsey? What if we go broke chasing this green dream?"

Digby grasped Lindsey's point and jumped in. "No, Lucy. What if we create a situation where anyone who wants to get into fusion energy has to go through us? Right?"

Lindsey nodded. "That's what I'm thinking."

Lucy sank in her chair. "How would that even happen?"

Sergei said, "We leverage the licenses Con Fusion acquired from universities and national labs for superconducting magnets, materials, exhaust systems, and grid connectivity. That gives us a piece of the action, no matter the method that finally wins out."

Lindsey said, excitedly, "I'm warming to this idea. Perhaps we scoop up any additional enabling technologies we see out there while they're relatively cheap."

Armani shook her head. "That will take budget we simply don't have."

Lindsey said, "Then we have to find the money. This is an investment in our future."

Lucy scoffed. "You're starting to sound like the government."

"Exactly," Lindsey said. "The Secretary of Energy is demanding we get with the program. Let's ask her to pay for it." There was murmuring around the room as Lindsey put her hands on the table and leaned forward to make sure she had their attention. "Hacksaw Harry and his allies want our heads on spikes out there on Broad Street. So we have a choice. We can lose this company and go down in history as climate villains and failures. Or we can leverage what appears to be an advantageous position in nuclear fusion to save Crowe Power. At worst, we live to fight another day. At best, who knows? We might look like heroes."

Digby said, "Seems like a no-brainer to me."

Lucy muttered to Armani. "You can say that again."

"What if it doesn't work?" Lucy asked.

"We're trying, at least. And we're giving people hope. It seems to me that people want a sense that we're actually doing something about climate change. If we can develop a credible story that's uniquely ours, I'd call that progress."

Lucy persisted. "And how do we do that?"

Lindsey looked around the room. There were experts in technology, finance, and business administration, but nobody who could lead the kind of PR campaign she had in mind. Coming up with a convincing story might be harder than fusion. "I've got an idea," she said.

* * *

The usually unflappable Digby followed Lindsey out of the meeting and into a pantry, phone in hand, looking very tense. As Lindsey poured herself a coffee and reached for sweetener, Digby added a dollop of sour cream: "Bentley set up a meeting with Harold Crenshaw for next week."

Lindsey's jaw went slack. "We're not ready. We're just starting to get our story together."

Digby sucked in his breath. "Then we have to get ready. Quickly. If he senses we're not responsive, he'll go public."

"Can't we ask for a little more time?"

"I don't think so. It's like negotiating with the Taliban," Digby said. "You know what he'll do. Beheadings in the public square. Starting with you."

"Where are we meeting?"

"A restaurant in the Village," Digby replied.

She shook the packet of Sweet 'n Low and tore off the top. "How are we to convince our critics fusion is a real possibility?"

Digby shrugged. "I don't know. I see almost nothing about it in the media."

As other people approached the coffee counter, Lindsey indicated a quiet corner of the pantry. They walked over. "Who was that guy who ran communications under Robbie?"

"Marty McGarry?"

Lindsey nodded. "That's it. Marty. He's totally full of shit, right?"

"He could sell snake oil to snakes."

"Sounds like a useful skill. Isn't that what we have to do?"

Digby said, "Robbie couldn't stand him."

"I consider that an endorsement," she said. "What did you think?"

Digby said, "I thought he was great. He worked some magic around here."

Lindsey nodded. "Okay. Give Marty a call. Tell him I'd like to see him ASAP. Do you have that background report on Hacksaw Harry yet?"

"Still working on it."

"Speed it up if you can. I need to know what I'm up against."

12. UP WITH THE CHICKENS

The night sky was giving way to a morning blush of pink clouds over the Upper West Side neighborhood around Lincoln Center when Marty's new virtual assistant, Kiley, started chirping at him from a speaker on the nightstand next to his bed. "Time to get up, Marty."

Marty rolled over. *What the hell?*

"This is a friendly reminder," Kiley said cheerfully. "You wrote in a text message to your son yesterday that you would get up early this morning and work out."

Marty sighed. Did Kiley listen to instructions? "Shut up, Kiley."

Kiley failed to process the command, or maybe she just didn't want to. "Time to get up, Marty," Kiley said again.

Whatever happened to a good, old-fashioned clock radio with a snooze button? Marty pushed aside his pillow and fumbled behind the nightstand for Kiley's plug. He yanked it out of the wall, then rolled over on his back. *There. Just give me a few more minutes...* His eyes closed again, and he was nearing the outskirts of dreamland when Kiley called from his phone on the kitchen counter. "Time to get up, Marty. Answer, 'Yes, I'm getting up,' or, 'No. Please ignore my promise.'"

Who the hell programmed this system to be so aggressive? Was there no escaping these connected devices? He had just pulled his pillow up around both ears when the TV turned on, trumpets blaring and bass drums pounding, heralding the opening of a video from YouTube. Marty sat up and rested on his elbows. What the hell was this? There, on the screen, was a 45 RPM record, "Chicken Fat," with the name of the actor Robert Preston below. Marty had downloaded the novelty song from the 1960s on his phone once as a joke, and now Kiley had weaponized it against him. Preston sang:

"Push up, every morning…Ten times!"

"Push up, starting low,

"Once more on the rise, nuts to the flabby guys…

"Go, you chicken fat, go away. Go, you chicken fat, go…"

Body-shamed by his own TV? This was truly humiliating. Marty found the remote, clicked off the television, and rose from his bed to stretch. He had to admit, Kiley had him dead to rights: he was avoiding a workout. Every other time he'd committed to an exercise regimen in recent months, a work issue had intervened. He had to get to the office early for a meeting. He was wanted on a Zoom call with Asia or Europe. He needed to write a speech for Walker, track down a reporter to correct a story that ran overnight, or meet someone for breakfast. Now, with nothing on his schedule but white space as far as the eye could see, there were no excuses. It was time to get in the best condition *of his life!*

He picked off the heaps of clothing hanging on the Peloton in the corner of his bedroom and tossed them onto the bed. He tapped the Peloton tablet to look up the live class schedule and found one coming up a mere forty-five minutes from then. *Perfect!* He changed into his gym shorts and a t-shirt and stretched by the floor-to-ceiling window, bending this way and that as he looked out at the traffic on Columbus Avenue and the people scurrying to work, many of them carrying coffee or paper bags with something to eat.

And now that he thought about it, wasn't that exactly what was missing from this new routine? Nourishment? How could he complete a rigorous Peloton class without something in his system? Why, he could get dizzy and fall off his bike, cracking his head open! Worse, with the blood thinners he was on, Marty could bleed to death on the fresh white carpet! Nobody would find him for days or weeks until neighbors noticed a smell and… *That does it.* For health reasons, he needed a breakfast sandwich to awaken his body and prepare it for the rigors—if not the complete shock—of a workout.

He grabbed his wallet and phone and headed to the elevators, listening to the news on 1010 WINS through his AirPods. *"Our top stories at this hour: Local residents up in arms today as the city council votes to put a prison on Park Avenue and 63rd Street as part of its plan to distribute criminals equitably throughout the five boroughs. Speaking of criminals: Manhattan's prosecutor announced today he will offer cash to lawbreakers for the inconvenience of being arrested. And, the United Nations called for a global Climate Lockdown today as it warned in a report that the Earth's temperature will rise three-point-two degrees centigrade by 2100 if nations fail to agree to a plan to address climate change. Now for today's weather on the ones. Well, Jamie, that's a bit harder to predict. The forecast calls for a high in the range of seventy-two to seventy-nine degrees, or maybe eighty, depending..."*

Marty headed out of his building for a short walk to his neighborhood's new outpost of Café Che, a franchise of the downtown shop known to locals as "Commie Coffee." Café Che's capitalist model was doing so well that it was now exporting its revolution throughout Manhattan, one soy latte at a time. Marty carefully stepped over a zonked addict sprawled out on the sidewalk on Broadway, eyes staring up into space, and entered the shop, which was busy with a crush of students, Lincoln Center artists and performers, and retail workers from nearby shops getting their own morning fix.

Marty was greeted by a chipper barista with a name badge that read Becky. *"Viva la revolucion,"* she said, cheerfully. "May I take your order?"

Marty scratched his chin as he looked up at the menu board. "So," he said, "tell me about the Bay of Pigs Breakfast Bagel."

"Oh, that's wonderful. It's egg, cheese, and Possibly Pork on an onion bagel, with a chimichurri schmear."

"And 'Possibly Pork' is... what exactly?"

"A pork-like product."

"I see. Pork-like. What does that mean?"

Becky moved in for the sale. "It has all the taste of pork, but there's no meat. It's, like, totally vegan."

Marty was intrigued. "What do they use instead of meat?" he asked.

"I think it's just, you know... fats and salts."

Marty asked, "Anything else?"

"I'm not sure." She looked over to a young man mopping the floor behind the counter. "Dayquan, do you know what's in Possibly Pork?"

"I think it's like, fibers or something?" Dayquan said, wringing his mop. "Might be, like, recycled shit."

Becky smiled through her bafflement. "Whatever it is, it's really yummy. You should try it."

Marty nodded. "Well, okay. Give me one of those and a regular Guerilla Grind coffee."

"Sure thing," she said cheerfully. "Would you like to buy a Café Che t-shirt or red star beret? A Hero of the Soviet Union coffee mug? We have a Grand Opening special with all socialist merchandise twenty percent off."

Marty thought over the offer. "Shouldn't it be free?"

She frowned. "Someday, maybe, when we have a better world. Just not today. Would you like to round up your purchase to donate to the Planetistas?"

"*Nyet.*"

"Okay, then. That's twelve-fifty-seven. Just tap your phone there and... name?"

"Fidel."

"Okay, Fidel. Your order will be right up."

Marty took a seat by the windows overlooking a vest-pocket park and glanced at a discarded copy of the *New York Times*. The top story said that experts reported that climate change was causing disparate impacts among migrants pouring over the country's porous southern border, forcing them to wade through even deeper water to reach Texas. The Fenwick Administration wanted to rush life preservers to the Rio Grande but was having difficulty sourcing preservers that didn't contain petroleum-based materials.

"Fidel!"

Marty picked up his order, bit eagerly into his sandwich, and... yuck! *This is a worse disaster than the Bay of Pigs. It isn't even plausibly pork. It's not even possibly food.* He set down the sandwich, rinsed his mouth with coffee, and picked up his phone to read the *New York Post*. He skipped past today's photo of Cardi B and was quickly engaged in a story detailing the never-told-before beauty secrets of Megan Thee Stallion, whom he thought looked nothing like a horse, when his phone buzzed with a text from Digby Pierrepont.

Digby

Today 9:25 AM

Hey, Marty. Hope you're doing well. Want to check
your interest in something we have going on here. It's
rather urgent, so please call me as soon as you can.

Marty hit the callback number and was pleased to hear Digby answer on the first ring. After an exchange of comments about how good it was to reconnect again, Digby asked, "Tell me, Marty. How are things going with you and Walker?"

Marty paused. Should he admit he was fired? Or should he wait? "To be completely honest with you, Digby, we're not seeing eye-to-eye on certain things."

"That's not exactly hard to believe."

"Right? We got into it yesterday over some of those crazy little details he focuses on. Like whose name goes on press releases. You remember how persnickety he can get."

"Maybe it's a good thing I called," Digby said. "Would it be absurd for us to ask you to think about working with us at Crowe Power again? I know you've got a great gig at Staminum and your life here was somewhat, shall we say... tumultuous?"

"A better word might be farcical," Marty said. "You were a witness to the daily beat-downs. Happily, I can finally report that with the passage of time and an intensive gin therapy program administered by Dr. Hendrick's, I've been able to reintegrate into the world without unduly drooling."

Digby laughed. "Sounds like you're ready to come back."

"Let's not get carried away," Marty said.

"Could you at least have a conversation about it? Maybe find an hour to steal away today?"

"Today? Gosh, I don't know right off the top of my head," he said with a heavy sigh. "Let me have a look at my calendar." Marty paused and glanced around him, picking a fleck of egg off his gym shorts, stuffing his preposterous pork into an empty coffee cup, and idly craning his neck to see who was walking through Dante Park. "Let's see... looks like I've got time to see you late this afternoon."

"Actually, it's not me. It's Lindsey who would like to see you."

Marty's heart fell. Could he really stand to deal with another entitled member of the Crowe family? He'd had more than his fill with Robbie. Now another wealthy dilletante? "Does this job report to her?"

"Yes, which should tell you something about its importance. This is a very big deal."

"I don't know, Digs." Was it possible Lindsey would have any idea what she was doing as chairperson of Crowe Power?

"Look," Digby said, "if this is any help at all, Marty, she's a far cry from Robbie."

"I figured as much."

"Why is that?"

Marty said, "She dumped his sorry ass, which speaks to some level of intelligence."

"Well, now she needs a little of that Marty magic. Can you see her?"

"I can."

"Great," Digby replied. "She's out of the office right now, but she'll be back at four. Can you come in then?"

"Yes, I can." Marty hung up and reconsidered his original plan for the day. Alas, now he'd have to go home, pretty up, and head downtown. The Peloton would have to wait yet again. Not that Kiley would understand.

13. ALL CHUCKED UP

Lindsey found Uncle Chuck, the *eminence grise* of the Crowe family, at his posh multi-story apartment on Park Avenue. He looked fresh from the golf course, wearing a white sport shirt with a club crest on the breast, perma-pressed gray gabardine slacks, and black Gucci horsebit loafers. At eighty-five, he had been reduced to playing fourteen holes from the closest tees, but he still managed to get out three times a week.

"It's the only goddamn place I can smoke anymore," he grumbled, as he ushered Lindsey through the foyer. "Sylvia won't let me light up in the house. And God knows there's no place they let you take a puff in public. Marijuana's okay, but good old-fashioned American tobacco isn't?" He shook his head sadly. What a world. "You ever play Pine Valley, Lindsey?"

She shook her head. "Sorry, Uncle Chuck. I don't golf."

"I don't either," he said, dismissing the notion with a wave. "But that doesn't stop me from playing. Or from investing a fortune in a game at which I pretty much suck."

He led her down a long gallery of priceless modern art to his study, a windowless library lined with black walnut shelves stacked with books on war and business, endeavors he found strikingly similar. He smoothed his thinning silver hair across the top of his freckled head and motioned for Lindsey to take one of the caramel leather Paris club chairs. She took her place on the other side of an antique side table topped with a vintage Wisteria lamp from Tiffany Studios. A long-faced woman from a Modigliani painting stared dolefully at

Lindsey from across the room, almost as if she sensed Lindsey had a serious problem and empathized with her.

"I'm sorry to bother you, Uncle Chuck," Lindsey said.

"Well, let's see," he said, looking at his watch. "Two-thirty. I think all I'm missing is *Let's Make a Deal*."

Lindsey smiled. "Sorry about that."

"Don't be," he said.

"Thank you," she said. "I want to get your advice on something."

Chuck pulled a Winston Light from a sterling silver cigarette case bearing his monogram and lit it with a lighter he kept stashed in a drawer of the table between them. "If Sylvia comes in here, I'm handing this to you, okay? Can you fake it?"

"I've had lots of practice," she said.

"Alright," he said. "Tell me what's going on."

Lindsey explained the barrage of criticism she was getting from the White House, the news media, protesters, and now, investors. She read Chuck excerpts of the letter from Harold Crenshaw and conceded that many of his points were incontestable: Crowe Power had almost nothing to show for its efforts to develop green energy, and that was a threat to the company's survival. "It's not that we haven't tried. As I've told the board, I know a transition to green energy is inevitable, given the increasing animosity toward fossil fuels. It's just that our efforts are blocked at every turn."

Chuck sat forward with his chin resting on his fist, much like the man in *The Thinker*, the bronze statuette by Auguste Rodin, a miniature of which rested on the table behind him. At last, he looked up. "Perhaps all these attacks aren't a coincidence."

Lindsey leaned forward. "What do you mean?"

"Have you considered the possibility that Hacksaw Harry is behind the opposition to your green projects? And that he, in turn, is ginning up all these protests charging that we're not green enough?"

Her eyes widened. "I hadn't thought of that."

"It seems to me the two go hand in hand," Chuck said, blowing a stream of smoke away from her. "I wouldn't be surprised if he lobbied the White House to kill our pipeline, too. In all these instances you've mentioned, you have to think of who stands to gain if we lose."

"I think you just said it was Hacksaw Harry."

"He may just be the front man."

Lindsey blanched. "For whom?"

A sudden knock on the study door panicked Chuck. "Oh shit." He handed his cigarette to Lindsey. "Hold this." She took it and held it awkwardly. Then he called. "Yes?"

A servant entered with a sheepish look on his face. "*Señor Crowe.* You want?"

Chuck snatched his cigarette back from Lindsey and cupped it in his hand. With a limited vocabulary in any language other than English, Chuck responded with a muddled combination of English, French, and Spanish. "*Si,* José. I do want. Uh, *je voudrais un scotch.*"

José blinked rapidly. "Voo-dray?"

"No. I don't want voo-dray. I want scotch. *Scotch!*" He shook his head and muttered to Lindsey, "This may be hopeless. Maurice is on vacation and Jose and I aren't quite on the same page. Would you like something to drink? I'm not promising results."

Lindsey wanted to get back to the conversation. "Nothing, thanks."

"Oh, c'mon," Chuck said.

"Okay. How about an iced tea?"

"I'll give it a shot," Chuck said, speaking in a deliberate cadence as if he were addressing an Alexa, or a small child. "José. *Elle voudrait un té froid.*"

José's eyes fluttered. "*Qué?*"

Chuck said, much louder, as if the issue was Jose's hearing, "*UN TÉ FROID.*"

José shook his head and appeared to break a sweat. "*Perdón, señor Crowe. No entiendo.*"

"Sorry, Linz," Chuck grumbled. "I guess we're out of that."

"I'll take water."

"*Agua, por favor.*" José nodded and skedaddled as Chuck stubbed out his cigarette and leaned back in his chair, settling into the cushions. "So, let's think about this," he said, pushing his fingertips together. "What does Hacksaw Harry want from you—apart from what he says in his letter? I doubt he gives two shits whether we're green enough. That guy's a vulture capitalist from way back. And up until now, he hasn't cared who knows it. That's why his company's called Carrion. So, we have to ask ourselves: what's he really after?"

Lindsey sat up straight, all her senses on alert. "I assume he wants control of the company so that he can drive up our share price and sell out."

"How would he manage to do that?"

"Break up the company and sell off the pieces."

Chuck nodded. "Right. And who would benefit?"

"His investors, of course."

"Okay," Chuck said, rolling his hand. "Who else?"

Lindsey shook her head. "I'm not following you, Uncle Chuck."

"Think of our competitors' footprints," he said. "Who would like nothing more than to get control of our refineries in the Eastern United States and in Europe to complement their networks in the Western U.S. and Asia?"

She fell back in her chair and sighed. Why hadn't she seen this coming? "Staminum."

"And who would want to block our pipeline so that they get a monopoly on the major pipelines from Canada?"

She rolled her eyes. "Staminum."

"And who would want our power plants all over the world?"

She gently slapped her forehead. "Of course. Staminum."

"Not to put too fine a point on it, Lindsey, but who's got a bug up his ass about Crowe Power because your ex-husband drove him out even though he was doing a great job? The same guy who'd like nothing more than to take back control of our company on his terms—and kick our family to the curb."

Lindsey put her elbow on the armrest and dropped her forehead into her hand. "Walker B. Hope," she said, sullenly.

"From what I read in the *Journal* today, he's building up a cash hoard," Chuck said. "It's not a stretch to figure that Hacksaw Harry wants to cut into Crowe Power so he can carve Walker Hope a slice or two."

Lindsey laid her head back on the headrest and looked up to the intricate laurel moldings along the ceiling, her eyes darting from side to side as she thought this through. "It's so obvious. Why didn't I see it?"

Chuck leaned over and patted her knee consolingly. "Because you haven't been around as long as I have. This isn't my first rodeo, you know. Do you have any idea how many times people have made a run at our company?"

Chuck recalled the bid by a power company from the South in the 1960s that had been thwarted by the Department of Justice with a push from the Crowe lobbyists throwing money all over the capital. He told her of the coup attempted in the 1980s by Crowe Power President Adam Oakley, who had commissioned a private study by a renowned investment bank to wrest control away from the family and make himself chairman. Fortunately for the Crowes, Oakley approached the wrong banker—a drinking buddy of Chuck's brother Les with whom Les was tight. Les fired Oakley before the study was stapled together, bought the bank's files, and burned them. And when oil prices collapsed in the 1990s, Crowe Power's financial situation grew so dire that it went so far as to draw up bankruptcy papers. The company was twenty-four hours from filing Chapter 11 when the family collateralized personal assets to secure a last-ditch line of credit. Oil prices revived not long afterward, as did the company stock, and Crowe Power was saved from the executioner.

Chuck said, "I'm sure a Staminum acquisition of Crowe Power assets would thrill Steady Stamper and his family. We've beaten them like a rented mule for the better part of a century. Now that they're getting competitive again under Walker, it's no surprise they're coming after us."

Lindsey reminded Uncle Chuck that she'd deflected Walker's earlier interest in taking over Crowe Power by promising that she would beat him to the punch—and bid for Staminum instead. But there was no chance of that now. The company stock was too weak to use as equity, her cash was needed for operations, the company's lines of credit were nearly exhausted, and all the big banks were under increasing pressure from regulators to avoid lending to oil and gas firms.

Chuck settled back in his chair. "It looks to me like they've executed their strategy perfectly—so far. Our low share price is a consequence of Hacksaw Harry's campaign against you. Now they're moving in for the kill."

As Lindsey settled back in her seat to contemplate the situation, José returned, placing a scotch on a silver coaster next to Chuck and a glass of water next to Lindsey. As he turned to leave, Chuck called after him. "José, *ferme la porte.*"

José, baffled, turned back to Chuck. *"Qué?"*

"Shut-o the goddamn *door-o!"* he blurted, impatiently, and pointed to the door.

José caught the drift and hurriedly closed the door behind him. Chuck watched him go, then lit another cigarette and exhaled two streams of smoke through his patrician nose. Lindsey took a sip from her glass and practically spit. "This is *vodka.*"

Chuck laughed a big phlegmy laugh. "Oh, shit. I forgot to warn you about that. José used to work for Maggie Clayton before she died. Remember her? Maggie started drinking every day right after breakfast, but always called it her 'water' so nobody knew for sure what she was drinking. At least until she passed out. Then they kind of figured it out." He chuckled. "Sorry about that."

"Not that I couldn't use a drink," she said, setting the glass aside, "but I can't afford to pass out right now." Lindsey looked at her watch, then leaned close and spoke in a near whisper. "With all this going on, I'm hoping you can help me hold the family voting bloc together. I expect this will be a rough go. Hacksaw Harry has built this new clean image for himself, but by all accounts, he still plays dirty. If he goes public with his complaint, he'll have the media and the institutional investors on his side and the pressure will be intense. The family may be my last line of defense. If they don't back me, we could lose the company."

Chuck leaned over and patted her knee to console her. "In the end, the family always sticks together."

"I'm not so sure this time," she said, wringing her hands. "You've heard about Missy?"

He shrugged. "If I'm not mistaken, she doesn't have a vote yet."

"No, not until she turns twenty-five. But she can influence others in that generation. I don't know any of them who are proud of our company. They think we're evil. And then, of course, you have Robbie."

He nodded, grimly. "Right. Robbie…"

"He's the wild card. He blames me for losing his job. I'm sure he would love nothing more than to humiliate me in some fashion."

"Let's do the math here," he said. He added her twenty percent of the family votes to his fifteen percent, the twelve percent share owned by Bits and Digby, and Aunt Lizzie's seventeen percent. "She backed you for the job, so I expect she's a lock." He ticked through the other votes, which Lindsey counted in her head.

"That's ninety percent of the family bloc," Lindsey said. "I may need Robbie's chunk, too. God help us if he has the deciding vote."

Chuck pulled on his cigarette and nodded. "I'll talk to him."

"Would you do that?" She fought back a tear, leaned over, and patted his hand. "Oh, thank you, Uncle Chuck. He might listen to you. He surely won't listen to me."

Chuck shrugged. "I'm not sure he listens to anybody, but I'll give it a shot." Chuck looked affectionately at Lindsey. "I have all the confidence in the world in you, Lindsey. You're the best thing to happen to this family since Homer rolled out his original dynamo. If you hadn't taken over when you did, we'd already be finished."

She took a deep breath, trying to calm herself. "I'm doing what I can. Wish I thought for sure it was enough."

"One word of advice: try to keep ol' Hacksaw from going public with this. Once it's out, it's Katy, bar the door, and he'll come at you from all angles. The Crowes don't like to litigate publicly. We're not common. And thank God, neither is our stock. Preferred shares in CRO may once again be our saving grace."

Lindsey smiled, grateful for the support. "Thank you, Uncle Chuck. You don't know what this means to me."

"You manage Hacksaw Harry. I'll manage Robbie," he said, taking a pull on his cigarette. "As long as I'm on the green side of the fairway, we'll be fine."

14. BLUNT ASSESSMENT

In the basement of the Crowe Power Company headquarters, the last loyal soldier from Robbie Crowe's toppled regime was holed up in a janitor's closet, sniffing solvent glue he had pulled from the supply shelf, when his phone vibrated in his pocket. Howard J. Doolin, known to associates as Howie-Do-It, saw Robbie's name pop up on his screen just as the glue hit him with a euphoric high, followed immediately by a disturbing hallucination. The closet was suddenly teaming with mice. Hundreds of them! Crawling all over the floor and the walls! He bolted from the closet, stumbled into the hallway, and slammed the door behind him. *Fucking A! That was weird…*

"Dude," Howie said breathlessly into the phone. "Wassup?"

"You alright?" Robbie asked.

"Yeah. It's just… vermin, man. This place is, like, infested."

"I'm not surprised in the least," Robbie said. "Everybody tells me the company's gone to hell since I left."

"So true."

"Well, I'm glad the Orkin man hasn't exterminated you. I need your help on something."

In previous years, Robbie had sent his trusty henchman on myriad black ops missions. Howie had bugged and placed cameras in the office of former Crowe Power CEO, Walker B. Hope. He had spied on and attempted to intimidate a dissident shareholder who was waging a Twitter war against Robbie's poor leadership of the company during his tenure as chairman. He had hacked into the computers of Robbie's critics and shared their personal information on the web. And he had delivered numerous checks to people whom

Robbie wanted to either speak up or shut up. That this thickly muscled, buzz-cut thug was still employed at Crowe was a testament to the justifiable fear that firing him could lead to violence. The company's safest option was to keep him in the basement with minimal responsibilities and far, far away from the C-suite.

"Lindsey's up to something," Robbie said, "and I need to find out what it is."

"Whoa," Howie said as he headed back to his cubicle in a dark corner of the basement.

"Did you think of, like, asking her?"

"Oh, hell no. She hates me," Robbie said. "I have no idea why that is. You know I was nothing but good to her for so long…" Robbie choked up as he recalled how she'd coldly dumped him —*for practically no reason!*—then rallied the family to take away the job that rightfully belonged to him. *Oh, the injustice of it all!* "I'm the one who should be pissed, right? She screwed me royally."

"Absolutely," Howie assured him with a growl. "You want me to take her out?"

Robbie was alarmed. "On a *date?*"

"No," Howie said, then in a lowered voice, *"out."*

Robbie sighed. "No, no, no. Nothing like that."

Howie was itching for a scrape of some kind. He hadn't assaulted anybody in months. "Has she got a new boyfriend? I can straighten him out."

"I have no idea," Robbie said. "But if you hear anything like that, let me know. I'll kick his ass myself."

"Oh, man! I'd *pay* to see that, boss."

"Yeah? Well, it would be worth it, let me tell you," Robbie said. "I want you to look into something else. Remember when I was chairman and I bought Greeneron and all of those incredible energy technologies?"

Howie hesitated. Everything beyond last week was a bit hazy. "Kinda."

"They're down to just one technology in that portfolio. I need to know which one. Do you think you could find out?"

"What's the dope?"

"It has something to do with clean energy."

"That sounds kinda cool."

"Yes, it is, but they want to take credit for my vision!"

"That's definitely *not* cool," Howie protested.

"It wasn't enough for her to take my job, my house, my family. She wants more. She wants to take my greatest contribution to Crowe Power—and, for that matter, to the world—and say it belongs to her. Well, whatever that is, it's grand larceny! I set it all up, but everyone will think it's her. What kind of bullshit is that?"

"Can't let that happen, boss," Howie said. "I'm on it."

***

It never took much to wheedle information out of the guys in the Building Department, but it made things quicker when Howie offered a little inducement—in this case, a special blend of his Weed o' the Week. As the in-house marijuana dealer for the Crowe Power Company building and custodial staffs, he liked to keep the market stimulated by offering variety, usually with a dab of creative flair. So today he mixed in Blue Dream, in honor of the Crowe Power Company's Broad Street Blue color, and Green Crack, since this mission was all about Earth-friendly energy, and headed for the break area near the boiler room.

"Yo," Howie said, as Hector, Santos, and Merle drank coffee, chatted, and played cards. Luis stood by a vent, blowing cigarette smoke up between the metal slats. "I come bearing gifts."

The men met this welcome news with exclamations of "alright!" and "about damn time!" Howie looked over his shoulder before laying a couple of blunts on the plywood table. "Papa's got a brand new buzz, boys. And this one's on the house. Let me know what you think."

With a shuffling of folding chairs, the building crew headed for the vent to fire up Howie's latest masterpiece. Sucking in the smoke, Santos closed his eyes, his mouth forming an 'O,' and passed it on to Merle. "That's some fuckin' good shit there, brother," Santos declared as he exhaled a skunky gray plume up the vent. "I don't care what they say: you still da man."

After they passed the joints around twice, Howie made his ask: The company was working on a new energy project aside from the usual refineries, pipelines, and power plants. Had they heard of anything?

Luis said, "We got a crew out in Jersey City doin' some painting. Chairlady Crowe gonna pay a visit today so they had to clean it up a bit, you know?"

"I was over there yesterday, man," Santos said, taking another hit. "They got some crazy shit goin' on. It's on some back street behind the Statue of Liberty."

Howie moved in and took a hit of a joint, then blew smoke up into the vent. "Tell me about it."

"They got this machine? Looks like some big fucking pressure cooker or something." Santos said. "Dude was tellin' me they heat up this shit to, like, a hundred million degrees Excelsior."

"You mean… Celsius?"

"Yeah! That's it."

Everyone else in the group laughed. "Oh, right!" said Luis. "A hundred million degrees! Take that blunt away from him! Dude is *way* too high."

Santos shook his head. "I'm tellin' you man, this shit's for real."

Howie regarded him skeptically. "A hundred million degrees?"

"They said it was, like, way hotter than the sun. For real! They call it fusion, or somethin' like that. And they were sayin' it could power the whole fuckin' world, man."

Luis, starting to weave a bit, was impressed by the cosmic possibilities. "That is fucking *awesome.*"

Santos scoffed. "Yeah. As long as it don't blow up. Know what I'm sayin'?"

Howie asked Santos, "So what were you doing out there?"

"Bro, they needed some part for an exhaust system they were making. They said this machine gives off, like, helium gas. They didn't want it spillin' in the room. I guess that would make everyone talk like fuckin' chipmunks, right?"

"No way!" Luis said, laughing. "You mean, like, *Alvin?* The cartoon?"

"Exactly!"

Oh, man! This was wild! Howie struggled to keep all the details straight, but he had a general sense of things. This must be what Robbie was looking for. He was going to freak the fuck out!

15. RETURN TO SPLENDOR

Marty peered through the glass door of the corner suite on the top floor of the Crowe Power Company to see a familiar sight: the smiling, matronly assistant, Winnie, craning her head to see who was coming. Recognizing Marty from his previous tour of duty, she reached under her desk for a button, which buzzed the lock, clicked open the door, and set off a Pavlovian alarm bell in Marty's brain as his encounters with the volcanic former chairman, Robbie Crowe, came rushing back.

Straight ahead, he could see the doorway where Robbie had flung a *Fortune* magazine at him because of its cover story praising Crowe's former Chief Executive Officer, Walker B. Hope, as the best CEO in America and dismissing Robbie as a feckless dilletante. Beyond that was the inner sanctum where a few of Robbie's balled-up speeches had been aimed at Marty's head or his retreating back, and the ornate antique desk where Robbie would slump behind mountains of paperwork he never touched, bemoaning his heavy workload and lack of support. How many times had Robbie threatened to fire Marty and everyone else in his organization? Robbie's lackluster reputation was never the fault of his own laziness, questionable judgment, or reckless behavior, but always to the underlings who failed their overling.

It was quickly apparent to Marty that neither trauma nor drama was in the offing today. The vibe was decidedly calmer and more businesslike, starting with Winnie's warm, "Welcome back," as if he were returning to a favorite seaside resort rather than a torture chamber. He was cheerfully ushered into Lindsey's office, where he was met with a kind smile from the new Crowe Power chair. With a bearing that projected a surprising degree of authority, Lindsey led him to the casual sitting area away from her desk and offered him coffee from a serving set.

"I imagine you've spent a fair amount of time in this office," she said.

"Home of my greatest hits," Marty replied, "most of them upside my head."

Lindsey laughed. "All of us who dwelled in Robbie's inner circle probably suffer from at least a mild case of PTSD."

Marty wondered what the Immersive Robbie Crowe Experience had been like for her. Had she suffered the same bullying and temper tantrums? Or was Robbie indifferent, which could be just as emotionally devastating for a spouse? Everything Marty had seen in his years of working with him suggested his chief interest in his relationship with Lindsey was to stay married to avoid the financial and professional calamity that would be triggered by divorce. Seeing her now, so attractive and personable, Marty couldn't understand why he had treated her so dismissively and disrespectfully. But then again, he was Robbie, which explained everything.

Lindsey folded her hands on her lap and sat up straight in her chair. She asked, "Do you remember the last time we met?"

"If I'm not mistaken, it was at an event at your home in the Hamptons."

"Robbie and I hosted a fundraiser to build community support for BlowCo's offshore wind power project," she said, stirring her tea as well as her memory. "We invited a hundred friends and neighbors but only eight people showed up."

"Parking was easy, as I recall, once you got past the protesters out front."

"Everyone we knew was incredibly enthusiastic about wind power, at least when we talked about it casually at cocktail parties and they had no real skin in the game. But when they learned they might see turbines from their verandas, that was the end of that." She picked up her tea and sipped. "They called their lawyers in from Manhattan and invented all kinds of excuses why a wind farm couldn't possibly work. There would be diesel fumes, hazardous chemicals, noise, fires—everything but a tsunami. You'd think we were proposing a toxic waste dump next to the duck pond. The whole thing was a debacle that left me questioning their sincerity."

"As Kermit proved."

"It's not easy being green?"

"Yes," Marty, replied, "but he also proved it's easy to sing about it."

She put down her cup and leaned closer. "You wrote the speech Robbie gave that evening. You made a very compelling argument for wind power."

"Oh yeah. That was a doozy," he said. "I almost believed it myself."

"It left an impression on me," Lindsey said. "I need to make a strong case for a different kind of green power, but with one critical difference this time."

"You have to persuade."

"I have to *win,*" she said sharply. Then, "So tell me: how are things for you at Staminum? Are you happy there?"

There was something so disarming about her direct approach that caused Marty to reject his natural impulse to offer Bullshit Answer No. 62. Under normal circumstances, he would moan about how difficult it would be to leave Staminum during their time of need, and that he really loved his job, and that it would have to be just the right situation to cause him to leave, and... *Aw, fuck it.* "I was fired yesterday," he blurted.

Lindsey pulled back in surprise. "You—*what?*"

"Surprised me, too," Marty conceded. "Walker needs to show more diversity in his leadership team, which I admit is probably overdue. Not sure why it landed on me, or why he decided to punish my replacement by giving her the job, but there it is. I'm unemployed, as of today. By the looks of things, diversity doesn't appear to be an issue here."

Lindsey shook her head. "Oh, no. Not at all. We have diversity coming out the wazoo." She paused and looked away a moment. "Are we allowed to say 'wazoo' in an office?"

Marty shrugged. "You may want to ask HR. I'm not even sure what a wazoo is."

Lindsey said, "Come to think it, I don't either."

Marty rubbed his chin. "It could be like a... a ying-yang?"

"Not sure what that is, either."

"I could Google it."

"Forget it," Lindsey said, waving it off. "I never was very good at anatomy. Or slang. But I do know diversity is not an issue with us. One of our board members said our management team looks like a brunch table at Balthazar."

Marty laughed. "Maybe you need a man on your team."

She offered a mock frown. "Let's not get carried away."

"Fair enough."

"What I do need are certain skills that my team doesn't possess. Do you still want to work? You're not retiring or anything?"

"Oh no," Marty said. "I figure I've got a good ten years ahead of me. Then maybe three or four crappy ones after that, followed by a rapid decline before I start swirling the drain. So yes, consider me interested and available—sooner rather than later."

Lindsey went on to explain about Harold Crenshaw trying to take over the company, possibly to benefit Walker Hope and Staminum Energy. While the Crowe family's stock accounted for a great number of shareholder votes, there were two issues that troubled her. One was that the family stock trust was up for renewal, and it was far from assured that every member of the family would support it—especially Robbie and the younger generations.

"I saw the story about your daughter protesting yesterday," Marty said. "Is it possible she would defect?"

"She's deeply resentful—of what, I'm not sure," Lindsey said, grimacing. "But it's a worry."

"What about Robbie?"

She inhaled deeply. "I'm not counting on his support. You know he thinks I stole his job. There's no doubt in my mind that he'd like to get even somehow."

"Even if it costs your family the company?"

"You know him well enough. He would sell Crowe Power to ISIS if it could somehow vindicate him."

Marty absorbed that. "What's your other concern?"

Lindsey explained that the big institutional investment funds that held Crowe Power stock, such as Spearhead Partners, Gemstone, and Fourth Street, were under increasing political and financial pressure to push the climate agenda, too. "We can't ask these funds to support us unless we at least give them cover," she said.

"So, let me see if I have this straight," Marty said, sitting back. "You believe that Hacksaw Harry and his investor pals are all pretending to be green so they can take control of your company?"

"Correct."

"So you have to pretend you're even greener to save it."

"More or less."

"So you need to tell a story."

She threw her head back and raised her arms. "A big, bold, beautiful green story."

"Do you have a story to tell?"

Lindsey finished her tea and dabbed her lip with a linen napkin. "We might." She told Marty that she was planning to visit Crowe Power's Consolidated Fusion offices the following day and that the subsidiary held at least some potential to revolutionize the energy business. "I hope there's enough there that we can stitch together into a defense of our business."

"And if you can't?"

"That's not an option. I could lose the company." She sighed and leaned back in her chair. "Can you imagine how I'd be viewed? A woman finally gets control of this company for the first time in its hundred years of history and immediately runs it into the ditch? That's not an outcome I can live with."

"So you're putting all your chips on fusion." Marty considered that as a strategy. "I'll admit I'm not a student of physics. In high school, I thought physics was spelled with an 'f', which not coincidentally was my grade."

"I'm less interested in your knowledge of science than your imagination, Marty. As I recall, you helped make Walker Hope into the most admired CEO in America. That took some creative storytelling."

"Walker tells me any idiot could have done that. But then, I don't regard myself as just *any* idiot."

Amused, she suggested, "You're a special idiot?"

He nodded. "I like to think so."

"So knowing all this," she said, "would you be comfortable taking a job here?"

"A job?" Marty said. "No. I've had enough corporate jobs for one lifetime. They always end in disappointment."

She sat back in her chair. "I'm certainly sorry you feel that way."

"I'm not talking about me," he said. "I'm talking about my bosses. I'm like the sand in their oyster shell. I make a pearl, eventually, but they get sick of the irritation. That said…"

"Yes?"

He leaned forward. "Why not make me a consultant? I'll be yours, full-time, available twenty-four-seven whenever and wherever you need me. I just won't keep office hours or fill out personnel evaluations or attend corporate re-education camps or any of that other crap. I'll charge you by the hour and you can give me a success fee if we beat the bastard."

"How much?"

"If I help you get Hacksaw Harry off your back, my bonus is two million dollars."

She nodded. "I hope to pay you that bonus. Come with me tomorrow to Consolidated Fusion and see what we have to work with. We'll pick you up at 10."

They both stood and shook hands. "I'll be there."

"Make me a pearl, Marty," she said. "But don't kill the oyster in the process."

16. BALL OF CON FUSION

Robbie, pacing in front of his office windows at the Crowe Institute for the Greater Good, slapped his forehead as Howie delivered what passed for an intelligence report. "Fusion! Of course!" Robbie said. "It's so *obvious*. I was on to that *years* ago. I'm sure I mentioned it in one of my speeches or something."

Howie earnestly offered his usual uncritical support. "You're always ahead of the curve, bro."

"I mean, fusion… it's… it's—" Robbie paused at the window and turned back to Howie. "How would you describe it exactly?"

"You're asking *me?*"

"Well, no," Robbie said. "Just testing you to see what kind of public awareness there might be out there. I'm thinking this might require work on my part to educate people. I mean, this is a bold vision for the future and not everybody is going to get it."

Howie searched through his memory bank, which was largely empty, except for the moment when he'd walked through the door. "I know it involves heat."

"Heat—right!" Robbie exclaimed. "Lots and lots of heat."

"Oh yeah," Howie said. "My boys say this big oven thing could, like, vaporize a pizza."

"No doubt," Robbie said. "What else?"

Howie stood up and slowly approached Robbie at the window. "It's nuclear" —*nuke-ya-ler*— "maybe."

Robbie shook his head, dripping with impatience. "Duh, Howie. Everyone knows that. It's called *nuclear* fusion, for Christ's sake."

Howie squinted, thinking. "I'm pretty sure it uses balloons."

"Balloons?"

"No, wait… not balloons—*helium* is part of the deal somehow. I guess everyone out there at the lab talks funny. Like chipmunks or something." Was that it? Howie couldn't remember exactly. It was all so confusing. *That weed was da bomb, man…*

"I've never heard that before, but okay," Robbie said. "Do you recall anything else?"

"They said it comes from plasma."

"Like what, a plasma TV?"

"I guess so. Maybe that's how you watch it, or something?"

Robbie addressed Howie as if he were an uncomprehending child. "Now, Howie. Think back. Do you know where they have this fusion lab?"

Howie looked out the window across the Hudson. Wasn't it over there someplace in Jersey? Somewhere near that marina across the way? That sparked a thought in Howie's diminished brain. "Dude," he said. "You need a fuckin' party boat."

Robbie said, "I'm trying to get some important information about my old company, Howie. Why are we talking about a party boat?"

"So we can party, man. Invite some chicks. You know."

Robbie despaired. Whatever drugs Howie was doing had damaged what little gray matter he had left. "Howie, please. Focus. Okay?"

"Yep, yep, yep," Howie muttered.

"You were going to tell me: where is Lindsey's fusion lab?"

Howie blinked slowly and nodded his head. "It's, uh…" *It was coming to him…*

"Well, where is it?"

Coming… coming. "It's, uh," Howie nodded out the window. "Oh! Damn! You know what? It's right over there, bro. Jersey fucking City!"

Robbie looked out the window. "Jersey City? Seriously?"

"That's what my fellas tell me. They were out there painting or something, getting ready for a visit from your ex."

"No *shit!* This must be a really big deal."

"Oh yeah," Howie said, making up for ignorance with enthusiasm. "Huge!"

Robbie paused, dwelling on the absurdity of this situation. It was patently unfair for Lindsey to get credit for Crowe Power's push into fusion. Without Robbie's incredible vision to drive the company into its bold green future, Crowe Power would have no plan other than plodding ahead with its fossil fuel business, waiting for the executioner's axe. And without his daring acquisition of Greeneron, fusion would never have been something they would even consider. The credit belonged to him, and him alone. Lindsey could not deny him his rightful glory.

Howie sidled up to him. "What are you thinking, boss?"

"I'm thinking she's crazy if she thinks she gets the credit for this. I thought of it first."

"Obviously," Howie said. "What do you want to do about it?"

Robbie turned to him. "What else? I'm going to take it back."

"You mean… just the fusion part?"

"Maybe," Robbie said, rubbing his hands together. "But if the only way I can get it is to take over the company again, then, damn it, that's what I'll have to do."

17. MIDTOWN FUNK

Walker's receipt of the preliminary earnings forecast had put him in an edgy mood. *Wasn't anybody in this company gonna do their dang job? This was not a good time to be within a three-foot radius of his simmering* temper, lest it boil over, but Shanelle Pruitt had no choice. The click of her red Louboutin heels on the terrazzo floor echoed off the walls of the corridor leading to Staminum Energy's Media Center as she struggled to keep up with Walker's long stride. They were headed toward the Employee Town Hall and Walker was clearly on a mission.

"How are you going to address the layoffs?" she asked.

Walker kept his focus straight ahead. "I'm not," he replied.

"You're not going to mention them?"

"That's all in the rear-view mirror, Shanelle."

"It's still very much on people's minds," she said.

Walker shrugged. "Then they need to get it off their minds, don't they? We're a business, sweetie."

Shanelle winced. *Sweetie? I'm not your damn sweetie.* "I know what we are."

Walker continued. "Then you know stuff happens. Anyone who's wobbly-kneed out there needs to grow up. Like now."

Shanelle, aggravated by his flippant responses, persisted. Wasn't it her job to help make sure he didn't look like an arrogant ass? "Walker, fifteen thousand people just went 'poof.' Here one day, gone the next. It's not like our employees didn't notice that the person next to them disappeared. You know what they're all wondering now?"

"I have no idea," Walker said.

"They wonder if they're next."

Walker laughed, bitterly. "Well, now. They will be if they don't get on with it, right?"

Shanelle thought of Marty, who would roll his eyes at such a remark, and then get fired. She struggled not to repeat his mistakes with Walker. This called for a more constructive level of tact. "Walker, I think it would be helpful to acknowledge the elephant in the room."

Walker stopped in the hall and looked down at Shanelle, who stood nearly a foot shorter. "This isn't about me hearin' from them. This is about *them* hearin' from *me*. Don't you think they want to know what's on *my* mind? Because that's what I'm goin' to focus on. And my biggest concern is that we're not hittin' our numbers. Not on costs. Not on revenues. Not on safety. Nothin'. That is the pachyderm on the premises, Shanelle. Me wringin' my hands at a Town Hall about folks who don't work here anymore isn't goin' to fix our performance." He pointed toward the auditorium. "They have to fix it, or they will be next. It's been almost a week. Time to stop feelin' all weepy about their lot in life and get back to work."

He began to walk again, and Shanelle followed. "I hear you, Walker. But I worry you're going to miss an opportunity to win hearts *and* minds."

He waved that off. "I'm more interested in profit and loss. I haven't missed a quarterly earnings report in ten years, and I'm not goin' to start now. We're at a critical point in this company's history, Shanelle. We have a chance to grow—significantly—but we can't do it unless our share price remains strong. We miss earnings, we miss our opportunity. That won't be good for Staminum, for me, for you, or anybody in this Town Hall. You understand?"

Shanelle avoided eye contact, lest her facial expression betray her disgust. She should have asked for another bag of money. *Where's Marty when I need a buffer? I don't know how much of this shithead I can take...*

Walker pushed hard through the heavy metal side door to the auditorium stage and Shanelle followed. They walked to the curtain, where a stagehand put a lavalier microphone on his shirt while they looked out at the people filing into their seats. With all the departures in recent days, there were lots of empty chairs behind the management team, which had dutifully filed into the first two rows to ensure that someone up front would enthusiastically applaud the boss.

"You're goin' to introduce me, right?" Walker asked.

Shanelle looked at him quizzically. "I wasn't planning on it."

"Then why are you here?" he asked, sharply.

"I'm doing what I always do." *Damn fool!* She pointed to a table at the side of the auditorium where the production crew sat with headsets in front of computer screens. "I sit with the production team directing the cameras and selecting people for the Q and A."

"No, no," he said. "I want you to sit on the stage with me." He turned to the stagehand. "Get a chair for her, will ya?"

Shanelle protested, "Walker, this is your show, not mine."

He pulled his cuffs from the end of his jacket sleeves and stretched his neck. "We have important goals for this company, Shanelle, includin' diversity, equity and inclusion. People need to see evidence we're makin' progress, even if the numbers don't prove it just yet."

She bristled, fixing Walker with her withering stare. "You think I'm some kind of trophy to hoist for the crowd? Is that what you're saying?"

He gathered himself and turned to her. "Let me ask you somethin', Shanelle." His eyes narrowed. "Did you see how Staminum stock jumped when I got hired? Huh? That's because Staminum had just picked up a shiny new trophy—me. And it was rewarded immediately by investors. That's the way the world works. I don't write these rules. I just play by 'em. And whether you like it or not, you play by them, too. You might like to think you're above it all somehow, but none of us are, not if we're lucky enough to still work here. Now, if you've got something to say, I suggest you keep it to yourself. I don't have time to argue this point. Are you joining me on stage?"

"I'll make the introduction," she said. "Then I have to go."

Walker sucked in his breath and bounded across the stage with his customary zeal, clapping his hands and grinning and waving to applause from the assembly, including the standing ovation in the first two rows. Shanelle tentatively stepped to the lectern and offered a brief introduction, then pointedly walked off-stage, casting an icy stare at Walker as she left.

True to his word, Walker focused his remarks entirely on the need to meet the company's performance metrics. The energy business was consolidating rapidly, Walker said, and staying strong and united through a common sense of purpose was the only way Staminum could control its destiny. And wasn't that the best job security any of them could have?

"Okay," Walker said. "Let's get to your questions."

He opened by pointing to pre-approved questioners tossing softballs that he could easily smack out of the park. What do you see as our greatest asset? (*Our people!*) Can you talk about our progress in diversity, equity, and inclusion? (*We're workin' on it every day!*) What's the key to reaching our goals? (*Teamwork!*)

"Sis, boom, bah," Shanelle muttered into her headset. This was not what people wanted to hear from their leader, regardless of what Walker thought. She told the director. "Cue that guy in Texas."

The director said, "I thought you said we should avoid him."

"Yeah, well," Shanelle growled. "I changed my mind."

"Alright," Walker said, looking to the director, who pointed to a monitor. "I guess we're callin' on, uh, Jorge! Jorge down in Corpus Christi. Jorge, what's on your mind today, my friend?"

Jorge Suarez, a foreman at Staminum Energy's refinery, faced the camera and said, "I hope you don't consider this out of line, Mr. Hope. But I'm just wondering how you lay off fifteen thousand workers and say we're all about people."

Walker shot an angry look toward Shanelle, who stared right back at him. He stepped to the front of the stage and looked over the heads of his designated clappers to the cameras in the back of the auditorium. "Oh, Jorge, I'm *sooo* glad you asked that," Walker said, almost as if he meant it. "Let me just take just a minute to say I appreciate how difficult it was to bid farewell to so many very fine people this week." Walker glanced to Shanelle. "I know it's very much on people's minds. We all hurt for them. These were our colleagues and friends, and I just want to wish them all the best in their future endeavors, whatever they may be. Of course, they can't hear me right now, but still… if you see any of 'em, that's the message here—and you can say you heard it from me: *I care.* They are on my mind, and they are also right here." He tapped his chest, where a heart should have been located. He then looked down for a moment, as if in silent prayer, mourning, or perhaps suppressing a burp. He stepped to the front of the stage and clapped his hands.

"Alrighty then. That's behind us now, so let's all start thinkin' about what kind of future we're goin' to have together. I hope that everyone in this room, and everybody listenin' all over the world, understands that the continued success of our company is the best job security in the world. Staminum Energy is changin' in profound ways to meet the challenges of our industry. And the money we are savin' through these personnel adjustments will help power our growth for a bright future ahead. That's good for all of us. You. Me. The guy in the control booth back there. Everybody—includin' our many people of color, who, I'm proud to say, now comprise twenty-two percent of our workforce, bigger than ever before!"

Jorge cut in. "I don't understand, Mr. Hope. We've had a hiring freeze for more than a year."

Walker spoke more slowly. "I hear ya, Jorge. But, see, the vast majority of people who were separated from our company happened to be males of a, shall we say, pale persuasion."

"So… you didn't hire no more people of color?"

"No."

Jorge said, "You just fired more people who didn't have no color?"

Walker, indulging this impertinent dumbass, nodded. "That's one way to look at it, Jorge. Think of it as diversity addition by subtraction."

"That doesn't help me run the plant. I—"

Shanelle knew she had taken this exchange as far as she could. She cut Jorge's mic and signaled to Walker to wrap it up. He drew the meeting to a close by offering an email address for further company questions with a jolly hand-wave. "So long, Stamini! See you next quarter!"

Exiting the stage, he hustled down the steps to the auditorium floor to find Shanelle, who was taking off her headset at the production table. "Walk with me," he commanded. She followed him out a side door to an empty corridor and headed toward the elevators.

"Now, Shanelle. I know this is early days for you. But why did you let that Jorge nincompoop hijack my meetin'?"

Shanelle looked at him blankly. "You said you valued diversity of people and diversity of opinion, Walker. I thought you would want to hear questions from someone out in the field."

"Those weren't questions. That was an interrogation—and a deeply disrespectful one."

"If that's what people are thinking, don't we have to deal with it sooner or later? To me, it makes sense if we get it on the table, deal with it, and move on."

Walker spoke sharply. "I expect better from you, Shanelle," he said, putting his arm around her shoulders.

Shanelle shook her shoulders and spoke to him sharply. "Please take your hand off me."

Walker dropped his arm and stopped in his tracks, while Shanelle kept walking. She didn't look back.

18. MISSY THE MARK

For one of the few times in her life, Missy had garnered public recognition for her own initiative and point of view, rather than from her status as a member of one of the richest families in the world. And here, before her, was her prize: a Detox Green Juice on the house, delivered to her table personally by an admiring Ernesto, spiritual leader of the Planetistas and assistant general manager at the original Café Che in New York's Financial District.

"You showed incredible courage to support us in our protest march," Ernesto said as he leaned close, with a few bits of organic scone trapped in his Brillo-y beard. "Consider this a gift from the People. *Salud!*"

Missy felt a thrill run up her leg. This tribute meant so much coming from Ernesto, whom she regarded as something of a sexy beast, despite the disgusting beard detritus. But it was more than him. All around her, Missy sensed appreciative glances from others in the revolutionary café as they sucked down thirteen-dollar juices and eight-dollar lattes. So what if her ire had been misplaced against Larrabee Industries? Surely, they all understood it was the *intention* that mattered most, as it always does in righteous causes. These people, struggling against an oppressive system, clearly got it. She was rising up against the Man. And, in the case of Crowe, the Woman—who happened to be Mumsy. Nobody had told her to take such a bold stand. She charted this path entirely on her own. It was her achievement—not Homer Crowe's, or Charles Crowe's, or any other Crowe's—and this lovely plastic cup of weird juice was, quite literally, her *pièce de résistance.* She raised the cup to her lips and sipped cautiously, rolling its repugnant flavors around her mouth and trying not to gag. *Yuck! This swill tastes like asparagus soaked in hookah water.* Nevertheless, with the adoring eyes of the People upon her, she would take it all in, happily, with a gracious smile, even if it prompted a case of the shits. *I'm with you, common people!*

Ernesto, meanwhile, slipped back behind the counter and into a quiet corner of the kitchen. He sent a message to his financial backer, Harold Crenshaw, at his office in the Trump Building on Wall Street three blocks away.

El Comandante

Today 10:10 AM

Missy's here. I gave her a free drink so she sticks around.

Harold broke off a meeting with his portfolio managers to adjust his wardrobe. He took off his tie, removed the cufflinks from his shirt, rolled up the sleeves, and licked his fingers to pat down a hair plug gone haywire. He moved in close to the mirror to check for poppy seeds in his teeth, then walked hurriedly to the express elevator to the street, down the narrow sidewalks of William Street and Beaver, and then up to Broad. He pushed through the door to find a bustling coffee shop offering the usual array of pastries, espresso drinks, and cleansing juices, along with an extra splash of commercial-grade communism, on sale today only. He looked around at the tables, which were supposedly communal but lacked actual communing, as everyone was glued to their electronic devices. The walls were emblazoned with Warhol-style portraits of Che Guevara, the bloody Latin American revolutionary who was presumed to be a hero to these customers for reasons none of them could cite. That this fashionable bastion of commie stylings was situated in the heart of New York's dog-eat-dog financial world struck Harold as high comedy.

He caught the eye of Ernesto, behind the counter, who nodded in the direction of a young woman sitting at the end of a long table, engaged with her phone and nursing a tall glass of green sludge. Ernesto arched an eyebrow and handed Harold a double espresso. He said quietly, "Good luck."

Harold walked slowly to the table where Missy sat. This grungy dust bunny was one of the richest women in the world? Seriously? Maybe she was just dressing down for Commie Coffee. From the looks of her—ragged denim overall shorts over a pale orange t-shirt, an upper left arm full of indecipherable tats, and unkempt hair pointing in every direction—she could easily pass for a professional dogwalker on a break from rich clients' wheezing French bulldogs and cute little cavapoos. "Excuse me," Harold said, affecting astonishment, "but aren't you Missy Crowe?"

Missy looked up to greet the gabardine-garbed geezer with a scowl. "Who are you?"

"My name is Harold Crenshaw. I just want to say I'm a fan."

She eyed him suspiciously. "You don't say."

"Actually, I *do* say. It requires guts to take it to the streets like you did. And to oppose people in your own family? I know how hard that is. I've done it myself," he said, sitting down across from her. "But when principle is involved, you have to do what's right. Right? That's what I believe."

Was this guy bullshitting? Missy slapped her phone face down on the table. "What principles move you, Harold?"

Harold was taken aback. Principles? *Shit.* He searched his memory. Were there any principles in there? *Wait! Yes!* There had been something interesting on his fortune cookie at lunch yesterday, beside his lucky numbers. Searching... searching... *Aha!* "Well, right at the top of my list," he said quietly, "is the idea that if you know the right thing to do and you don't do it, well, that's the ultimate form of cowardice."

Missy nodded. That was plausible—admirable, even. "I actually agree with that."

Phew! Harold leaned back and threw his left arm over the back of the chair next to him. "Of course, you do. You wouldn't have done what you did otherwise. I'm trying to do the right thing now too, regarding Crowe Power."

"What is that?"

"I bought stock in the company."

Missy slumped. "Oh."

Harold sat up and leaned toward Missy. "Don't misunderstand. It's not because I believe in the company. It's because I *don't.* They're on a perilous path, endangering all of us on this damaged, abused planet that so desperately needs healing. I bought shares to force Crowe Power leadership to change its ways."

She scratched her head. "Like how?"

"Exactly what you and—what's your group? The Planetistas?" Reflexively, he glanced over at Ernesto, who was working the espresso machine.

"Yes," she said.

"It's what you and the Planetistas were demanding out there on Broad Street. Crowe Power needs to demonstrate it has a credible plan to wean itself off fossil fuels. This is no time for excuses. They need to go green—and fast. Otherwise, frankly, I don't see why they should still be in business. There are many more responsible operators out there right now who are beginning to move in the right direction."

Missy picked up her phone. "You said your name is Harold Crenshaw?"

He nodded. "That's right."

Missy typed furiously on Google. Who was this guy anyway? *"Hacksaw Harry?"* she asked, incredulously. "Is that *you*?"

Harold put a hand on his chest. "That's hardly a nickname that I endorse, but yeah. And so be it. I make no apologies for fixing obsolete companies that fail to keep up with the times. Crowe Power was a great enterprise back in the day. I know. I was an investor long before we were ever aware of the climate emergency that was coming. No disrespect to your mother, of course, but times are different now. Crowe needs to adjust, but they haven't, and I don't see any sign that they will."

"So… how are you going to get them to change?"

He shook his head. "First, I'm going to have a conversation with your mother. Nice and polite. Respectful. I want to reason with her and see if I can get her to see the light."

Missy scoffed. "Good luck with that."

"If that approach fails, I promise you: I won't give up. I'll escalate—and do whatever it takes."

Missy pursed her lips, then asked, "Like what?"

He looked around to see if anyone was listening, but found the gaggle of students and gig workers immersed in their own devices. He turned back to Missy and spoke in low tones. "I intend to nominate my own slate of directors for the Crowe Power Board. I want people who are committed to sustainability and who understand the true meaning and effects of energy. Scientists. Educators. Activists. Philosophers." He paused, as if thinking deeply. "Frankly, someone like you would be perfect."

"*Me*? Why me?"

"Because, frankly my dear, you give a damn."

Missy laughed. "My mother would never approve. She's, like, totally pissed at me right now."

Harold shook his head. "This is not up to her. It's up to all the shareholders. We just have to line up the votes."

We? Missy gulped. What had she unleashed with this protest? Marching was one thing but backing it up with aggressive direct action against the family firm was another. Would she really participate in a revolution against her mother? What would that mean to her revocable trust and her ability to give away all her money while keeping a few mil for herself? Maybe it was better to take Mother up on her offer to work at the company. Maybe she really would see things differently. She looked across the table at Harold, who was studying her like a bug. If she declined to help him, she could be portrayed as making a half-hearted push against the company.

She picked up her phone and brought up her search again. "This whole thing is a little hard to believe," she said. "Are you for real?"

Harold crossed his arms. "Maybe you think investing five hundred million dollars isn't a sign of serious intent," he said. "If so, my hat's off to you, Ms. Crowe. But where I come from—a poor neighborhood on the south side of Boston—a half-billion is serious scratch."

Missy pointed to the screen on her phone. "It says on Wikipedia you made most of your fortune investing in oil and gas and coal."

"Guilty as charged," he said, raising his right hand as if taking an oath. "But that's certainly not the case anymore. You'll also see in there that I came to a point where I realized I couldn't do that any longer. I had—what would you call it? A crisis of conscience. How could I live with myself if I were contributing to the problem? My mission now is to fix those companies that I used to invest in and make them responsible corporate citizens."

Missy put the phone down. "I'm not promising anything. But give me your number."

"And?"

"I'll call you, maybe."

Harry nodded. Then he leaned across the table. "Do you think we could interest your dad, too? I understand he works over at Brookfield Place. Shame, the way he was booted so unceremoniously to the curb—especially when he had such a magnificent vision. Maybe we could all have a strategy session out on my boat."

Her expression showed deep apathy, if not antipathy, so Harry decided to sweeten the pot. "Maybe I can coax Ernesto to join us, too. I know he's a big fan of yours."

She seemed surprised. "He is?"

"That's what he tells me."

"I can't believe you know him."

"I'm a huge supporter. Huge! So… whattaya say?"

Missy perked up. "I think we could probably arrange something."

19. POWER TRIP

Two idling Cadillac Escalades parked in front of Marty's apartment building on West 62nd Street with windshield wipers slapping away the rain from a sudden downpour. Marty dashed out of his vestibule as Andrei, the uniformed driver, opened the rear door of the first car to let him into the back seat.

"It's amazing," Marty said, snapping the water off his hands. "Scientists can predict with absolute precision how climate change will cause the world's temperature to rise in eighty years. But they couldn't predict that it would rain today." Marty buckled in and the driver pulled away, and Marty looked to Lindsey. "Sorry. Looks like I'm late."

"Not at all," said Lindsey. "I think we were early."

That certainly never happened with Robbie. When he was running the show at Crowe, he made it a point to be late for meetings, corporate jet flights, and limo rides so that everyone would be reminded that he was the center of the known universe. "Thanks for picking me up," Marty said. "I can't wait to see what all the Con Fusion is about." He gently slapped the head rest on the front passenger seat. "Morning, Digby."

"Hey, Marty," Digby called over his shoulder. "Glad you could join us."

"Almost didn't make it," Marty said. "I was up half the night learning everything I could about nuclear fusion. Some of it even stuck."

"Like what?" Lindsey prompted.

"The good news is that everyone calls fusion the holy grail of clean energy. Clearly, the company that gets there first is in a great position."

"And the bad news?" she asked.

"I have no idea how it works."

Digby said, "Join the club. I don't understand it either."

"I'm counting on the team at Con Fusion to know everything there is to know about it," Lindsey said. "We may be betting the company on them."

Sheets of rain caused southbound traffic on Ninth Avenue to congeal and clog, leading to a stop-and-start snarl in the lanes to the Lincoln Tunnel. At times like this, Robbie would typically instruct the driver to illuminate the red-and-blue police lights embedded in the grille of the car, sound a pulsing siren, and blast his way through. Lindsey, however, seemed unbothered by the traffic jam and placidly scrolled through messages on her phone. She looked so elegant and above it all. Was she up for a knock-down street fight with someone as ferocious as Hacksaw Harry? Marty prayed she was nothing like her ex, who typically escaped conflict by running off with his mistress du jour once it became apparent that the scrape might require effort on his part.

Lindsey put her phone down in her lap and looked out the window, giving Marty an opening to ask a question. "If you don't mind my asking, Lindsey, how did you happen to settle on fusion for your green strategy? It's not exactly the flavor of the month."

Lindsey sighed. "Wish I could say I picked it because I'm certain of success," she said. "The truth is, it's my only option. You recall Robbie bought Greeneron from Staminum for five billion dollars."

"I remember well. Walker was giddy about unloading it."

Lindsey continued, "I assigned a task force to evaluate every one of its technologies. They panned through it all and found only fool's gold—crap, crap, and more crap, sometimes literally. Energy from manure. Energy from pond scum. Energy from everything but lightning bugs. There are three reasons I can think of why Robbie bought it."

"First?"

"He truly believes we need to go green, and he thought it would get us there," she said, as the vehicle entered the tunnel. "Secondly, he was desperate to be love by the activists. For some reason, he craves the esteem of people who want to tear down the system. He seems to think they're his comrades-in-arms against the establishment, of which he's a charter member, by the way."

Marty nodded. "I don't get it, but I certainly see it. What's the third reason?"

She shrugged. "He's an idiot."

Marty nodded at the obvious. "Well, yeah. That's pretty well documented."

She shook her head. "We had written off almost all of Greeneron and were just about to dump the last bit of it when Harold Crenshaw entered the picture. Aside from our wind and solar projects, Consolidated Fusion is all we have left in our green portfolio."

"So why were you going to shut it down?"

"Nobody could see a return on investment—at least not for the foreseeable future."

Marty sat back in his seat and folded his hands on his lap as Andrei exited the tunnel and maneuvered onto southbound Willow Avenue in Hoboken toward Jersey City. "I'm sure you've noticed that the most successful companies of the past twenty years—Amazon, Apple, Google, Facebook, Microsoft, Tesla—were developed off technology platforms that once seemed like a distant dream. Even in their early days, they built huge valuations before they could turn a profit or even generate much in the way of revenue."

"So I've noticed," Lindsey said. "Could that same phenomenon apply to our efforts in fusion, too? We'll see." She turned to face him. "The main thing is, we have to make people believe it's going to work. That's why I called you, Marty. I need you to sprinkle some of that pixie dust on this story and bring it to life."

Marty gulped. "As Kris Kringle said in *Miracle on 34th Street*: it's a tall order. The only media paying attention to fusion right now are technical journals. They're giddy about it, but it appears to be largely off the radar of the mainstream media, which are more in the mode of wait-and-see. That's good in a way."

"How so?" she asked.

"We can define the incredible possibilities of fusion on our own terms. But you do recognize we're not just defining a technology. We're defining you, too. History may remember Lindsey Harper Crowe as an industrial genius like Henry Ford—or a carnival barker like P.T. Barnum."

She sighed. "I know."

"Are you okay with that?"

She shook her head. "Honestly? No. Not at all. It's not my nature to promote myself and talk to reporters. It only invites invasions of my privacy. But what choice do I have if I want to keep our company alive? We have to take risks. And there's no doing it half-assed. Robbie tried that and you saw the results. If I'm in—and I *am* in—then I'm all in."

Marty nodded. "Good."

She patted the seat between them. "I trust you are, too."

"All the way," he said.

The car pulled off the turnpike behind Jersey City's glittering new skyline and wound its way through congested streets toward Con Fusion. In the distance, Marty could see the back of the Statue of Liberty, and it struck him that this could be the perfect place to tell a monumental story. If this fusion project were credible at all, perhaps Lindsey could be imagined as a modern-day Lady Liberty, garbed in green, lighting the way to a promising new era of energy. *Give me your tired, your poor, your huddled energy companies yearning to be clean...* It definitely had possibilities.

20. MATTER OF TIME

Bespectacled engineer Wesley Williamson, known as PC for his resemblance to the dough-faced geek in the old Apple commercials, walked with trepidation to the doorway of his fusion laboratory in an industrial park in Jersey City. With a heavy sigh, PC opened the windowless metal door and scanned the damp pavement. Until this moment, he had treasured the anonymity of his skunkworks far from the Crowe Power fortress on the other side of the moat. The distance, both in terms of geography and interest, allowed him to continue his fusion research unbothered, without fear that the big bosses in the city would sell the company, shut it down, or smother him with management.

There was no hiding now. Two black Escalades glistening with raindrops made their way down Morris Pesin Drive and pulled up in front of his building. The best PC could hope was that Lindsey Harper Crowe would appreciate that he was making progress and go away, leaving him to continue his research.

A voice came close to PC's ear. "I did not know we were supposed to wear a tie."

PC, wearing a short-sleeved white shirt and a plaid brown-and-orange tie that nearly reached his navel, turned to see Pranit Khatri, an India-born scientist nicknamed Mac only because that was the other guy in the Apple commercials. Otherwise, he bore no resemblance whatsoever to the actor Justin Long.

"I'm just trying to look like the kind of person who's acting responsibly with their money," PC said. He appraised Mac, who was dressed in his standard black pants, black hard-soled shoes, and blue plaid shirt. "You're fine."

Mac fidgeted and looked at his watch. "I do not like this. What do these people want from us?"

PC grimaced. "They're either going to close us down or get involved. I'm not sure which is worse."

"Should we order food?"

PC shrugged. "Like what?"

"I do not know. Subway?"

PC practically spat. "No way. Bigshots like this don't eat Subway."

"What do they eat?"

"You're asking me? I have no idea. I just know they don't go to Subway."

Mac nodded. "So… what are you thinking? Jersey Mike's?"

Now PC was annoyed. "Stop it, will ya? Let's not keep them here any longer than necessary. I want to give them a tour and point them back to the city."

A pair of uniformed drivers scrambled out of the front seats of the Escalades and opened the rear doors, allowing Lindsey, Marty, and Digby to emerge from the first car and executives Lucy Rutherford, Armani Jones, and Sergei Baranov to exit the second one. The appearance of Crowe Power's leadership team made PC gasp. He could envision fifteen years' worth of research into harnessing the power of the sun and stars coming crashing to earth, leaving a giant crater where his career used to be.

Lindsey stepped briskly over the curb, smiling broadly, and extended a hand. "You must be PC," she said.

Wesley was surprised, and a bit shaken. "How did you know?"

"Just a guess," she said, brightly, before turning to Pranit. "I'm thinking you're Mac."

"Some people call me that," he said. "I do not know why."

PC and Mac led the Crowe Power brain trust into the inner sanctum of Con Fusion: a cavernous room whose main feature was a machine that resembled a giant metallic pressure cooker, which in some ways it was. Stairways and catwalks crisscrossed the room, and a swirling network of pipes, hoses, cannisters, cables, and meters connected the machinery. A trio of scientists sat on rolling chairs, staring impassively at computer screens on a large console, white light reflected in their eyeglasses.

Lindsey felt a sense of wonder as she circled the machine, her team in tow. "So, this is the future."

Lucy mumbled, "God help us."

Lindsey ignored her and wondered, "What do you think we're looking at?"

Marty said, "If I'm not mistaken, I think it's the Flux Capacitor."

She laughed. "You really did do your research, didn't you?"

"I fell asleep on the chapter about stellarators. When I woke up, *Back to the Future* was on TV."

PC explained that the machine was called a tokamak, also known as an "artificial sun." It featured a donut-like ring, inside which hydrogen isotopes were superheated to make a circulating plasma, or ionized gas, and confine it using magnetic coils. As the isotopes fused, they created helium, releasing energy. The goal was to create a self-sustaining reaction, called ignition, that theoretically would produce at least ten times more energy than it took to heat the plasma. Nobody, to date, had extracted more energy from a tokamak than they put in.

"Has anyone come close?" asked Lucy.

"Oh yes," PC said. "Every year, we get substantially closer. With the advances we're seeing in materials, magnets, containment methods and new approaches to heating the plasma, we know now fusion energy is possible. It's just a matter of time."

"And money," Lucy added.

PC winced and shot a glance to Mac. This skepticism, while understandable, was unsettling. He said, "We look at it this way. The company that gets there first will make it all back—and conceivably, a great deal more. That's why you're seeing money moving into this space from some of the world's richest people. And of course, all the biggest countries in the world are racing after this. They know the possibilities are unlimited. Do you realize how many inquiries we've had lately from China?"

Lindsey was alarmed. "Seriously?"

"They're calling every day," PC said proudly.

Lindsey and Marty shot each other a look as Sergei walked to the base of a perforated metal staircase which rose to a platform overlooking the tokamak. "Can we go up there?" he asked.

"Of course, Sergei," PC said. "You know your way around."

They all trudged up to the top and looked down at the complex machinery.

"How long have you been working at this?" Lindsey asked.

PC summarized his journey from PhD candidate at Princeton to Consolidated Fusion, which licensed technology from universities, America's national labs, and other fledgling fusion companies it had acquired and subsequently advanced. Despite Con Fusion's expansive portfolio of intellectual property, the company was now on its fifth owner in fifteen years. Armani reminded Lindsey that three previous owners had run out of money in the so-called "Death Valley curve" between enterprise start-up and revenue generation. A fourth owner sold the company to Winesta Capital for pennies on the dollar, and Winesta sold it at a huge profit to Greeneron, a Staminum Energy subsidiary that Robbie acquired for Crowe Power.

Lindsey pressed on. "So tell me," she said to PC. "Why should we continue to fund this project when so many companies have failed to make money?"

"Because you're in energy and this is the single best solution to the world's energy problems," PC said. "Start with the fact that it is based on hydrogen, the most abundant element on Earth. We apply the same process of fusion that powers the sun and the stars to create clean energy. You end up with an abundant source of energy with very little waste and no carbon emissions."

Marty said, "So… why don't we call it that?"

"Call it what?" PC asked.

"Star power."

Lindsey growled, "*Ooh!* I like that!"

PC winced. "I don't know. It sounds a little too simple."

Lindsey said, "What if it's the price of getting funded?"

PC nodded. "It's sounding better to me."

Lindsey turned back toward the machinery. "And this tokamak can create it?"

"We'll know soon. I assume you've heard about the ITER project in France. The learnings we get from that project should help us understand the pathway to commercialization. In the meantime, little companies like ours are springing up around the world, hoping to find a shortcut, because they know the prize is huge."

Lindsey folded her arms and soaked that in. "So, tell me. What's next on your agenda?"

"Our plan is to fire it up next week. We want to go for the world record for a controlled plasma burn."

Lindsey sagged. "Wouldn't the results take months?"

"Not exactly," PC said. "The record is seventeen minutes."

Lucy was unimpressed. She practically spat, "That's it?"

PC huffed, "Do you have any idea how long the Wright Brothers' first flight at Kitty Hawk was? Twelve seconds. But it was a start. By their fourth flight, they were up to almost a minute. They kept going from there, just as we intend to go from here."

Lindsey stepped in to calm the rising tension. "Okay," she said. "Suppose you hit the record. Then what?"

Mac said, "We want to build a pilot plant to demonstrate how fusion—or, if you prefer, *star power*—can be commercialized. We see a pathway to producing energy within the next ten years. But it will take a great deal of money. We barely have enough now to run our experiments."

"How much do you need?" Lindsey asked.

PC said, "To really do it right?"

"Yes."

"Five hundred million dollars."

The Crowe Power leadership team exchanged glances, with Lucy and Armani shaking their heads as if to say, *out of the question.* Finally, Lindsey said, "Suppose I get the money for you."

Lucy's jaw dropped but PC looked to Mac and they both smiled for the first time all day. "We would be cooking with gas."

Lindsey turned to Marty. "Do you see enough here to tell a fantastic story?"

Marty shrugged. "Getting there." He turned to PC. "Would your plasma burn create any electricity?"

PC looked to Mac, who answered. "It would take a few additional steps, but yes. It's possible."

"How much?"

"I don't know," PC paused, calculating. "Using heat, steam, a turbine... maybe enough to warm a tea kettle."

Marty nodded toward the window and New York Harbor. "What about her? Could you light up the Statue of Liberty?"

PC looked grave. "Oh... I don't know about that."

"How about just the torch?"

"If that's what it takes to get approval, we'll give it our best shot," PC said.

Lindsey asked Marty, "What are you thinking?"

Marty replied, "To paraphrase W.C. Fields: If we can't dazzle them with brilliance, baffle 'em with bullshit."

Lindsey laughed. "How's your supply?"

"Brilliance or bullshit?"

"The latter."

"Like hydrogen," Marty said. "Abundant."

***

By the time Lindsey and her team emerged from Con Fusion, a bright fusion-powered sun was turning the puddles of water on the street into steam. There was no parting of clouds for Armani, who was responsible for Crowe Power's budget. She appeared highly stressed as she approached Lindsey.

"Lindsey, with all due respect, you know we don't have the money for this."

Lindsey stopped on the sidewalk and turned to Armani. "Then we have to find it," she said calmly.

Armani sighed. "Lindsey, I barely have enough cash to keep our pipelines, refineries, and power plants operating. I don't have an extra five-hundred million dollars lying around for such a highly speculative venture. Every dollar we've got in this company is committed."

"Then we go outside the company."

"Where? All the big lenders have been scared away."

"Where does anyone find money for green initiatives?" Lindsey asked. "Washington, D.C. It's where money grows on trees." As the rest of the group gathered round, Lindsey stepped into the middle. "Alright, people. We need to move very quickly. Digby, you said you and the Secretary of Energy have a bit of history, right?"

Digby looked around at the group waiting to hear the story and decided this was better communicated privately. He pulled Lindsey away from the group. "We both grew up in D.C." He looked sheepish. "I even dated her briefly in college."

"How briefly?"

"Let me think," Digby said. "I guess it was... almost an hour."

Lindsey regarded him incredulously. "An *hour?*"

"It was a strange thing," he said, quietly. "We were just finishing our first beer when she got a phone call from her roommate that her cat was sick. Obviously, she had to leave right away."

"Uh-huh." Lindsey nodded solemnly. "Does she still hate you?"

"I don't think she ever did," Digby said, defensively.

"A sick cat? Seriously? The date was not going well, Digby. Trust me."

Digby sniffed, "Well, we're friendly enough now."

"Think you can get us an audience?"

"Possibly."

"Let's meet her down in D.C., ASAP."

They turned back to the group and Lindsey addressed Armani. "We're going to separate Con Fusion from your Crowe Power budget, Armani. Get your team to structure a spin-off. Call it the Star Power Company. Get us a stock symbol people can remember. Like STAR, or something. Crowe Power will hold all the shares, so that if somebody buys our stock, they get Star Power, too."

Armani brightened. "I like that."

"Thought you would," Lindsey said, patting her arm. "Sergei, I need you to figure out which technologies make the most sense as part of Star Power, and what should stay with Crowe."

Sergei nodded. "Got it."

"And Lucy," Lindsey said, "I need you to find engineering support for PC and Mac. We're going to need to demonstrate how they're going to squeeze electricity out of this tokamak. People have to see how it works."

"And if it doesn't?"

"Not an option," Lindsey said.

Lucy nodded. "On it."

Lindsey turned to Marty. "And Marty, I want you to develop our talking points around Star Power. When Digby and I go to visit his old girlfriend in Washington, I want to have a presentation that puts a puddle under her chair. And then I want you to figure out how we're going to announce this thing. We need a really big show."

"I was thinking of Lady Liberty as our celebrity spokesmodel."

Lindsey laughed. "Robbie was right about one thing."

"What's that?"

"You really are full of shit, aren't you?"

"I am," he said. "And so far, I've made a pretty good living off it."

She regarded him skeptically. "Let's see how you do over the next week."

21. TAKEN FOR A RIDE

A hazy morning sun reflected off the windows of the skyscrapers of Lower Manhattan as Robbie strolled along the North Cove Marina along the waterfront in Battery Park City. He pulled his Oliver Peoples sunglasses from the breast pocket of his sport jacket and squinted at the names of the boats.

At the end of a slip along the breakwater, he found a gleaming new eighty-foot Viking yacht, *My Float Option*, with a listing of New York City. The vessel was the smallest in Harry's fleet, which was dispersed in ports of call around the world, but suitable for easy access in and out of the smaller marinas of the city. Robbie spotted Missy sitting at a table on the stern, having coffee with Harold Crenshaw, who was clad in white jeans and shirt, a blue blazer, and sockless canvas deck shoes.

Spotting Robbie, Harold rose from his chair and waved cheerfully. "You found us!"

Robbie broke into a grin and walked to the foot of the jetty. "Permission to come aboard?"

"Absolutely!" Harold said.

Robbie stepped over cables and hoses laying on the dock, grabbed Harold's outstretched hand, and jumped onto the deck. He offered a hug to Missy, who practically glowed as she introduced the legendary Ernesto, Castro-bearded field comandante of the Planetistas and notorious latte whiz at the original Café Che, who emerged from the cabin holding a large paper cup of coffee.

"I remember you," Robbie said, offering a hand.

Ernesto shook Robbie's hand and raised his chin, striking the defiant pose of Latin American revolutionaries. "I remember you, too," Ernesto said, peering through his aviator sunglasses. "You are… large Bolivian Jungle Roast, two ounces of soy milk."

"Good memory!" Robbie said.

"Perhaps you would like one now," Ernesto said. He handed over the cup with Robbie's special blend.

"Impressive," Robbie said, gratefully accepting the cup and taking a small sip. "Perfect temperature, too."

Missy explained to Harold, "Dad can get a bit cranky if his coffee isn't just right."

"That's understandable," said Harold, as he indicated they should all sit down at the deck table as the ship's crew untied the ropes and the captain up on the bridge throttled the engines. Ernesto offered a plate of freshly baked Banana, Kale and Crabgrass muffins from Café Che, and the boat pulled away from the dock, heading out to the roiling Hudson River, and turned north toward the piers of Tribeca and the West Village. The thrum of engines and the rush of the water against the hull drowned out the sounds of the city nearby and left the rest of the world behind.

"Thank you for joining us this morning, Robbie," Harry said. "I know how tough it is to break away from the office."

Robbie waved his hand as if to say *forget it*. "They can live without me for an hour or two. We'll see how hard they work when they think no one's looking."

"Which reminds me," Harold said, "I've been chatting with Missy and Ernesto here about your old shop." He leaned forward, consoling. "And I must say, we're all saddened to see what's become of Crowe Power since you stepped down as chairman. For a great company like that to fall so hard. It must be particularly heartbreaking for you, considering your incredible vision."

Robbie shook his head. "They've completely lost their way," he said sullenly.

Harold said, "I truly thought that under your direction, Crowe Power was on the precipice of greatness—an energy company that would show all the other energy companies out there how things should be done in the modern world. But they can't seem to do anything. All their projects are stalled, from pipelines, to solar farms, to wind turbines. When the feds finally lower the boom on fossil fuels, I don't know how Crowe Power's going to stay in business."

Robbie turned crimson with rage. "They can't!" he said. "And here's the worst of it. I left them the damn playbook! All they had to do was follow it. But I guess, because it was my vision, they felt they had to throw it away, regardless of its value. Can't have any vestige of ol' Robbie still around! Oh, no! It's pathetic that they purged my legacy just to spite me. Now look at the share price. There are your results! They've only hurt the company—and themselves."

Harold shook his head, as if the Crowe saga pained him deeply. "So sad and so true. I hate to see waste like that, especially for such a once-great enterprise. I remember the days when Crowe Power was known as the industry's great innovator. Now all they do is provide energy the old-fashioned way, the obsolete way. They're as fossilized as the fuels they use." He threw up his hands. "The pity of it is that you know and I know it doesn't have to be like this. Not if the people who really care about Crowe Power and what that name has meant for more than a century step forward and say, 'Damn it! Enough is enough!' I've got to believe there are others like you who don't want to be associated with this embarrassing decline in social responsibility."

Missy shook her head. "Dad," she said, "Harold is so right. We have to do something. It's humiliating to be associated with this lumbering dinosaur. It's bad enough that my name is Crowe. Now Mother wants me to work there, to be complicit in her crimes against the planet."

Robbie was taken aback. "You're not going to work there…"

She practically spit. "I *can't*. I'd rather get down on my hands and knees and clean latrines in a homeless shelter."

Harold appraised her jewelry and determined that was unlikely. "Fortunately, I don't think that's necessary, Missy," he said. "If we all work together, we can take this company back and show that Crowes are still responsible citizens of the world, willing and ready to do the right thing."

Robbie, knowing Harold's record, found this blatant pandering a bit much. Still, if he offered a chance to restore order in the realm, so be it. He took a deep breath and prepared himself for Harold's pitch. "What do you have in mind?"

Harold explained his plan to nominate his own board of directors to the company, backed by key institutional investors and just enough members of the Crowe family to ensure election. These hand-picked directors would replace the over-the-hill gang currently rubber-stamping Lindsey's governance with a panel of leading thinkers from business, academia, foundations, and political science who would hold Lindsey's feet to the fire. No longer would she simply talk about her green intentions; she would need to demonstrate real progress to help prevent Earth's imminent immolation.

"That makes total sense, Harold," Missy said. "It's, like, so obvy!"

Ernesto nodded, solemnly, as he stroked his beard. "I will serve on the board if you need me, Harold."

"Thank you, Ernesto," Harold said, patting him on the shoulder. "I think your revolutionary spirit would be indispensable. Ultimately, the makeup of the board will be up to the person I believe will become the next chairman."

Robbie looked at him expectantly. "And you're thinking?"

"Who else could it be but Lester Robertson Crowe the Third."

Whoa! Robbie had known this was coming, yet it still hit him like someone fired a dozen of those hideous vegan muffins at his chest. With Harold's backing, he would return from exile in triumph. The idea was bracing, exhilarating, and entirely appropriate. And it was about damn time! Nobody else had his unique qualifications: superior breeding, education, experience and, above-all, direct descendant Crowe-mosomes. That special genius that made Homer Crowe famous was still alive in Robbie's DNA and flitting through his system, infusing him with a certain unique brilliance.

"From your lips to God's ear," Robbie said. At last, he could chuck his useless, boring-ass foundation and get back to the office where he belonged. He would rule the energy world once more, commanding a global empire, and everyone everywhere would know his name, from heads of state to captains of industry. He would light the path to climate virtue for all to tread, capturing the swooning admiration of comely baristas at Commie Coffee shops all over town. There would be no more "Wobbies" written on his cup! "Let's do it!"

Harold clapped his hands together in glee. "So glad to hear it!"

"How do we get this done?" Robbie asked.

"Next step is: I will meet with your ex and present her with her options," Harold said. "Should she resist, then we dispense with the niceties. We do a full-court press: media, investors, the works."

Missy embraced Ernesto and Harry suggested champagne to celebrate their agreement. He retrieved a bottle of Louis Roederer Cristal Brut he had on ice in the cabin and poured a glass of bubbly for each of his guests. Ernesto offered the toast he imagined Che might say: *"Salud, diner, y amor!"*

The boat picked up speed as it passed Diller's Pillars, the new park known as Little Island that had been built on stilts over the river, sending a three-foot wake cascading over a flotilla of kayakers along Chelsea Piers. Ernesto and Missy walked to the gunwales and watched the kayakers struggling to keep their balance over the bounding main. *Aw, that's kinda too bad ...* Ernesto called back to Harry. "What kind of mileage do you get on this rig?"

"Do you want one?"

Ernesto sipped his champagne and shrugged. "You know, if I had the means, this is exactly the kind of boat I would have. Not too big. Not too small. I think if we're going to sell communism to the masses, we need to show them that it doesn't necessarily lead to poverty. Everyone can prosper—especially those who sacrifice to lead the revolution. That's fair, right?"

"Why not?" Harold guffawed. "Worked for Castro."

"I just wonder about the fuel consumption. We don't want to appear, um, ostentatious."

Harold shrugged. "Let me think about that a second, Ernesto. At a speed of thirty-five knots, you'd have to figure, oh... roughly two hundred gallons per hour." Sensing a skeptical eye from Missy, Harold added, "I assure you we won't use more than five hundred gallons this morning. I've told the captain to throttle it down if he has to."

Robbie nodded, approvingly. "That's not bad, when you think about it. My buddy out in Sag has a Lürssen. That thing takes four-hundred gallons just to back up."

Harold held an index finger in the air. "And that's exactly why I bought a smaller yacht like this," he said, looking at Missy, then Ernesto. "We *all* need to do our part. Until people start taking this climate challenge personally, we're never going to make progress. No one gets a pass when it comes to saving Mother Earth."

Robbie sighed. "I couldn't agree more."

Missy looked uncomfortable. "I'm not sure I totally get this. How does having a yacht square with a green vision?"

"Well," Harold said, "sometimes, we turn off the engines."

"When?" she asked.

"Well, like when we stop."

"Oh," Missy said.

Harold continued, "Compare this little trip around the Hudson to flying to Florida, *then* getting on a helicopter, *then* into an SUV, and then—*finally!*—onto a boat. If you look at it on a net emissions basis, I'm slashing my carbon emissions by keeping my yacht in Manhattan."

"Okay. Okay." Missy nodded. "I can see that… I guess."

As Missy turned her attentions back to Ernesto and snuggled up against him along the railing, Robbie leaned back in his chair, cocking his head to catch the wind in a way that would avoid a hair disaster. He addressed Harold. "You know, Lindsey does have a green strategy."

Harold scoffed. "She sure can't seem to execute it. From what I've seen, all her wind and solar projects are at a standstill. But I'm sure you have better intel than I do."

Robbie scratched the back of his head. "I've got a guy inside the company who tells me there's another green program that she never talks about. At least, not yet."

Harold, alarmed, "What do you mean?"

Robbie pointed to an area on the south side of Jersey City behind Liberty Island. "She has a fusion lab right over there."

"Fusion?"

"Yeah," Robbie said. "Of course, like everything else, it was my idea. She's trying to make a go of it. Pretty pathetic if you ask me."

Harold scratched his chin. He had noticed that big investment money was beginning to dribble into fusion. If Lindsey had a decent position there, it was all the more reason to move on Crowe Power and monetize it. "I don't understand how that's fair," Harold said. "You had the idea, and she tries to take credit? That's just wrong."

"No kidding!"

"Morally, ethically wrong!"

"We've got to do something about this."

Harold reached over and patted him on the knee. "And we will, Robbie. We will."

As the boat approached the Statue of Liberty, the captain slowed the engines so they could all get a good look.

"I've seen the Statue of Liberty a million times," Harold said. "For some reason it still fascinates me."

Robbie nodded, absently, then looked up and studied the monument, cocking his head from side to side. "You think she has a nice ass?"

"Lady Liberty?"

"I mean, she's dressed like the Taliban, so it's hard to tell," Robbie said. "But sometimes I wonder: what's behind the curtain? You know?"

Harold didn't know. Nor did he want to know. He'd never lusted after a statue before. But then, he wasn't Robbie, who apparently chased everything that moved, and even things that didn't. "Not getting out on dates much these days?"

Robbie grimaced. "It's been a while." Which was all the more reason to get his old job back. Time to get back in the game!

22. MRS. CROWE GOES TO WASHINGTON

A deeply inconvenienced administrative aide for the Department of Energy yawned and shook her head as she led Lindsey and Digby down a dreary corridor in the bleak James V. Forrestal Building in southwest Washington, D.C. Lindsey, glancing about at the warren of dark, empty cubicles and offices, noted that the aide and the building exhibited few signs of energy, despite the department's purported mission—at least until they were deposited in a conference room and the petite blond Secretary of Energy, Jessica Holtgren, arrived.

"Lindsey Harper Crowe!" she chirped, as Lindsey entered the conference room. "What a pleasure to finally meet you in person!"

Lindsey blushed and offered her hand. "It's an honor to meet you, Madame Secretary."

"*Please!* Call me Jessica, I insist!" she said in a breathy purr as she peered up at Lindsey through her reading glasses. She then turned to Digby and stretched up on her tiptoes to offer a hug. "And Digby! My dear, *dear* friend! How long has it been?"

Jessica flopped dramatically into a chair at the end of the table. She shook her head at the wondrous miracle of this meeting, and her regret that it had taken so long. *Why* hadn't she kept in better touch with Digby? *Why* hadn't she made it a point to see him in New York, at least once on her fifty or so trips to the Big Apple? Sure, she was busy as any cabinet secretary, especially one charged with such a challenging conundrum as solving climate change, but that was absolutely no excuse, given their long history, to not stay connected with her beloved chum. She recounted how fondly she remembered their childhood in the privileged enclave of Chevy Chase, Maryland, their summers at the country club and at the Cape, their educations at the sister schools of Landon and Holton Arms, and the classes they had taken together at Cornell.

"Oh," she said. "And who could forget that date we had at the Pines!"

It was Digby's turn to blush. "I certainly can't."

Lindsey couldn't resist. "It's just too bad about the cat."

Jessica looked puzzled. "Cat?"

Digby shook his head—*don't go there*—but Lindsey continued. "I understood that you had a sick cat at the time."

"I did?" she said. She put her head back on the chair and looked up at the ceiling, thinking. Then she smiled. "Oh, *that*," she said, waving it off. "Well, enough about the good old days, right, Digs?" She reached over and shook his upper arm. "Let's talk about the future, shall we?" She tapped the folder on Crowe Power's nuclear fusion program that Marty had sent by express courier, entitled:

STAR POWER
America's Fusion Future

Harnessing the Forces of the Universe!

"Whew!" Jessica said, "First off, I have to tell you that I am impressed by how fast you have pivoted from fossil fuels to clean energy. I love, love, *love* this idea! And calling it 'star power?' I get *chills!*"

Puddle accomplished! Lindsey said, "So happy to hear you say that."

"Oh yes," Jessica said, peering over her reading glasses at Lindsey. "Of all the green energy ideas we have, this one—" she stabbed the folder with her finger, "is my absolute favorite." She reposed. "You know, I've been keen on fusion for a very long time. Many people around here think it's a hopeless long shot. But I'm thinking, as a nation, we have to shoot for the moon." She shot a hand in the air, then spread her fingers apart. "*Whoosh!*"

Lindsey nodded enthusiastically. "And for the stars, right?"

Jessica continued, "*Exactly!* There's absolutely no way we can afford to lose this battle to the Chinese or the Russians—or for that matter, the French, British, and Japanese. Every day, I wake up worried that one of them is going to come out with an announcement about a breakthrough in fusion. And then where will we be? I'm afraid the last one in this energy pool may be a rotten egg. And I..." she punctuated each word with a stab of her index finger on the table, *"don't. Want. To. Be. That egg!"*

"That would stink," Digby said.

"Especially for someone in my job," Jessica added.

Lindsey was relieved at her interest. What a change in attitude from their last call, when the secretary had killed Crowe Power's pipeline and threatened investigations. This was going far better than expected. "I am so glad you sense the urgency as we do," she said.

Jessica continued, "Oh, yes! Between you, me, and the lamppost? We need a new story. Much as I'm a fan of solar and wind power, it's never going to be enough to wean us off fossil fuels. There are just too many variables we can't control. The minerals and precious metals required. The land. The shorelines. The local rights-of-way. Battery storage. Waste disposal. Whether the wind blows or the sun shines. All the back-up power required from fossil fuels." She shook her head. "We need alternatives for a truly sustainable future. And, this part is *really* important, we need to give people *hope*—no matter how far-fetched or fanciful— that we have a solution to this climate crisis. I mean, we can't keep sounding the alarm that we have an emergency on our hands and scaring people half to death without offering a solution. We need a better answer than we have now, right? And this," she said, holding up the folder, "this sounds just fantastic enough to do the trick. Imagine! Harnessing the energy of the sun and the stars!"

Lindsey nodded. "There's a long way to go, of course, but we're quite excited about the possibilities."

Jessica rested her chin in the palm of her hand and stared intently at Lindsey. "So tell me," she said, "how do we make this happen?"

We? Lindsey heard. *That's a good sign.* She explained to Jessica that the fusion lab in Jersey City needed money for further research and testing to overcome hurdles to commercial viability, and for a demonstration plant to show that it all worked. She intended to create a spinout of a new subsidiary called Star Power that would have its own listing on the New York Stock Exchange, and that the firm could have a trove of valuable assets in the form of its technology licenses. "We think this stock will be very attractive to social investors and politically-oriented pension funds."

Jessica slapped the table with both hands. "Are you *kidding*? You'll have a gold rush on your hands! Oh, my god! Yes, yes, *yes!* I mean, people will be shouting from their solar-paneled rooftops, 'Where do I sign?' And, frankly, I'm one of them. This is *sooo* exciting!" She leaned back in her chair, eyeing Lindsey and Digby. "How many green jobs do you think we can generate from this?"

Lindsey squirmed. She hadn't really considered that part. "It's difficult to say at this point," she said.

Jessica considered that answer a moment, then held up her hands, palms out, as if to say, *that's okay.* "Let's game it out, shall we, because this will be an important part of our pitch to the American public. How many people are on the job now? Couple hundred?"

Lindsey counted on her fingers. "Well, let me think. There's Wesley..."

The Secretary's face fell. "Wesley?"

"We call him PC. There's Pranit..." said Lindsey, now on her middle finger. "His nickname is Mac."

Jessica suddenly looked grave. "You can name them all?"

Lindsey nodded. "I guess we have about six."

Jessica's jaw dropped—not in a good way. "Six people. Not... six *thousand?*"

"No," Lindsey said, picturing the lab in her mind. "Pretty sure it's just six."

Jessica wearily stood up and paced. "Still," she said, thinking. "The promise is there, right? I mean if this catches on—like we absolutely *know* it will—you could extrapolate and... I could see a million green jobs out of this eventually. Maybe two million. So let's just call it that."

Lindsey winced. "I don't know what all those people would do, exactly..." She looked at Digby, whose eyes widened as he shook his head. His expression said, *This is no time for candor.* "Of course," Lindsey continued, "as long as you're speaking theoretically, anything's possible, I suppose."

Jessica gripped the back of a chair. "Understand this. The president wants to give people some sense of optimism. They're losing jobs in coal mines and power plants all over this country. We have to give them at least a promise of getting something back. They can't all make solar panels. Especially when the Chinese do it cheaper."

"Right," Lindsey said.

Jessica shook her head. "What I wouldn't give for autocratic rule some days. Just ordering things done, you know? I mean, if we're going to compete with people working for pennies on the dollar…" she sighed. "Ah, well. Could these be union jobs?"

Lindsey flashed a puzzled look to Digby, who asked, "All two million?"

Jessica nodded vigorously. "Uh-huh."

Lindsey said, "I don't see why not." *It's all make-believe anyway!*

The secretary clapped her hands together. "Alright! Now we're talking." She brushed a hand across the air, as if she were reading something in the sky. "I can see the headlines now. 'Fenwick Administration finds holy grail of clean energy!' 'Two million good-paying green union jobs!' Oh my God!" She paused, thinking. "You know what we need to do? Let's call it *one-point-nine* million so that it sounds like we really scrubbed the numbers."

Lindsey replied, "Entirely your call, Jessica."

Jessica was ecstatic. "The president will be *very* pleased. He's giving a speech in San Francisco next month and he's hoping for some big news to announce. This could be—well, let's think about that. Why not make star power a *mandate*? Huh? Say thirty percent of our electricity must come from fusion?"

"By when?"

"I don't know. Say 2040."

"That seems a bit soon."

"Okay. Then 2050."

Lindsey nearly burst out laughing. *This was ridiculous!* Jessica was clearly getting way ahead of herself. How could they mandate a fusion solution that wasn't yet proven? Then again, they had done it many times already. "That's pretty aggressive, considering where we are at the moment," she said.

Jessica leaned across the table, resting on her knuckles. "Moonshot, Lindsey! *Moonshot!* Think JFK in 1962."

Digby interjected, "It probably makes sense to have a stretch goal."

"Heck yeah!" Jessica exclaimed. "We'll be outta here by then anyway." Jessica sat down and leaned forward, folding her hands together. "So tell me: what do you need? You know I've got all kinds of dough in my big ol' taxpayer cookie jar—federal tax credits, grants, and loans. What flavor would you like?"

Lindsey steeled herself for the hard part. "Well, Madame Secretary—excuse me, *Jessica*—as you would expect, Crowe Power has already invested significantly in star power," she said. "But given the public's clear interest in this, we think five hundred million dollars from the federal government would help us advance our technology significantly."

Jessica gravely shook her head. "No."

Lindsey was crestfallen. After all this buildup? *No?*

"Make it a billion," the secretary proclaimed, slapping the table.

Lindsey sat up a little straighter. "Really?"

"Of course! Could you use it?"

"I'm, I'm… I'm sure we could."

"Lindsey. Please," Jessica said. "On a project this important, I don't want the government to look like pikers here. I want an investment large enough to underscore our confidence that this will work. And a show of confidence requires a show of cash. So I'm gonna show you the money!" She began a little samba in her chair, as if she heard dance music.

Lindsey watched her with wonder. "Thank you so much."

"This isn't *my* money, mind you," Jessica said, grandly. "It's *our* money. The American *people's* money. And there's an endless supply if we spend it—ahem, *invest it*—in projects for the public good. This is for our children and our grandchildren, right? So, in that spirit, I have absolutely no qualms about going into more debt and making them pay for it, because they're the ones who will eventually benefit. Besides," she said with a chuckle, "I think I owe Digby for that aborted date way back when. A cat! *Ha!* And I *hate* cats! I don't know what I was thinking."

Lindsey flashed a glance at Digby, who seemed to sink into the cushions of his chair. She said to Jessica, "All I can say is, 'wow!' We'll do everything we can to justify your faith in us. We can provide metrics to measure progress and—"

"Nah," Jessica said with a backhand wave. "There's only one number anyone around here is worried about right now, and that's November 8. Just make us look good, my friends. Don't go bankrupt between now and then. Hear me? Our opponents would have a field day."

"Understood." Lindsey gathered her things to leave, but Jessica sat back in her chair.

"Before you go, I want to ask you one other thing—just between us chickens."

"Of course."

Jessica jumped up from her chair, peered into the hallway to see if anyone was around, and closed the door. She returned to the table, sat forward eagerly and spoke in a hushed tone. "Any idea what this new Crowe Power subsidiary will be worth?"

"Star Power?" Lindsey looked to Digby, who scratched his neck as he spoke. "Hard to say, really. I'm sure you know our country spends about a trillion-and-a-half dollars a year on energy. Imagine the market value of a company that leads such a huge industry on a new path forward."

Jessica nodded solemnly and pressed her fingertips together. "Some people are going to get very, very, *very* rich off this investment." She sighed and shook her head. "Not me, of course. I'm just a poor public servant. And I'm totally okay with that. I didn't sign up for this job to get wealthy like some people do in this town. I came here to serve the people of this great land of ours."

Lindsey nodded vigorously, almost as if she believed her. "Thank you for your service," she said.

Jessica reached over and patted her hand, then leaned back in her chair. "On the other hand, you may have heard that my husband, Steve, is involved with a firm that dabbles in energy stocks. I don't know a thing about it—we have a Chinese wall in our house, and we keep these things entirely separate, of course— but I'm sure he would be keenly interested in getting in on the ground floor of a company like this, as would a few of his select clients."

Lindsey looked to Digby to respond. He was rather terse. "We have to be careful not to disclose anything to outside parties that could constitute insider knowledge," he said. "I'm sure you understand."

"Of course!" Jessica said. "Don't think twice about that! I would never suggest anything untoward."

"Of course not," Lindsey said.

"Frankly, I only know the broad outline of this Star Power spin-off, or whatever you call it," Jessica said. "I don't really understand the concept. All that high finance stuff goes right over my head. What I do know is that Crowe Power is a highly responsible company, and it would be smart for some people to load up on CRO right now, to show faith in your leadership."

Lindsey said, "That's a judgment you would have to make. As Digby suggested, we can't offer investment advice."

"Please," Jessica said. "Not another word about that. The billion dollars you're about to get from me has absolutely nothing to do with my husband's interests. You realize that, right? There's no quid pro quo here. None whatsoever."

"Of course."

"That said… the sooner I hear from you about the timing of this spin-off the better. I'd hate for there to be some sort of bureaucratic snafu to get in the way of your payment. We need to get moving on our path to a bright clean energy future for our nation."

"Thank you again," Lindsey said, standing.

Jessica clasped her hand. "God bless you, Lindsey." She turned to Digby. "And you, too, Digby."

"Thank you," he said.

Jessica added, "And God bless the United States of America."

* * *

"Not a word until we get to the plane," Lindsey said with a shudder as she and Digby left the Forrestal building and headed toward their waiting car.

Digby nodded. One never knew who or how they were listening to conversations in this town. They climbed into the back of the vehicle and sped off to Reagan National Airport, where they were ushered through a gate onto the tarmac and dropped off at the stairway to Crowe Bird I. Safely strapping into their seats, Lindsey said, tartly, "Your girlfriend's a total whore." She turned to him and shook her head. "And now, it seems, I am, too."

"Lay down with swamp creatures, you get slimed," Digby said.

She looked at him and shook her head. "How did you not manage to get laid by that chick?"

Digby sighed. "I was the only one in my frat who didn't."

"She dumped you for a *cat?*"

Digby's head fell back on the seat. "Please. Don't rub it in. Did you think it wasn't humiliating enough to learn that the cat didn't even exist?"

"Come, now," she said, leaning across the aisle and patting his arm. "You're probably better off. Who knows what sort of cooties you might have picked up. I need a Silkwood shower when I get home. Maybe some penicillin, too." She settled into the seat. "Are we doing the right thing?"

Digby shrugged. "Getting in bed with the federal government. What could go wrong?"

"That's what I'm wondering."

"Here's the thing, Linz: I don't know where else we could get this kind of money. I can't imagine a bank of any repute would lend to us for a project that's so high-risk. And we certainly can't divert cash from operations. We have to pay for turnarounds at the refineries in Mississippi and Guatemala, patch up the pipeline in Montana, and decommission our power plant in Germany. No wonder Armani is so scratchy about all this."

"Oh, I know," Lindsey said, shaking her head. "It's just, Jessica's offer seems too good to be true, you know? A billion dollars? No strings attached?"

"It does seem a bit loose," Digby said. He picked up his phone and typed into the browser.

She paused, thinking. "What sort of sleazy operation do you think her husband is running?"

"I'm looking him up now," Digby said. "He has a website, Steven Stump Investments, but there's almost no information about him. Not even a photo. And there's nothing about the kinds of investments he does."

"Do you think he even exists? Or is Steven Stump a DBA for your girlfriend there."

"No, he definitely exists," Digby said, dropping his phone. "I met him in at a lunch here at the Met Club a couple of months ago. Handshake like a wet fish. Limp and slippery."

"That's appropriate."

"Definitely a swamp creature."

"Him or her?"

"Take your pick," he said.

The flight attendant, Charles, laid placemats on the tables in front of them, took orders for tea for Lindsey and bourbon for Digby, then returned to the galley. Lindsey looked out the window toward the Washington Monument across the river and sadly shook her head. "I've never been more cynical about government in my life."

"If you think there's something you can do to change it, forget it," Digby said. "Our best option is to go with the flow, even when it's sewage."

"What happens when they ask to see what they got for their money? She thinks there are two million green jobs out of this," Lindsey said, shaking her head in wonder. "So far, we've got a half-dozen geeks in lab coats. In another year or two, I'd be shocked if we had more than fifty people working on fusion."

Digby shrugged. "It doesn't matter, Lindsey. In Washington, good intentions trump results every time. We have good intentions, right?"

"Good enough," she said.

As Charles returned with their beverages, Lindsey needed something to break the tension besides hot tea. She leaned across the aisle and picked up Digby's glass of bourbon. "Would you mind if I had just a little sip of this?"

"Help yourself."

23. EVERYBODY MUST GET STONED

In the heat of a mid-afternoon summer day under a canopy of honey locust trees, Missy, Blair, and a few dozen activists awaited the start of a "Save the Planet" rally on a granite bench in Zuccotti Park, historic home of the Occupy Wall Street protest camp in 2011. Missy fired up a silver lighter pilfered from her mother's townhouse to light a marijuana cigarette and took a deep drag. She threw her head back and slowly exhaled, looking through the billowing smoke curling through the trees at the lights in the surrounding buildings. As the marijuana took hold, she was lifted on a magic carpet ride, transported back to the Occupy camp as she imagined it: teeming with tents and righteous people committed to changing the world by replacing capitalism with something else. She could see tables laid out for petition drives to end oppression in all its forms, teams of people painting signs for marches, and speakers standing on the benches, punching the air with soaring rhetoric and inspiring the throng with a Utopian vision of a just future.

In her mind, there was no trace of the luxe lifestyle that characterized her own upbringing. Nor were there any of the rapes, robberies, and assaults that were inflicted on the Occupy crowd and their hygiene-challenged contingent by the predators in their midst. She imagined an atmosphere of Woodstock-style peace and harmony and love, sweet love, which is *exactly* what the world needed now.

"This is where it all happened, Blair," she said. "I was here."

"Weren't you, like, nine?"

"Eight. But, you know, I was paying attention. We drove by it once on our way to the helipad. I remember asking my mother, 'What is going on there?' She wouldn't tell me, but I had a sense it was something important. I even asked if we could stop and see. But she was in a hurry to get out to the Hamptons."

Missy took another pull on the joint and passed it to Blair, who closed her eyes and took a half-hearted pull before coughing it up in a violent spasm. "I don't know how you can stand that stuff, Missy," she said, handing it back. "Give me a nice glass of wine any day, preferably at a bar or a club."

Missy shook her head, pitying poor Blair, who was so hopelessly uncomfortable outside her bougie bubble. "Let's not become our parents, okay?"

Blair shrugged. "What's so bad about that? I mean, I wouldn't want to be *exactly* like them, but my parents have had a decent life. They seem happy."

"If you ask me, I'd say they just pretend. Look at my parents. They were miserable together." Missy took another toke as a bedraggled, snaggle-toothed man approached, his filthy pants belted beneath his butt. He jingled coins in a paper coffee cup. "Help me out," he mumbled.

Missy looked up at him, blankly. Help him *how?* "Look. I know this may not be possible, but do you, by any chance… take Apple Pay?"

"Apple *wha*—?" He scowled at her. "I don't want no damn *apple*. I want some *money*, bitch."

"I'm really, *really* sorry, sir. I don't have any cash," Missy said. She nodded toward Blair. "I think she does."

"Oh thanks!" Blair said under her breath, as she glared at Missy. "What is *wrong* with you?"

"What?" Missy said. "I just want to help him."

"Then help him. Don't volunteer me."

"*Come on!*" the man yelled, rattling his cup again, harder. "Give me some *money!*"

She held up the smoking joint. "Here," she said. "You can have this."

He snatched it out of her hand and stumbled away, puffing on the joint. Blair said, "Why would you give him anything after he called you 'bitch?' If somebody said that to you at school, you'd have them expelled."

Missy shook her head, exasperated. Blair was such a naïve waif. "Don't you understand? He talks that way because he's angry at the system."

"What do you mean?"

"*We* did this to him."

"*Who* did?"

"*We* did. Our families. We may not have created the system, but we went along with it because it protected us and our privilege."

"Well, yeah," Blair said. "That's the way it's supposed to work. It's called 'society.'"

Suddenly, squeals of delight poured from the crowd as three black cars came to a stop on Broadway and a squad of security personnel appeared to survey the park, heralding the arrival of glamorous Congresswoman Evita Manolo, the "Socialist Sensation." A fourth car followed, and out came the sleek and stylish congresswoman, smiling broadly and waving to her peeps—the grubby proletariat.

Missy grabbed Blair by the upper arm and squeezed. "Oh my God! There she is!" Her heart raced as she and Blair pushed their way through the crowd. They watched Evita get helped up to stand on one of the benches to address the gathering, and wobble momentarily on her stiletto heels. Missy exclaimed with wonder, "You know what's so great about her? She makes socialism look like fun."

"Oh yeah," Blair said. "Lotta laughs."

"Before, when you'd think of radicals, you'd think of glowering old bags like Emma Goldman," Missy said. "But Evita is so fresh and so different. She smiles. She laughs. She proves you don't have to wear a burlap bag to speak truth to power."

"I like that sleeveless dress," Blair allowed.

"She's got the shoulders for it, don't you think?"

"Very chic. You think it's Chanel?"

"Could be."

Wearing bright red lipstick, Evita smiled broadly as she surveyed the hundred or so people in the park. Missy estimated that half of them were there for the rally. The rest were skateboarders videotaping their exploits, nannies taking a break, men who managed the hot dog and falafel carts along Cedar Street, and scruffy drug addicts wearing saggy parkas on an eighty-degree day. It was difficult to make out what Evita was saying, given the muffled megaphone and the echo from the buildings, but Missy was getting the gist of it.

"Oh no!" Missy said, standing on her tiptoes to look over the man with the knit cap in front of her.

"What?" Blair asked. "I can't hear."

"She said the world is going to end in *twelve years!*"

Blair folded her arms over her chest. "How does she know that?"

A bearded man standing behind her said grimly, "It's true, man. You'll totally understand if you smoke fentanyl."

"Yeah. Great tip," Blair said, then turned to Missy. "Did she say exactly which day the world will end? I'm scheduled for a huge installment from my trust fund around then. Maybe I should accelerate my payouts."

Missy ignored her and cocked her head to hear.

"…our struggle is urgent, people!" Evita bellowed. "Climate change was, like, practically invented here in New York—right down the street from where we stand. And I want it to end here, starting today, starting now. We must take action! No more empty promises! These companies that don't comply to our demands will be, like, totally taken down to the ground, and crushed under the heels of our boots!"

Blair leaned toward Missy. "Nice boots."

With a hearty wave and a broad smile, Evita was helped off the bench and ushered back to her waiting black car. Her entourage rumbled down Broadway, leaving the assembly in a shroud of reignited marijuana smoke.

As Missy and Blair turned away from the rally, Blair said, "I don't understand something. Why do they call them fossil fuels? Is that because only old people use them?"

Missy shook her head. "No, no. It's because they were formed from the buried remains of animals and plants that existed millions of years ago."

"Got it."

"Let's take a walk," Missy said to Blair. "I want to show you something."

"Oh no," Blair said, rolling her eyes. "Not another Missy Mayburn Crowe Oppression Tour."

"Come on," she said, taking her hand.

"Can't we take the double-decker bus?" Blair muttered. "They point out nice things."

They walked up the hill through the park to Broadway and headed south past coffee shops, ornate building lobbies, and shuttered storefronts papered over with "For Lease" signs, the lingering scars of a pandemic that never quite went away. Nearing Bowling Green, they looked both ways for speeding delivery motorbikes and carefully crossed to the other side of the street. Missy gently pulled on Blair's arm as they stood in front of 26 Broadway, which was once the address of Alexander Hamilton and his family. Now, in its place, stood a massive limestone edifice.

"There it is," Missy said.

"Okay. I give up," said Blair, growing weary. "There's *what?*"

"The evil empire that started it all: the Standard Oil Trust," she said. "Long before there was a Rockefeller Center, there was a center for the Rockefellers' business. And this was it. Twenty-six Broadway was Standard Oil's headquarters after they moved here from Cleveland in the 1880s. If you go around to the back on New Street, you can still see the original red-brick building where John D. Rockefeller worked. He was, like, Big Oil's original gangsta. That's why my great-great-great—" She paused. "How many greats is that?"

"Three."

"—grandfather, Homer Crowe, built his own headquarters around the corner on Broad Street, so he could be close to the first great industrial monopoly in the world. Even after the trust busters went after them, Standard was still the big dog in the business. Look at all the companies they spawned—it's virtually the entire industry that exists today: ExxonMobil, Chevron, BP, Marathon… All were once little birds that fell out of this nest. It's no wonder Rockefeller's descendants have divested from fossil fuels. I know what a colossal embarrassment it is to realize your family weaponized energy against our planet."

Blair regarded Missy with dismay. "That seems a bit harsh, Missy. I know you're guilt trippin' about oil and gas, but haven't they served some useful purpose?"

"Sure, Blair. But at what cost?"

Blair shook her head. "I don't know. I mean, if things warm up a bit, is that so bad? I think the winters here are too freaking cold already. So we rise a couple degrees. I don't think that means they'll be growing bananas on Staten Island and pineapples in the Bronx."

Missy shook her head sadly. Bougie Blair was so incredibly hopeless. Why even argue? She needed to spend her time with more like-minded individuals. "I'm meeting with Ernesto tonight to talk about his plan."

"For climate change? Or for you?"

Missy smiled. "Both, I think."

24. GOING STEADY

alker wasn't sure if he was supposed to continue pretending that his septuagenarian boss, Staminum Chairman Steadman "Steady" Stamper, wasn't having an affair with his twenty-six-year-old personal trainer, Elyse. But the fact that this comely young lady from a middle-class family on Long Island suddenly had an apartment on Park Avenue, a personal driver, and a string of Fitness by Elyse studios in Manhattan was a clue. So, too, was the fact that she was practically sitting on Steady's lap in the corner of the Fitness by Elyse juice bar on 61st Street when Walker stepped through the door for his meeting.

Steady, in black Paulie Walnuts garb and a Fitness by Elyse-branded towel around his neck, looked like he might have been working out, or possibly just thinking about working out, or maybe just watching Elyse work out, which excited a few beads of perspiration on his brow. At the sight of Walker, he roused himself to stand and smile, gleaming white dentures providing high contrast to his perma-tan skin and silver hair. Elyse slithered out of view without so much as a glance Walker's way. Apparently, the charade was still on.

"Walker, my dear fellow," Steady said, grandly. "How are we this morning?"

"I know one of us is good," Walker said. "I trust you are as well."

"Indeed," Steady said. "Won't you sit down?" As they settled into the corner booth, Steady suggested a beverage as the waiter approached. "Perhaps you would like a glass of cranberry juice? A pomegranate smoothie? Good for the prostate, you know."

"Water's good for me, thanks," Walker said.

The waiter asked, "Flat? Sparkling? Bottled? Filtered? Purified? Fortified—"

"More like mystified," Walker said, holding up a hand in surrender. "Tap is good enough for me."

"Coming right up," the waiter said.

Walker looked around at the rustic-chic surroundings: lots of distressed wood and iron, and black-and-white photos of New York City from the early twentieth century. If Walker wasn't mistaken, these were photos he had seen in Walker's library in his mansion out on Oyster Bay. Perhaps they were on loan to Fitness by Elyse from the Steadman Stamper Collection, as was Steadman Stamper himself.

"I have to tell you I'm rather fascinated by this pressure campaign you're running against Crowe Power. It's rather ingenious in a way," Steady said. "How do you think it's playing out?"

"So far, so good," Walker said. "Between Harold Crenshaw, the Planetistas, and the media, I believe we're boxin' them in every which way. Harold tells me he might have even picked up some unexpected allies in the Crowe family."

Steady laughed. "You don't say! I can't imagine Lindsey Harper Crowe has many friends in the family right now. It appears she's even lost the support of her own daughter."

"If we continue to do this right," Walker said, "I don't see any way out for her but to accept the new board. They'll vote to break up the company, and we can move in to pick up the pieces."

"What parts are you most interested in acquiring?"

"I'd like to get our hands on their refineries in the Gulf. After that, my priorities would be their pipelines in Europe, and their power plants along the East Coast."

"That would leave the Crowes with what?"

"A big building on Broad Street," Walker said.

Steady nodded thoughtfully but said nothing.

Walker read the silence and said, "You seem concerned."

"I concede that I am," Steady acknowledged.

Walker leaned forward and stabbed his index finger into the table. "Don't be. We're goin' to win this fight."

Steady nodded. "That's what concerns me."

Walker was stunned. "How so?"

Steady leaned back in his seat, creating a little extra distance between them. "I've studied your integration plan," he said. "It all makes perfect sense—if this were 1995."

Walker struggled to contain his impatience. "What do you mean?"

"It seems to me as if it's based on assumptions that this industry will continue to hold a license to operate. I'm not so certain that's true," Steady said. "Doubling down on fossil fuels when they're increasingly out of favor seems very risky to me. Between disinvestment campaigns, pressure on suppliers, and one new regulation after another, I wonder whether we're just putting a bigger bullseye on our back. What happens if a breakthrough technology leaves us with an obsolete business model?"

Walker practically scoffed. What did this man know about the business? He sat out there on his big ol' estate, collecting his paychecks and his dividends, and chased his personal trainer around the pool. "I know there's all kinds of speculation out there about this technology or that one, but I don't see that happening," Walker said. "But if—and that's a very big if—if that were to happen, that's okay. We'd be in position to acquire it."

"How so?"

"Because all this pressure on oil and gas will reduce supply and raise prices. We'll make so much money over the next ten years, we'll be in position to buy anything that emerges. I don't care about bein' the first one into the next big green technology that's unproven. I'd rather be a fast follower on somethin' we know works. In the meantime, the world will still need somebody to provide basic energy. That somebody will be us—bigger and better than ever before."

Steady rubbed his hands together as he warmed to the idea. "I hope you're right, Walker. There's nothing I'd like more than to take down the Crowes. Those smug bastards have been a thorn in my family's side for four generations. But I only want to do that if it makes business sense."

Walker smiled. "I'll take care of my end of the bargain, Steady. Then you can take care of yours."

"When should we know if the Crowes are giving up?"

Walker looked at his watch. "Harold's meetin' with Lindsey Harper Crowe an hour from now," he said. "I'll have a status report for you this afternoon."

25. CROWE ON THE MENU

A black car weaved its way up Sixth Avenue through bicycles, delivery trucks, scooters, and pedestrians—everyone seemingly going the wrong way all at once. As the car came to a stop at the light at Canal Street, the driver eyed Lindsey in the rearview mirror. "Are you okay back there, Mrs. Crowe?"

Lindsey met his eyes and forced a smile. "I'm fine, Andrei," she said, knitting her hands. Already on edge about her forthcoming meeting, the driver's question unsettled her even more. Was her anxiety that obvious? She couldn't let that show with Harold Crenshaw. He'd pounce.

"Temperature alright?" Andrei probed.

"I suppose," she said, with a nervous yawn.

Andrei looked away for a moment, then back again. "If you don't mind my saying so," he said, "you seem a little, I don't know… tense. Would you like a little nip?" He blindly reached into his console with his right hand and pulled out an airplane-sized bottle of vodka. "You know—take the edge off a bit?"

Now she had one more reason to be concerned: her driver kept a stash of booze next to his seat. Lindsey waved him off as the light changed and the car lurched forward. "I appreciate your concern, Andrei, but no. I'd just rather, um…" *Hmm.* Truth is, she'd rather do anything other than sit in this car right now heading to a lunch meeting with the man who wanted to destroy her company. "I just need a moment to collect my thoughts."

What in the world was she doing anyway, putting her head on the block before a merciless executioner like Hacksaw Harry? Would Crowe Power's fusion project be enough to at least cause him to hesitate before he chopped the company into pieces? Should she even mention fusion at all? Heart galloping, she took a deep breath: *I can handle this*. She told herself that she had successfully faced down another business titan when she took control of the Crowe Power Company. Then again, that was Robbie, and he was a feckless weenie.

Hacksaw Harry was in a different league altogether: a cunning, ruthless predator with a track record of wealth creation through corporate destruction. If he were successful, the storied Crowe name would be consigned to history's dumpster. Walker Hope would emerge triumphant once again and thousands of jobs would be lost, many of them belonging to people whose families had worked for Crowe Power for generations. She would lose her own sense of purpose, which had been to lead her company into a new era of energy, a goal that had reinvigorated her after her marriage to Robbie had whimpered to its sorry conclusion. She sighed and shook her head, looking absently out the window. There was no escaping the sense of impending doom, if not humiliation. Losing a century-old business after just one year in charge would be a failure on every level—personally, socially, and financially. Maybe she should be relieved that it might soon be over, and all the pressure would be off. She could repair to the veranda of her beach house in East Hampton with an Irish coffee and a blanket, watch the piping plovers skip across the sand, and listen to the waves lapping the shore.

Andrei turned right on Bleecker Street and again on Thompson, a tree-lined avenue crowded with narrow storefronts, rickety dining sheds, and buckling sidewalks teeming with students from NYU. Andrei pulled to a double-parked stop in front of a storefront Italian restaurant once called Rocco, a name still vaguely visible on the distressed red-and-white metal sign hanging over the sidewalk. Neon script running across Rocco's name now spelled out Carbone, the moniker of the chic hideaway known as much for its hard-to-get reservation as its spicy rigatoni. Andrei scurried out of the driver's seat to open the rear door and offer his hand as Lindsey stepped to the curb, then pulled open the door to the restaurant for her to enter. "Good luck," he said.

Lindsey found Bentley Edwards waiting for her in the vestibule, elegantly dressed as always.

"Thank you for coming, Bentley," she said, patting the dapper lawyer's arm. "I do appreciate the support."

"Of course," Bentley said. He gestured toward the back room. "Your lunch date is already here."

Lindsey shuddered. "Oh lord. Did you speak with him?"

"Just a quick hello." Sensing her tension, he added, "Don't worry. He won't bite."

Lindsey nodded and smoothed her skirt. "How do I look?"

Bentley appraised her tweed Chanel suit, with three-quarter length sleeves and a slim skirt. "Like a million dollars."

She arched an eyebrow. "I hope more than that."

"Why do you say that?"

"I want him to think I'm unaffordable."

Bentley led her over a black-and-red checkerboard tiled floor in the front through a velvet curtained archway to the back. Harold stood at a table in the corner to greet Lindsey, surprising her with his height and lean frame. He smiled as they shook hands, but in a strangely menacing way. Perhaps it was his bear-trap mouth and oversized incisors, which looked like they could hack through wood, or possibly her leg. Otherwise, he appeared more rugged than she imagined, with bulging muscles that suggested strenuous daily workouts. Was Harold her age? Thanks to spas and plastic surgeons, it was impossible to tell the age of anyone in New York's elite circles anymore; they were all on needles and pins.

He gestured for Lindsey to take the blue velvet banquette. "Please." He sat across from her while Bentley took a chair between them. A recording of Dean Martin crooning *Sway* wafted softly over the sound system. *"Like a flower bending in the breeze... Bend with me, sway with ease..."*

"Such a pleasure to meet you at last, Lindsey," Harold said as pleasantly as a TV weatherman announcing sunshine for the weekend. "I'm glad we can sit down and discuss our situation like adults."

"I couldn't agree more," Lindsey said, warily.

"Good to hear," he proclaimed. "No sense fighting in public unless it's absolutely necessary, right?"

Lindsey interpreted that as the threat it was intended to be, but Bentley nodded to her as if to say, *See? He's not so bad!* Still, she couldn't resist a jab of her own. "Shall I call you 'Mr. Hacksaw?'" she asked with a smile. "Or just 'Harry?'"

He smiled back. "Don't believe everything you hear," he said. "Harold will do just fine." At the approach of a sommelier carrying a bottle of wine, he said, "I hope you don't mind. They keep a few cases of wine from my cellar here on the premises. I asked them to bring up a Brunello for the table."

Lindsey put the linen napkin on her lap. "Whatever your pleasure. I won't be having any."

The sommelier peeled off the foil from the top of the bottle. "Signor Crenshaw," he said. "Always wonderful to see you, sir." He carefully opened the bottle, examined the clean cork, and poured a splash for Harold, who lifted it toward the light and swirled the bowl, appraising the wine's purplish hues and long legs. As he brought the glass close to his nose and inhaled deeply, Lindsey imagined the inviting aromas of black cherry and licorice. *Ahhh...* She could swan dive into a glass like that and swim for hours.

"Lovely," Harold said, eying her over the rim.

Lindsey forced a smile. Was he referring to the wine? To her? Or how much money he expected to squeeze out of Crowe Power?

"Signora?" the sommelier asked as he poised the bottle near her glass.

Lindsey reflexively placed her left hand over the top of the glass. "I'll, um, I'll pass for now, thank you." Reducing her alcohol consumption had been getting more difficult every day. Declining now was torture, but the fate of her company required a sober approach. As the sommelier finished pouring for Harold and Bentley, it took all the willpower she had to stop him before he turned away and ask for a splash.

Harold noticed her hesitation. "*Salute,*" he offered with a broad smile.

Lindsey lifted her water glass, clinked with both men, and said, "*Cin-cin.*"

A waiter appeared and they put in their orders for entrees. As he departed, Harold took a slow sip of his wine, then leaned across the table. "I hope you don't take my critiques of your company personally, Lindsey. This intervention on my part has nothing to do with my regard for you or your family. In many ways, I admire your leadership. It's amazing how much progress you've made, considering the difficult circumstances you inherited. Walker Hope's sudden departure. The unfortunate Robbie debacle." He shook his head, almost as if he cared. "It was quite a mess down there and I know you're doing what you can to clean it up."

Lindsey noted the backhanded slap but chose to ignore it. "Profit-wise," she said, "I'm happy to say we're doing well. We have our challenges, as all companies do, but I think they're manageable, especially with the leadership team we have in place. They're very good at what they do. Our performance metrics are the best they've ever been."

"Right." Harold nodded solemnly. "But if things are going so well, why do you think that's not reflected in the share price?" he asked.

"What would you have us do?" Lindsey asked.

"It's all in the letter I sent you," he said. "Do you really need me to enumerate them again for you?"

"Not really," she said. "I just wanted to watch you say it with a straight face."

"Crowe Power hasn't kept up with the times, and it pains me to see it," Harold said. "You may not know this, Lindsey, but I was bullish on Crowe Power for many years. You had steady share appreciation, dependable dividends, stable leadership, and a sound business plan. Now we're in a very different era. Crowe Power hasn't adapted."

"You've certainly adapted—almost like a chameleon changing colors," Lindsey said, fingering her water glass. "And now, of course, I see that you're green. I'm curious how that happened. How did you arrive at the position of suddenly swooping in on a company like ours and pushing a social agenda as a virtue investor? It wasn't so long ago that people referred to you as a vulture capitalist and said that you cared only about one thing: money."

He scoffed. "What do vultures feed on, Lindsey? Carcasses. I make no apologies for that. I target companies where something has died."

"You don't say," she replied. "And what do you think died at Crowe Power?"

"Why, it's pretty obvious, isn't it? A sense of public responsibility."

Lindsey laughed out loud. "Oh, come now," she said. "When did you have this remarkable conversion to—quote, unquote—'responsibility?' Did you have some sort of epiphany on the road to Damascus? Or were you walking along Wall Street when pangs of conscience suddenly grabbed you by your manhood?"

Bentley squirmed uncomfortably in his seat while Harold tugged at his collar. "Actually, I was strolling down Broad Street near your headquarters," he said, his jaw clenched. "I passed the New York Stock Exchange and thought about all the companies whose values had plummeted because they let themselves become obsolete, and yours was at the top of the list. To my mind, that's not an inevitability. That's a choice."

Lindsey looked to Bentley for support, but he had purposefully buried his head in the wine list, avoiding the skirmish by studying Super Tuscans. "You do realize that fossil fuels still make up eighty percent of the energy consumed in this country and in the world," she said. "That's not going to change substantively any time soon."

"I understand that," Harold said.

"You also realize our company has begun a transition toward a more sustainable business model for the long-term, one that can withstand any sudden shift in the political winds," she said. "The fact is, we were making excellent progress on renewables until the very same environmentalists who bash us for failing to be sufficiently green put a stop to it."

Harold shook his head, sadly. "You've had bad luck."

Lindsey studied her adversary. Was he smirking? "Maybe there's more to it than chance," she said. "I get the feeling some people are doing everything they can to ensure we don't succeed—even on our best intentions—so they can take advantage of us. If you ask me, it's an orchestrated campaign." Harold flinched, ever so slightly, but Lindsey noticed, as did Bentley, who suddenly raised his head like a meerkat, peering over the top of the wine list.

"Lindsey, I'm sure there are times when things aren't going well where you suddenly feel the whole world is against you," Bentley said, quickly grabbing his glass and taking a slug. "I'm sure it's not the case. Maybe it's just your turn in the barrel."

A server laid down plates of crusty garlic bread, soppressata, and stracciatella di bufala, then refilled glasses, giving Bentley an opportunity to try turning down the heat. "Please, please. Why don't we have a little something to nosh on while we chat?" He lifted a serving plate and passed it to Lindsey. "Try the stretchy cheese. It's delightful."

Lindsey used tongs to pick up a chunk and passed the plate across to Harold, whose attempt at presenting a friendly countenance had failed under pressure. She looked away, lest her own hostility show more than it already had. The nerve of this man to waltz into her world and insinuate that he knew everything about the direction of her business—and that she did not—was deeply offensive. And Bentley's disappearance from the discussion was baffling.

"Look," she said, tapping the side of her water glass in her immaculately manicured fingers. "I understand we need to diversify into clean energy. A traditional fossil fuel-based company as big as ours is a big fat target. I know that in that sense, my goose is cooked."

As the waiter returned with three entrees, Bentley said, cheerfully, "The good news is: So is your chicken."

The waiter set down the plates and departed. Lindsey ignored her plate and addressed the larger issue on the table. "I would love nothing more than for this company to live long enough to be part of the long-term solution. Homer Crowe created a great company back in 1914, and we've had an incredible run. Lately, our reputation has been sullied—unfairly, in my view, but it is what it is. Can we change that? Yes. Could we again make our name something to be proud of again? I think we can."

Harold pushed. "You just have no idea how."

Lindsey said, sharply: "I do, actually."

"Really?" Bentley said, suddenly interested. "What do you have in mind?"

She eyed them both, who looked at her expectantly. Should she say it? "Well, I'm quite bullish on, um… fusion," she said, her voice cracking slightly.

Her hesitance was just enough for Harold to sense a lack of conviction. He couldn't help but break into laughter. "You can't be serious!"

Lindsey turned as red as the tablecloth. It was bad enough that Harold treated her with such condescension. Now he was openly mocking her? This was more than she could bear. She glanced at Bentley, who regarded her with obvious pity. Why, she wondered, had she invited him when he was not taking her side?

"You don't have the time or the money," Harold said flatly, swirling the wine in his glass. "If you think that will get the activists off your back, you're kidding yourself. But you're certainly not fooling me."

Lindsey summoned every bit of self-control she could muster. She pulled the napkin from her lap, carefully folded it in half, and put it on the table. "You don't really care about this, do you, Harold?" She looked across the table and into his blue steel eyes. "All you want to do is get your grubby mitts on our company and plunder it for cash. Your 'Hacksaw Harry' nickname is well deserved."

Harold practically snarled, "Insults won't help you."

"No? Well, I'm calling bullshit, Harold. I don't buy your green makeover. I don't buy your chummy chatter. The only thing I'll buy is your lunch." She stood and picked up her purse. "The bill is taken care of."

"I'm not bought off that easily," Harold huffed.

She turned back. "Neither am I, Hacksaw. Go fuck yourself."

***

Lindsey walked quickly to the door, her heels clicking on the tile floor. She exited the restaurant, found Andrei waiting in the car, and jumped into the back seat. The sanctuary of her car never had never looked so good. What a relief to extract herself from Hacksaw Harry's clutches, if only for the moment.

"The office, Mrs. Crowe?" Andrei asked.

"Please," she said, pulling her phone out of her purse and punching in Digby's number.

Seeing Lindsey's name flash on his phone, Digby excused himself from an outside table at Bobby Van's Steakhouse on Broad Street, where he was dining with three of his staff lawyers. Darting around the corner of Exchange Place, he answered, "How did it go?"

Lindsey bit the end of a nail. "Not great, frankly… I might have made a mistake."

"Uh oh."

She took a deep breath. "I snapped."

"How?"

"I told him off."

There was a pause before Digby replied. "That wasn't the plan."

She sighed as she looked out the window onto busy Houston Street. "If you'd have seen him, Digby, you'd understand. So smug. So superior. And not the least bit interested in what I had to say. He acted as if oil and gas were passe—while his SUV idled out on Thompson Street the whole time we were inside. And he laughed at our fusion idea—or maybe he just laughed at me. Either way, I could play nice for only so long. His veiled threats were more than I could take."

"What do you want to do?"

Lindsey fell back in her seat. "There's no other way around it: We have to prepare for war. He's going to go public. I can feel it."

Digby said. "It's going to get ugly. Are you prepared for that?"

"Worse than it is already? No," she said, flatly. "I'm not sure there's anything that can prepare you for an attack from this guy. I know it will be vicious. I know it will be cutting. And I know it will be scorched-earth," she said. "But I promise you this: I will fight back." She sighed. What else could she do? "How has your research gone? Do we have anything we can use against him?"

"We've combed through all the public filings, but so far… nothing."

Lindsey gasped. "What about private records?"

"You know I can't do that," Digby said.

"You can't or you won't?"

"Both," he replied.

There was silence on the line. Then, Lindsey said, "We're getting desperate here, Digby. He's going to fight dirty. We may have to fight just as dirty as he does."

Digby looked around to see if anyone could hear him, then cupped his free hand around the mouth of the receiver and faced the limestone wall. "I'm a lawyer, Lindsey. I can't fight dirty. If I'm disbarred, I won't be any use to you or anybody else."

"We don't want that," she said. "We'll play this on the up and up."

Digby exhaled. "Good," he said. "It's the only way I know how to play it."

"I know," she said. "You're a good, principled man, Digby."

She hung up and called her assistant. She needed help from somebody with fewer scruples. "Get Marty on the line for me, will you?"

26. STRIKE UP THE BRAND

Marty looked at his watch and yawned as the interminable Crowe Power marketing research meeting dragged into a second hour in the Homer conference room on the 24th floor. So far, the presentation had yielded nothing he could use in a campaign to defend the company. He didn't require polling numbers to tell him that the word "oil" wasn't popular with the American public, especially in urban clusters along the coasts of the Atlantic Northeast and the Pacific Northwest. He pinched himself to stay awake as the perky consultants from the jauntily-named Marketang Group skipped merrily through their lush meadow of data, picking out numbers like daisies and tossing them to the assembled crowd.

"New York City and San Francisco residents show generally low awareness of how much fuel a private jet uses," said Breeze Townsend, the agency's president. "Seventy-eight percent agreed with the statement: 'Celebrities flying around the world to lecture about climate change use electric engines in their private jets.'" She paused, thinking. "Obviously, there's some misunderstanding about jet propulsion. Might be an opportunity for consumer education there."

Marty nibbled from the ramekin of crackers next to his notepad and raised his hand. Breeze pointed to him. "Yes. You in the back there…"

Marty cleared his throat. "Where do the people you surveyed think electricity comes from?"

"Oh, that was a *very* interesting finding," she said, quickly thumbing through her massive binder on the conference table. "Unaided, sixty-six percent said either 'no idea' or 'a wall socket.' With prompting, some thought it might come from windmills and waterfalls. A surprising number thought their electricity was produced by burning recyclables—milk cartons, cardboard boxes, and the like."

Breeze's co-presenter, Milton somebody-or-other, piped in, "We thought that was an intriguing idea. Could be a new line of business for Crowe Power, if you're driven out of the fossil fuels business. You could burn recyclables."

Marty sighed as Breeze absently pulled and twisted on a chunk of long hair. "We do have some interesting findings about oil," she said. "Apparently, lots of people are still happy to use oil in their daily lives, but they just hate the word. When pressed, we found it stirs feelings of guilt about crimes against the planet. So, we asked people: What should oil be called? Is there a word or phrase that would make you think of oil in a better light?"

She hit her clicker and popped another slide on the screen. "'Schmoil' proved *very* popular, especially with our Brooklyn focus group. Unfortunately, it didn't test well elsewhere." She made a sad face and touched her cheek. "Too bad. I liked that one, too." She looked back to the screen. "We got a nice little bounce with 'Hy-C', short for hydrocarbons, but there was a trademark conflict. Apparently, Coca-Cola owns that brand of juice, and they didn't want their customers to think they were drinking gasoline. Understandable, I suppose." She clicked again. "We also tried 'oilio,' which we thought sounded like 'oleo'—you know, something you might melt and put on popcorn." She sighed. "Nobody found that very appetizing. But then, we tried this…" She brought up a new slide with bright green type:

earth milk

"And there it is!" she said, beaming. "Our team absolutely *loved* this concept. So did our focus group in Madison, Wisconsin." She let the wonderment sink in. "It's got such a wholesome quality to it, you know? It's not dirty old oil anymore. It's *earth milk*, like some totally natural liquid from the teat of Mother Nature. It's not drilled. It's not fracked. It's nourishment that is nothing but good for you and your family. And it's totally GMO and gluten free."

Marty resisted the urge to boo as Milton piped up again. "There's a historical precedent for this. It's like calling underwear Fruit of the Loom, which sounds a lot nicer, or tuna fish in a can Chicken of the Sea to make it more palatable. We want to get the entire industry to stop talking about oil as oil. Just let it go. That's yesterday's news. Call it pure unadulterated earth milk, full of one-hundred percent wholesome goodness."

"Oh my God! I love that idea," said Chloe Delaney, Crowe Power's vice president of Marketing.

Marty slapped his forehead. Was Chloe actually paying people to come up with this shit? Did they expect anyone to believe that America was a nation of gullible suckers? Then he remembered recent elections and conceded that they might be on to something.

"Another problem we have is how oil is produced," Breeze said. "People hate—and I mean, absolutely *hate*—the word fracking. To them it sounds like, you know," her voice went to a near whisper, "the f-word."

Chloe smiled. "It is an f-word," she said, prompting laughter around the room.

"F-word is fine," Breeze said, "but not if you're f-wording the earth."

"Oh," Chloe said.

"Yeah," Breeze said, somberly.

"But our company doesn't do any fracking," said Khalifa Said, a lobbyist.

"No. But your pipelines carry oil and gas that's produced from fracking. It makes you, like, an accessory to murder, you know—killing the planet."

Marty said, "So you're saying 'earth murder' didn't test well either."

"No," Breeze said emphatically. "That's why we need a new name for fracking, too. We tested a whole bunch of words and we got a very positive response from… 'caressing.'" She waited a moment for the people in the room to appreciate the ingeniousness. "See? We're kindly *caressing* the earth, coaxing a little bit of oil and gas to come out of the glands of the earth." Her voice went high. "Here, little earth milk. Come on out now…"

Marty wanted to stab his eyes with a pencil. Did they realize the peril this company was in? Why were they pretending they could save the fossil fuels business with some linguistic sleight of hand that everyone but a complete idiot could see through?

Sergei Badanov, the technology chief, offered a dose of reality to the marketing wizards. "You do realize that there's no caressing involved. Fracking is done with little explosions that blow up rock, which releases the oil and gas. And when they flare the excess methane, it creates fields of fireballs that you can see from the moon."

Milton shot a glance to Breeze, then looked back. "You know, you're right. We might have a bit more work to do on that one."

"Please understand," Breeze said, "that this is a long-term effort. We can't change perceptions about oil overnight. But we have to start somewhere."

Marty shook his head: Crowe Power didn't have a long term. The company was facing a existential crisis *right now*. He raised his hand again, and Breeze called upon him.

"Did you test the concept of fusion?" Marty asked.

"Oh yes," Breeze said, with a laugh. "Guesses were all over the place. Sixteen percent said 'fusion' was a car made by Ford, which was, much to my surprise, true not too long ago. Fifteen percent said it was a brand of razor blade from Gillette, which is also correct. And six percent said it was a disco, maybe in Philly. Only one respondent said it was a way to create energy." She looked at Milton and laughed. "I think we had a ringer in there."

Breeze put her paper down and picked up another sheet. "But when we asked our focus groups if they would be interested in getting their energy from, quote, unquote, 'star power,' like you asked, they lit up. 'Star power' sounds futuristic, cool. In fact, forty-six percent said they couldn't wait to see the movie."

Marty fell back in his chair. Ridiculous as it sounded, maybe this focus group was on to something. Make energy entertaining! Hard to turn a fifty-five-gallon oil drum into a barrel of laughs —regardless of what ridiculous name they gave it—but a theatrical presentation of star power had definite possibilities.

As the conversation drifted, Marty rose from his chair and wandered to the window. He looked across to Jersey City and searched the horizon. Just north of Con Fusion was a round dome. Wasn't that a planetarium? Where better to put on a dazzling show about star power? And a bit further south, across the bay was Liberty Island and the Statue of Liberty. Could he tie the two together somehow?

He felt a vibration in his pocket and pulled out his phone to see Lindsey's name on the screen. He left the room and found a quiet spot in the hallway. "I hope you found some ammunition to use against Hacksaw Harry," she said.

"I have," he replied.

"Good," she said. "Come up to the house. We're going to need it."

27. WHERE THERE'S SMOKE

Walker Hope found Hacksaw Harry on a sofa in the back of the darkly paneled Carnegie Club, where he was lighting a long, fat cigar to celebrate his impending triumph over Lindsey Harper Crowe and her company. A soundtrack of Frank Sinatra's greatest hits played overhead and a tumbler with McCallan 18-year scotch sat on the table beside him.

Walker took the overstuffed club chair next to the sofa. "Is that a victory cigar?" Walker asked hopefully.

Harold took several quick puffs and exhaled a long thin cloud toward the bookcases. "Not quite, but it's damn close," he said, examining the tip to see that it was evenly lit. "This is a Davidoff Royal Release Salomone from the Dominican Republic. One hundred and eighty-five dollars, but worth it. Would you like one?"

Walker shook his head. "I'm not much of a smoker. I have about one a year."

Harold stuck the cigar in his mouth and talked between clenched teeth. "Well, here's the way I see it. What better way to demonstrate my green bona fides than polluting the air? Right?" He growled with laughter.

"That's one way, for sure." Walker studied his partner and his remarkable incisors. *Was that man wearing some of them wax Halloween teeth? He was truly scary looking…*

"The good news is we've got her right where we want her," Harold announced. He recounted the conversation and the points he'd made. In his telling, Lindsey's flimsy defense of her regime had collapsed under his withering assaults before she eventually stalked off in retreat.

"I've softened the beaches," he said. "Time now for the invasion."

"What goes first?" Walker asked.

Harold ticked off the list: He would issue a news release within the hour announcing that he now held a five percent share of Crowe Power's common stock and that he was deeply concerned about the company's direction. The release would generate massive shock waves on Wall Street. That would be followed by calls to Lindsey from three powerful institutional investors asking that she give Harold's demands careful consideration.

By the close of trading, Harold predicted, investors expecting that Hacksaw Harry would "unlock" value in Crowe Power shares would send CRO stock soaring, giving his efforts further momentum. Then would come the kill shot the next morning: Veronica Sawyer's story on Buzzniss.com, portraying Lindsey as a clueless dilletante who was in over her head.

"Don't breathe a word, but I've seen the story," Harold said. "It's not pretty."

Walker shook his head. "I almost feel sorry for her, Harold. If this were a boxin' match, they'd have to stop the fight."

"Well, forget it. I'm not letting her off the mat. Especially after the way she talked to me at lunch," Harold said. "We'll ramp up the protests by the Planetistas and extend them to Crowe Power facilities in other parts of the world. The media is very sympathetic to a storyline about a greedy energy company willfully ignoring the climate crisis. You can expect lots of coverage that tilts in our direction. Then my guys will launch the campaign on social media, beating the daylights out of Crowe Power for its failure to get its wind and solar power projects off the ground."

"In no small part because of you."

Harold held the cigar in his teeth and pointed back and forth between the two of them. "Nobody but you and I need to know that."

"Roger," Walker said. "What about the Crowe family? Any progress prying away some votes?"

Harold laughed. "I wish you were there to see it! I played Robbie like a Stradivarius," he said. "That dumbass is giddy over the idea that he can become chairman again. He just has no idea how short his tenure is going to be. Wait until he sees new board. It won't be like that collection of doddering geezers they've got on his old board. Wish I could be in the room when he finds out they're busting up the company."

Walker stretched his arms over his head, thinking. "What's your view as an investor, Harold? Do you still think I should swallow the whole enchilada? Or just bite off a few pieces?"

Harold puffed on his cigar, thinking. He pulled a fragment of tobacco off his tongue and leaned forward. "I would say it's cheaper in the short term to pick off a few chunks. But you'd lose an opportunity."

"What's that?"

"Crowe Power and Staminum Energy are a perfect combination." He held up both index fingers and put them together. "And the beautiful thing is: regardless of all this happy talk about clean and green energy, the world can't break it's fossil fuel habit anytime soon. The companies that survive this shakeout will be needed more than ever, and your prices can go through the roof."

Walker took a deep breath. "You think they'll let us stay in business?"

Harold laughed. "They won't have a choice! I gotta tell you something, Walker. I've been making a killing on oil and gas since Evita Manolo and her fellow travelers conspired to reduce supply. I don't know why they think it's a terrible thing for the climate if oil and gas is produced in the United States, but it's somehow okay if it comes from Putin and the Crown Prince of Saudi Arabia. Once this country wakes up to the fact that it threw away its energy independence—and the geopolitical advantage that comes with it—it will be too late. But after these acquisitions, Staminum will be sitting pretty."

Walker blew out his cheeks. "What about Crowe Power's renewable energy? Is there anything there?"

Harold leaned forward. "That may be the best part," he said. "Their Consolidated Fusion subsidiary is positioned beautifully—right in the middle of what may be the next hot trend in energy. She's all giddy about it, but the market doesn't assign it any value just yet. The payoff is too far out in the future. So we get in now for a great long-term play. You would essentially get it for nothing."

Walker's brow furrowed. "Wait a second. Isn't that a company that I sold to them? Wasn't Con Fusion part of Greeneron?"

Harold chuckled. "It was indeed. So you win twice. Once when you sold it. And again when you get it back."

Walker said, "Alright. Let's play this out. Lindsey gets so rattled by our attack that she's relieved to sell. I buy all of Crowe Power. Does the market love it or hate it? You realize I have stock options at stake here."

"We make them love it. You slash costs. Cut jobs. Consolidate central staffs. Close their headquarters. You create pure plays by spinning out refining and pipelines into their own companies. And to top it off, you wave Con Fusion as your green banner to keep the activists at bay. The ESG crowd will eat it up."

Walker nodded. "I like it."

"Good," Harold said. "You give me the word and I'll unleash the hounds."

Walker smiled. "Let 'em go!"

Harold picked up his phone and punched in a number.

Walker sat back in his seat and relaxed, pleased that everything was coming together as they had planned it. "I think I will have one of those cigars," he said.

28. UNDERMINED

After being greeted by a servant in the vestibule of Lindsey's townhouse, Marty was directed to an ornate antique elevator with a sliding brass grate. He pulled on the handle, pushed the button for five, and rose to the top floor. There, he found Lindsey in an office larger than his entire apartment, with mansard windows poking out of the roof to capture the fading sun over Central Park.

"Oh, Marty. Thank God you're here," she said. Lindsey's face, illuminated by the white light of the computer screen atop the desk that had once belonged to her grandfather, was drained of color. Digby, more glum than usual, was slumped in an armchair, scrolling through his phone.

Lindsey hit a button on her computer, which started the printer behind her clacking and whirring. She pulled the print-out from the tray and handed it across the desk to Marty, who sat in a chair next to Digby and set his briefcase on the floor. "Here's the first salvo," she said.

FOR IMMEDIATE RELEASE

Carrion Investments Announces Five Percent Stake in Crowe Power
Continued   Underperformance   Demands   Change   in Governance

NEW YORK (PR Newswire) – Harold C. Crenshaw, Managing Partner of Carrion Investments, announced today that his firm has taken a five percent interest in the Crowe

Power Company, and that he will nominate a slate of directors to replace the company's current Board, including Chairwoman Lindsey Harper Crowe.

"It's plain to see why Crowe Power is underperforming the market," Crenshaw said. "The company's failure to begin a much-needed transition away from fossil fuels and do its part to resolve our climate crisis has shaken investors' faith in its future. We intend to jumpstart the company's transition with more responsible oversight. Sadly, the current regime demonstrates no capacity for getting it done."

Crenshaw said his slate would include business leaders, academicians, climate scientists, activists, and political philosophers culled from elite cultural institutions. "Crowe Power needs to broaden its thinking beyond the interests of certain entrenched family members to include its large community of stakeholders."

Before Marty could read any further, Lindsey said, "Our stock's up seven percent. Market seems to think he's going to succeed in getting a new board and booting me out." Lindsey's phone rang. She glanced at the name on her screen and looked to Digby. "Poundstone Partners," she said, with a shake of her head. "Yes, Ted," she answered, as she got up from her desk and walked toward an alcove, leaving Digby and Marty alone.

Digby stretched and yawned nervously. "That's the third institutional investor to call since the release went out thirty minutes ago. I don't think it's a coincidence."

"Hacksaw Harry lined it up in advance?"

"Of course," Digby said.

"What are they saying?" Marty asked.

Digby shrugged. "Surrender Dorothy."

Lindsey walked back to her desk and flopped in her seat. "That was Ted Papapanos. Surprise, surprise: he insists he's not picking sides, of course, but he wants me to give Harry's sock puppets careful consideration for our board. Which of course, I can't, and I won't."

Digby looked at his watch. "Fourth Street Partners is due any minute."

Lindsey nodded. "What do you think he'll pull next?" On cue, they heard a roar from a crowd outside, prompting all of them to rush to the window. "Oh no," she said. Down below, under the strobe of red-and-blue police lights, came a throng of fifty protesters, carrying signs and banners and rattling noisemakers. They settled in front of her house, where they faced the home and began to chant.

> *Climate change makes me cry,*
> *Please don't make our planet die!*
> *Let's get rid of oil and gas,*
> *So climate change won't fry my ass!*

"The neighbors will not be pleased," Lindsey said, turning away from the window. "On top of everything else, do I have to move?"

Digby sighed. "Where would you go?"

"To another planet, obviously," Lindsey said. "Based on what those people claim, this one's about to blow."

Lindsey retrieved a pair of binoculars from a nearby bookshelf and trained them on the street. There, in front, locking arms with a bearded man in a beret, was Missy Mayburn Crowe, daughter of the next American revolution, chanting along with her bedraggled comrades-in-arms while raising her fist in the air. Lindsey muttered, "Are you freaking kidding me?"

She handed the binoculars to Digby, who studied the street. "Is that… Missy taking to the barricades?"

"Les Miz Ms." Lindsey said, shaking her head. "Is there a way to contest maternity?"

Marty, awaiting his turn, was distracted from the commotion below by what appeared to be a couple having sex in the window across the street. Was he seeing what he thought he was seeing?

"Can you believe it?" Lindsey shook her head.

"Actually, I can't," Marty said. Taking the binoculars from Digby, he zeroed in on the grappling neighbors to confirm his suspicions. "Why, it's truly remarkable," Marty said, adjusting the focus. "Quite a show."

Lindsey returned to her desk and Digby followed. "Marty?" Lindsey called. "Are you joining us?" Getting no response, she called, "Marty? *Hello?*"

"Sorry," Marty said. He put the glasses down and returned to his chair across from Lindsey's desk. He folded his hands over his lap to conceal his excitement over the display he had just witnessed.

"Did you find out anything useful about Harold Crenshaw?" she asked.

Marty reached into his briefcase and pulled out a folder. He laid the folder on his lap and looked to Digby. "Are we under attorney-client privilege?" he asked.

Digby responded, flatly, "So far."

"Well, it just so happens that some internal documents from Carrion Investments landed on my doorstep earlier today," Marty said. "I, of course, have no idea how they got there, but I'm glad they did. It turns out that Hacksaw Harry is more cobalt blue than green."

Lindsey sat up in her chair. "How so?"

"As you may know," Marty said, putting the papers on his lap, "cobalt is a critical component of green energy. It's needed for batteries that power electric vehicles and store energy from solar and wind power."

Lindsey looked at Digby, who remained impassive. "Okay," he said.

Marty continued, "Harold is heavily invested in cobalt extraction, which—like oil and gas—is rarely found in the South of France. Cobalt is mined in the Democratic Republic of the Congo in central Africa, where tens of thousands of kids—many of them orphans as young as seven years old —are kept out of school to work in horrible, dangerous conditions. It turns out their small hands and fingers are very helpful for sorting rocks."

Lindsey asked, "How bad is it for the children?"

Marty handed over a stack of photos. "See for yourself," he said. "They work in rickety tunnels and trenches prone to collapse. The air is horrible, the water is worse. They have no helmets, gloves, or protective gear. Many of them live in camps rife with violence, disease, and sexual exploitation—all for the cause of making a dollar a day."

"Oh my!" Lindsey's mouth went agape as she looked at the photos of children covered in dust, emerging from holes in the ground, standing in filthy water holding burlap sacks, and picking through rocks with their bare hands. "This is so sad," she said. "I wonder what Harold's activist friends would have to say if they knew about this."

"They make a little bit of noise about human rights and pollution, but otherwise they give it a pass," Marty said. "After all, there's a bigger cause at stake here." He flipped over his paper. "Harry gives so much money to activist groups that none of them wants to see that his 'green' investments are centered on cobalt and rare earth minerals. He's mining rocks and minting money."

Lindsey crossed her arms. "And managing to create a new image for himself as an environmental crusader."

"Neat trick if you can pull it off," Marty said.

"Which he's doing," Lindsey said. "Are anybody's hands entirely clean in the energy business?"

"Not his," Marty said.

She slapped the photos on the desk. "Can we use this somehow?"

Digby simmered. "No," he said, sharply.

"Why not?" Lindsey demanded.

"Because it raises questions we can't answer about the provenance of these documents," he said. "Were they stolen? Hacked? Smuggled out of the company? None of this information is in public filings. If you give these to a reporter, it's quite obviously self-serving—and it gets traced right back to us."

Lindsey sighed. "That hardly seems fair."

"It doesn't matter if it's fair or not," Digby said. "That's the way it is."

The air went out of the room as they each pondered a solution. Finally, Marty said, "We can still fire a shot across his bow."

Lindsey sucked in her breath and raised her chin. "How so?'

"We let Harry know that you know."

"How do you propose we do that?" she asked.

Marty got up and paced the room. "Harold says Crowe Power is not a responsible corporate citizen, right? What if we announce that our company is setting up a school in the Congo? We'll partner with a human rights or educational group to save, say, a hundred kids from the horrors of cobalt mining and set them on a better path toward a better life. In fact," he said, "we will also offer scholarships to a few of the best and brightest for the study of clean energy at Princeton or MIT. We'll call it the Albert K. Harper Scholarship."

Lindsey brightened. "After my grandfather. I like that!" She patted her desk. "Are you hearing this, Grandpa?"

Marty continued, "Not only do we claim the mantle of good citizenship, but we put a spotlight on the problem of child labor, and we signal to Harry we know all about his investments. In the process, we undermine his ability to operate over there by depriving him of a cheap work force."

Lindsey laughed. "That should get his attention."

Digby took a deep breath. "Is it enough to put him off?"

Marty leaned against the bookshelf. "The school can be part of a comprehensive presentation on our outlook for the future, which begins with our incredible advancements in fusion. We'll show investors that Crowe Power is not only a very responsible company, but that it's leading the way toward a brighter, better, cleaner future."

Lindsey's angst was melting away. "*Oooh,*" she cooed. "I'm warming to this."

Marty looked to Digby, who nodded. "Credible enough, I suppose."

"Credible?" Lindsey scoffed. "Who's going to call us out, Digby? Harold can't. He's compromised. We're going to save the company—and maybe the world."

"Planet," Marty corrected her.

"Oh, right," she said. "I've got to get with the lingo."

"This may be a stretch, but okay," Digby said, standing up. "I'm meeting Bits at six o'clock. Text me if you need anything."

As Digby departed, Marty figured it was best that he should leave, too. But Lindsey said, "Let's flesh out your ideas a bit more. Can you stick around?"

***

Just a few hours earlier, it felt to Lindsey like her whole world was caving in on her. And maybe it still was. But, with a strong response to Hacksaw Harry taking shape, and a staunch ally by her side who indicated he would do whatever it took to protect her interests, she at least had a fighting chance.

"How about a glass of wine?" she asked, pushing away from the desk.

Marty smiled. "Twist my arm," he replied.

She walked to the pantry, opened the glass door to a wine cooler, and pulled out a shelf of red wines. She selected an Antica Terra pinot noir from the Willamette Valley, opened it with a corkscrew, poured a splash and swirled it in the glass before she inhaled its lovely aromas. She took two glasses to the tufted leather sofa in front of the sage tiled fireplace and handed one to Marty.

"For the first time since Hacksaw Harry darkened my door, I feel like I can breathe," she said. "Maybe we can beat the bastard."

"Cheers to that," Marty said. They clinked glasses and sipped the wine.

She set her wine down on a coffee table and pulled out her phone. She punched a few buttons, and the sound system came alive with Chet Baker's smooth trumpet pumping out the first riffs of "Let's Get Lost." She retrieved her wine and settled back again.

"I can't tell you how helpful it's been to have you working with me on this," she said. "Thank you."

"Glad to help," Marty replied, as he extended an arm across the top of the sofa.

"I have wonderful people on my team at Crowe Power. Lucy and Armani and Digby—they're all terrific. They follow the rules, which is what you want in a company like ours. We certainly don't need people taking creative chances with an oil refinery." She sipped her wine. "But this Hacksaw Harry attack is war, and my sense is the usual conventions go out the window. I don't want to be the Redcoats, honorably marching across the battlefield with bayonets drawn, while the Continentals pick us off from behind the trees." She shook her head. "Dying with dignity holds no honor for me. We need to win, even if we have to bend the rules." She looked at him with a glint in her eye. "I'm not going to ask how you got Harold's files."

"Good," Marty said. "I wouldn't tell you."

She held up a hand. "I understand."

"I hope you do. I need to protect my sources—and I need to protect you, too."

"Understood," she replied. "Plausible deniability, right?"

"Yes. That's the operative phrase."

Lindsey savored the wine, which sent warm waves of dopamine through her system, relieving her apprehensions. She'd almost forgotten how good wine tasted, and how it made her feel. She could handle this much without losing control; why not have a bit more? She went to the pantry to retrieve the bottle and brought it back to the sofa. Pouring for each of them, she said, "So tell me, Marty. How did you end up here, anyway?"

"As I recall, you said, 'Get your ass uptown.'"

She rolled her eyes at him. "Before that. How did you end up doing this kind of work?"

Marty explained that he had grown up in the Midwest, earned degrees in journalism from the University of Missouri and Northwestern, and worked his way through a series of newspapers before they were each rendered obsolete by the internet. "It became an endless series of staff cuts and pay freezes and all-hands meetings to meet the latest new owners from private equity firms. Most of them were more interested in buying distressed debt than news organizations. I could read the writing on the wall."

"What did it say?"

"'Jump.'"

Lindsey pulled her legs up under her and sipped her wine. "And you landed with both feet on Broad Street."

"I didn't have much choice," Marty recounted. "I had two kids nearing college, a wife who had left the work force to devote herself full time to playing around with our gardener in the potting shed, and I had a big mortgage on our house up in Westchester. Roger Barnes, my old editor at the Daily News, had left the newspaper business and ended up at Crowe Power. He tossed me a life preserver and I grabbed it. He said my work in one business nearing extinction was good background for another one. He assigned me to support Robbie, who at the time was failing his way up the corporate ladder. Roger said, 'He's slated for bigger things around here. Make him look like he deserved it.'"

"What did you do?"

"It was a challenge," Marty said, as he poured more wine for both of them. "Robbie didn't have any particular achievements or credentials. But he did seem to like grass and trees and a walk in the park, especially in the middle of the workday. So we decided to build a persona around his interest in nature: L. Robertson Crowe III, ardent environmentalist with a business sensibility."

"It certainly seemed to work."

"Oh yeah," Marty said. "It wasn't hard to sell to the media. Page thirty-eight in the journalist hymnal is a hallelujah chorus that sings the praises of anybody in big business who sounds like they want to save the planet. We wrung a ton of great clips out of Robbie's unusual conscience, and how he waged a brave, lonely battle against the establishment."

"You mean when he showed up for work."

Marty guffawed. "C'mon! A battle like that takes a lot out of a guy. He needed rest."

"Right," she said with a smile. "You really do spin gold out of straw, don't you? Can you spin some for me?"

"That's the plan," he said. "By this time next week, they'll proclaim you a Green Goddess."

Lindsey burst out laughing. "That's a hell of a stretch!"

"Of course, it is," he said. "But here's the thing: People want to believe. They're bombarded constantly with stories about impending doom from the 'climate catastrophe.' There's little they think they can do about it, especially if it involves personal cost or sacrifice. They would like someone to solve the problem for them. Now that someone is you."

Lindsey ran a hand through her hair, then shook it loose to fall on the tufted leather cushions and allowed herself to dream. "I would love for that to be true."

"I'd settle for a convincing story that gets us past Hacksaw Harry."

"Understood," she replied, turning to face him. "But... what if there were more to it than that? What if we really did chart the course toward a more sustainable future? I don't have the guilt that Robbie and Missy have about fossil fuels. Oil and gas and coal did a lot of good for a lot of people for a long period of time. They raised standards of living and gave people heat and light and mobility. But I know we can do better than digging materials out of the ground and burning them, releasing all that stuff into the atmosphere. Human ingenuity is better than that. We just have to find the way. Maybe we have an answer."

Marty nodded. "Maybe."

"If we fail," she said, "I don't want it to be because we didn't try. That's what our critics think—that we're not even trying." She paused. "I wonder what my little revolutionary is doing." She rose from the sofa and went to the window. Marty followed, taking his glass. "Looks like they're gone." She started to turn away, then noticed the window across the street, where the frisky couple was going at it once again. "Whoa!"

Marty sucked in his breath. "Yeah. Kinda noticed that earlier."

She looked at him and laughed. "Marty McGarry. Don't think I didn't know what you were looking at. You're a bad boy!" She grabbed the binoculars and focused them across the street. "They've been running the sexual Olympics over there just about every night for two weeks."

Marty smirked. "You must be appalled."

"Disgusted beyond belief," she said, with a smile.

"Have you called the cops?"

"Not yet," she said. "I'm still gathering evidence."

"It's your civic responsibility."

"Exactly," she said. She handed him the binoculars. "Check it out. It's even worse from the other window."

"Seriously?" he said. "This calls for an investigation,"

They walked to a second window and Marty trained the binoculars on the grapplers across the street. "My goodness," he said. "It's every bit as repugnant as you suggested."

She walked to a third window. "And from this angle, it's really ridiculous!"

Marty followed and peered through the glasses. "They seem pretty proud of their exhibition. There's just one thing I don't get."

"What's that?" she asked.

He put the binoculars down on the windowsill and faced her. "Did you see how he had his hand here?" He put his right hand on her waist.

"Yes," she said.

"I think it should go more like here," he said, reaching around her and pulling her close.

"I see what you mean," she said, looking into his eyes.

"Should we show them how it's done? You know, the right way?" He leaned in and kissed her neck. "Because if it were up to me, I would start right here."

She pushed him back a bit, albeit with a smile. "That's a wonderful place to start—but it's also where we need to finish for now," she said. "I don't remember all the particulars of our arrangement, Marty, but I think it's a little early for your success fee. Don't you?"

Marty's look expressed disappointment. "I expect to collect."

"I'm counting on it."

29. BUDDING ROMANCE

Fresh from her triumphant Millionaire Mom March, Missy fled East 67th Street with Ernesto for the wilds of Central Park. They wound their way past an expansive playground, down the steps to the Bethesda Terrace, and over the graceful Bow Bridge to the woodsy Ramble, climbing a hill to find a rustic bench overlooking the lake. Ernesto produced a joint from his satchel, and they began to smoke their way into a lazy summer haze. Ernesto let his hair down, doffing his red star beret and untying his man bun.

Missy watched Ernesto allow his curly tresses to fall to the shoulders of his black t-shirt and shivered with excitement. *How cool is this?* Here she was, in one of her favorite places on earth, alone with a genuine Latinx revolutionary in the mold of Guevara, Castro, and Chavez. She peered out over the lake, where rowers splashed about, and ducks paddled around them, scurrying at times to avoid their wooden hulls and oars. In the distance over the trees, she noted how much the skyline of Midtown had changed just in the time since she'd gone to college, with new skyscrapers whose stark outlines looked more like smokestacks than luxury living spaces. *Capitalism strikes again…*

Ernesto took a puff on the joint and passed it to Missy. "You seem, like, totally pissed off at your mother," he said.

She shrugged. "I'm not angry as much as I'm frustrated. She's in a position to actually do something about climate change and she's not doing it."

"What do you want her to do?"

"Go green," Missy said.

"I get that," Ernesto said. "But how?"

"I don't know."

"Oh well," he said. "If she can't hack it, maybe she should just go out of business."

"Wouldn't be the worst thing in the world." Missy shook her head, mournfully. "I mean, if Crowe Power is going to keep doing the same old, same old with fossil fuels, it's kinda like, what's the point? You know? All she's doing is destroying the planet. By the time the company figures it out, it will be too late. We'll all be drowned by rising seas. Or burned by raging wildfires. Or blown away by hurricanes and tornados."

"Or passing out from hyperventilation?" Ernesto asked.

"Whatever. It could be anything," Missy said. "It's so unpredictable."

Ernesto relit the bud and took a puff. "I could see alien invasions, you know? I'm thinkin' they're, like, looking at us from deep space and they see how Earthlings fucked it all up and they have to come and take over."

She took the joint from Ernesto. "Any way you look at it, it's bad."

Ernesto gazed vacantly out at the lake, lost in the amorphous ideology that was taking shape in his head. "Look, Missy. You know my feelings about this. Our society is totally rigged in favor of big businesses and billionaires. That has to stop. Right?"

"Oh yeah," she said.

"We should have, like, a central authority in charge of everything. Keep it simple, you know?"

"Makes total sense," she said.

"I actually talked to Evita Manolo about this at a fundraiser out in Queens, and she totally agrees with me."

"Really?" Missy said. "That is *sooo* cool."

"She says—and this is true—that the people of this country are too dumb to make good decisions about their lives. They only think of themselves when they should think of, like, all humanity, you know?" Ernesto said. "We need a big central committee of people like us, who actually care about what happens, to decide what's fair and equitable. And then we just tell people, 'this is what you're going to do and this is how you're going to do it.' I mean, I would be totally in favor of climate lockdowns, you know?"

"How would that work?" Missy asked, as she puffed the joint.

"Say carbon emissions are too high one day. The president just orders everyone to stay home. Nobody can go out. It's like we did with Covid, you know? Except this time, you use all this connected technology to turn down thermostats, or turn them up, and turn off air conditioners and furnaces. You could even lock people in their houses."

Missy's head went wobbly with the possibilities. "Wow. You are blowing my mind."

"And how about this?" Ernesto asked. "We could even do masks again."

"Oh," Missy said. "I loved the masks. I kind of miss them."

"It was great, right? This time," Ernesto said, "we take it a step further. We all have to wear these devices over our faces to capture carbon dioxide as we exhale."

"And what do you do with it?"

"I don't know."

Missy nodded. "Have you been thinking about this a long time?"

"Just since we sat down," Ernesto said.

"I see."

"Look," he continued. "Things are only going to get better if allocate resources based on what people need—not what they think they want because they saw it on TV."

Missy pondered that notion. "So you would take capitalism out of the equation?"

"Oh yeah. Just get rid of it."

"So with something like package delivery, instead of UPS and FedEx, all mail deliveries would be handled by… the Post Office?"

"Exactly."

"Wouldn't that kinda suck?" she suggested.

"No. Not at all!" Ernesto said, pulling on the joint and blowing a blue cloud. "'Cause, you see, when all the money for deliveries goes to the Post Office, then they'd finally have, like, the funds to do the job right. They wouldn't be going all postal and shooting each other and holding your mail for months and making you wait in long lines just to talk to surly people who can't help you. They would be, like, so happy. And that would make them want to deliver your mail."

Missy cocked her head. "How would that apply to energy?"

"We just issue orders. 'By such-and-such a date, we're pulling the plug on oil and gas.' *Boom!* No more gasoline-powered cars. We're yanking them off the road. Every vehicle must be electric, or we throw your ass in jail."

"But… most electricity still comes from fossil fuels."

"Well, yeah. But that's just, like, a technicality. Someday, it will all come from something else."

"Like what?"

He searched the horizon for an answer and came up blank. "I think… um, maybe it would come from…" He suddenly tired of the revolution. "You know what? I could really go for a slice."

Missy growled. "Oh yeah. I'm craving one of those thin crust pizzas at Fiorello."

Ernesto jumped up from the bench. "Let's do it."

They followed a trail down to the Oak Bridge and made their way through the crowds gathered at the John Lennon memorial at Strawberry Fields and crossed Central Park West. They arrived at Café Fiorello, decided on a table outside along the busy sidewalk under a green umbrella, and the host handed them menus.

"What are you thinking?" Ernesto asked, as he perused the menu. "That 'A Lot of Pepperoni' pizza looks awesome."

Missy hesitated. "I'm totally vegan," she said. "But…" She looked across at her revolutionary hero. "You could twist my arm."

"With a little extra mootz? That's kinda mandatory."

"Okay."

They slapped the menus shut, ordered the pizza along with glasses of a Sicilian red wine, Nero d'Avola, and commented on the passing parade of people on Broadway, whom they deemed largely bougie and oblivious to the coming climate apocalypse. "They don't even know what's going to hit them," Missy said, shaking her head. "You're so right, Ernesto. People like us have to make decisions for them."

The pizza arrived on a large tin platter and they each took a slice. Missy watched with delight as Ernesto folded his slice and took a bite, closing his eyes as the flavors hit his cannabis-excited taste buds. "Oh, man," he said. "That is so fucking good!"

"You probably didn't get much of this growing up," she said before taking a bite herself.

"No," he said, dabbing his mouth with a napkin. "We usually went to Ray's."

"Ray's… Pizza?"

"Yep."

Missy was confused. "They have Ray's in Central America?"

He spit little bits of cheese as he responded. "I didn't grow up in Central America."

"You didn't?"

"Nah," he said, with a pump of his shoulders. "Brooklyn, man."

Missy was completely baffled. "I thought you were, like, boat people."

"Well, yeah. I guess… I mean, my dad had a sweet little Chris-Craft bowrider."

"Bowrider?"

"Yeah. Twenty-four-footer. Kept it out at Brighton Beach."

Missy set down her pizza. She was having trouble keeping up. Was it the weed? The wine? What? "I must be missing something. I thought you were refugees."

"My grandparents were. My grandmother escaped from Poland in 1940."

"You're Jewish?"

"On my dad's side. My mother is Irish Catholic."

Missy was incredulous. "And they named you *Ernesto?*"

He shrugged. "Nah. They named me Ernest—Ernie for short. I use Ernesto as kind of a stage name. When the Planetistas hired me—"

"Wait. They *hired* you?"

"Of course. I can't afford to spend all this time running demonstrations without some compensation. I've got student loans to pay back, and the wages at Café Che only take you so far, even when you're an assistant manager. The Planetistas recruiter said I should adopt a *nom de guerre* with a South American flair." He raised the palms of his hands toward the ceiling and smiled at her. "So, presto: I'm Ernesto!"

Suddenly, Missy wasn't hungry. *What a disappointment!* Ernesto wasn't a socialist revolutionary from another country. He just was an ordinary schlub from another borough. She sadly picked the pepperoni off her slice of pizza, and the mozzarella. She was going back to being a vegan.

"So tell me," Ernie/Ernesto said. "What do you want to do after college? Are you going to follow in the family footsteps?"

She shook her head. "No," she said, sullenly. "I'm going to give all my money away."

Now it was Ernie's turn to be disappointed. "All of it?"

"Every last nickel. Except maybe a few million."

He sat back on the cushion. "I've never heard of any super rich person just giving away their entire fortune."

"I'm not like anybody else."

He nodded. "No. You're different. That's for sure." He took a deep breath, then returned to the pizza. "What about your friend, Blair? Is she giving away her money, too?"

"I can't imagine she would," Missy said. "She seems very comfortable with her wealth, regardless of how it was attained."

Ernesto nodded, thoughtfully. "So, like… does she have a boyfriend?"

"No," Missy said, fighting back tears. *And neither do I.*

30. THE MORNING AFTER

The night at Lindsey's townhouse left Marty's head swirling in the morning. What was he doing even thinking about getting involved with a woman who was effectively his boss? Throw in the fact that she was clearly out of his league in terms of wealth and status and about six or seven other categories, and the power dynamics were not in his favor. This couldn't possibly end well.

He left his apartment and hailed a yellow cab on Columbus Avenue to take him downtown. The driver suggested Seventh Avenue, since the West Side Highway was blocked by a climate protest, leaving thousands of cars backed up and idling on the road, burning gasoline, and emitting excess carbon dioxide while going nowhere. Marty agreed and settled into the cracked black vinyl seat, reading newspapers on his tablet, listening to a podcast on his phone, and glancing at the sights of the city.

As they passed ABC's *Good Morning America* studio at 44th Street, Marty checked out the latest headlines scrolling over the giant LED display.

...FRACKING RESUMES IN NORTH DAKOTA AFTER COURT CHALLENGE...
...ACTIVISTS FEAR GASOLINE PRICES COULD FALL...

No wonder the activists were concerned, Marty thought. If gasoline prices fell, people would drive their cars more often and for longer distances. They would use more gasoline-powered leaf blowers and lawn mowers and who knows what all. Carbon emissions would rise inexorably, putting Earth on Death Row. Seattle's famous sixteen-year-old climate guru, Rainwater Jones, insisted the world would die in 2030, and who was he to argue? She had passion, if not insight. So did cranky Senator Benjamin "Rusty" O'Toole and radical-chic Congresswoman Evita Manolo, who were pressing President Dewey Fenwick to clamp down on Big

Fossil. They called for an end to all oil and gas leases on federal lands and a shutdown of all transcontinental pipelines, hoping the ensuing scarcity would force people to rely on renewable energy. The fact that it didn't yet exist in sufficient quantities to keep America's lights on, cars running, and ovens warm was a detail that did not concern them. Once the citizenry became sufficiently cold and desperate in their dark, dank, and dreary homes, trillions of dollars of federal subsidies would incentivize the president's donors to plant the continental shelf from Florida to Maine with windmills, carpet the Great Plains with solar farms, and crisscross the country with extremely long extension cords.

Marty opened the *New York Times* site on his tablet. It had adopted a swirling, twirling, burning globe as the primary graphic feature on its front page, along with its daily lineup of stories highlighting more examples of climate change's dastardly effects, especially on the disadvantaged.

Climate Change Bakes Homeless Encampments
Sidewalk Tents Overly Warm
Governor Seizes Hampton Jitneys to Transport Victims to the Beach

Marty had to admit: Hacksaw Harry was smart for undergoing a green makeover; he had tapped seamlessly into the nation's dominant cultural narratives. There was no end to the media imagination tying every calamity imaginable to climate, with each new story outdoing the last. Editorialists found there was no cost too high, no action too extreme, and no sacrifice too severe to slow the terrifying ride. China and India had become the world's top carbon emitters, and emissions in the United States were trending downward for years, principally because of the transition from coal to natural gas, but rational discussions were not going to move the needle, which was trending toward 'E' regarding serious answers. Nor was it helpful to offer solutions such as carbon-free nuclear power, which was not sanctioned by the high priests of protest. Marty and Crowe Power had a choice. They would find or feign common cause with the so-called consensus thinking of selected scientists and their mysterious models, the media punditry, and the growing ranks of corporate philosophers, or they would risk extinction.

The driver, Najib, asked Marty a question, but between the hack's muffling mask and the plexiglass separating their seats, Marty had no idea what he was saying, even after three attempts of, "Sorry. *What?*" Finally, Marty simply said, "Yeah. Go that way," and the driver turned east to Broadway, then south again toward downtown. They passed battalions of tourists, a long line of people waiting to have their photo taken next to the Charging Bull's bronze balls, and a much shorter line for pictures near its head. Marty was let off at Beaver Street and walked the last block to Broad, where the Planetistas were again blocking the entrance to the building. He decided to wait them out across the street at Commie Coffee, where he found a booth in a dark corner. He opened his laptop and called up the planning document for his big event to announce Crowe Power's fusion initiative.

"Mind if I join you?"

Marty looked up to see Sergei Badanov, Crowe Power's Chief Technology Officer, holding a small cup of espresso. Marty gestured for Sergei to take the seat across from him. "Not at all," he said.

Sergei slid into the seat. "I'm not even going to try pushing through that crowd. I give them another ten minutes. They usually stop their huffing and puffing once the cameras leave."

Marty nodded. "Was Missy Crowe out there?"

"Oh yes," Sergei said. "Right in front. What an embarrassment for the family."

"They have more than one."

Sergei laughed. "Ah, yes. Robbie. He's certainly an idiot, but maybe not so useful."

Marty replied, "He has good intentions."

"Don't they all?" Sergei sipped his coffee then shook his head. "I don't understand these people. To have every possible advantage in life and become so angry about it. Do they have no idea how life is in most of the world? And then to clamor for a system that plainly doesn't work… It's insane. Are you a fan of Marxist-Leninist philosophy, Marty?"

"Me?" Marty shook his head. "Nah. I'm more of a Lennon-McCartneyist."

"Then you might be interested in life *Back in the USSR.*"

"You don't know how lucky you are, boy."

Sergei scoffed. "Hardly." He looked around at the wall posters of Che Guevara and Fidel Castro and their raised, clenched fists. "Do you know why I came to this country thirty years ago?"

"I'm thinking the Soviet Union was not a lot of laughs."

Sergei shook his head. "My father was a doctor. He came up with an ingenious invention to treat liver cancer. He could destroy tissue with virtually no surgery or radiation. He took it to the authorities for approval and they said, 'Yes! We love this! But, of course, it does not belong to you. It belongs to us. We paid for your education. We paid for your medical school. We provided you with a shitty car, a shitty grocery store, a shitty house.' They seized his invention. And then, being the bungling kleptocrats they were, they put it on a shelf and forgot about it."

"Wow," Marty said, shaking his head. "No wonder we beat them in hockey."

Sergei sighed. "Now look at where we are. Missy Crowe and her friends are clamoring for a failed system. They think calling for socialism makes them look smart and hip and caring and kind. But they can't see beyond the slogans on the t-shirts and coffee mugs. If she gets what she wants, they'll take her money and throw her in the trunk of a Lada."

"Have you ever met Missy Crowe?" Marty said. "I think she would prefer a car trunk to a townhouse on the Upper East Side."

Sergei winced. "Why would she want such a thing?"

"Simple," Marty said. "She's a nut."

"Ah," Sergei said. He drained his espresso then rapped the table with his knuckle. "I have to tell you something, Marty."

"Yes, sir." Marty shut his laptop and folded his hands on the table.

"I am very uneasy about this money we are getting from Washington."

Marty shrugged. "I thought you might be going there. And as the president would say, 'C'mon, man. It's free.'"

Sergei shook his head. "I know 'free.' There's no such thing when it comes to government. They always want something in return."

"This is the United States of America," Marty said. "It's not the Soviet Union."

"I don't care which government you're talking about. I'm telling you I've seen this movie before, Marty. You get in bed with them, you have their baby, and they take it. And they say, 'Consider yourself lucky we fucked you only once.'"

Marty said, "Sergei, I get that the politicians will make decisions for political reasons. But this puts them on our side. This check we're getting is the single biggest infusion of capital in any fusion company in history. That will accelerate our efforts and put us at the head of the pack."

Sergei crumpled his espresso cup and tossed it into a bin. "At what price, Marty?"

"There's one way to find out."

Sergei nodded, ruefully. "I'm not taking any chances."

"What are you talking about?"

Sergei smiled. "I'll let you know when the time is right." He glanced out the window and saw that the protesters had dispersed. "What is that saying? The coast is clear? I'll see you later."

Sergei left Marty, who restarted his laptop. Before he could reopen his planning document for Operation Star Power, a Google Alert popped up on the screen.

Crowe's Power Outage
Investors: Chairwoman Lindsey Harper Crowe Failing
See Buzzniss.com

Marty's heart raced as he clicked on the link to the story. Then it ran smack into his ribs when he saw who wrote it: his mistaken Tinder date, Veronica Sawyer.

<u>Buzzniss.com Exclusive</u>
This Crowe Won't Fly
Company's Fledgling Chairwoman Can't Get Lift

By Veronica Sawyer
NEW YORK – Just one year after taking the reins of
the Crowe Power Company, chairwoman Lindsey

Harper Crowe has shown even less aptitude for leadership than her disgraced ex-husband, Robbie Crowe.

Investors, led by legendary hedge fund manager, Harold Crenshaw, are clamoring for change at the notoriously stodgy firm, whose stock has slid precipitously over the past year. Environmental activists charge that the company's inability to transition away from fossil fuels is worsening the climate crisis. Even family members are growing restive, with the chairwoman's own daughter, Missy Mayburn Crowe, marching with protesters in front of the company's Broad Street headquarters, demanding change.

The mounting problems are not surprising to people who spoke with Buzzniss.com on background.

"She had almost no experience," said one insider close to the chairwoman. Prior to taking the top job, "her main expertise was brunch. The family, I think, just wanted someone to watch out for their interests. It was a desperation move, in my view. She was their last hope."

Marty's phone vibrated with a text message from Lindsey before he could go any further.

Lindsey

Today 9:53 AM

See the story on Buzzniss.com. Then see me.

ASAP.

31. COLLATERAL DAMAGE

Lindsey was visibly distraught when Marty found her in her office. Pacing the floor and shaking her head, her face drained of color, she struggled desperately to put this obvious hit job into some perspective. *I can't possibly be that bad.* Who were these unnamed "sources" in the story who could say such hideous things about her?

She looked up to see a stricken looking Marty standing in the doorway. "That story on Buzzniss.com," she gasped. "It's just... dreadful."

Marty walked over slowly toward the windows, his hands in his pockets, and leaned on the ledge. "A hit job, obviously," he said. "You know Hacksaw Harry's behind this."

Lindsey shrugged. "That doesn't make it any easier."

Marty sighed. "I know."

"Who are these people they talked to?" Lindsey asked, walking over to him. "Do you think they're real? Or did they just make it all up?"

Marty took a deep breath. He considered deflecting her concerns by assuring her it was all made-up nonsense. But his usual instincts were arrested once again by the expression on her face. She trusted him. And she was wrong. He was overwhelmed by a guilty sense that he unwittingly contributed to this attack on Lindsey by her most dangerous adversary.

"I'm afraid they actually talked to people," he said, taking her hand.

She looked at him quizzically. "How can you tell?"

He spoke in a near-whisper. "Because one of them was me."

She recoiled. "*What?*"

Marty rubbed his forehead with his fingertips. "I was ambushed by the reporter, this... Veronica whatever-her-name-is. It was in a restaurant. I mistook her for someone else. I was just making conversation, saying whatever came into my head, trying to sound knowledgeable about a subject that she was interested in, but in retrospect, I knew nothing about. I didn't even know you at the time."

She folded her arms tightly across her chest, her eyes showing more hurt than anger. "Then why would you say such a thing?"

"Because I was trying to sound like I was in the know. But I know now that I knew nothing about you…at all. It was reckless and stupid and careless, and I'm afraid, damaging. I'm sorry—deeply sorry."

"Couldn't you have at least warned me?"

Marty gasped. "I didn't know it was going to end up like this. I was hoping it would just go away."

"I… I'm at a loss, Marty," she said, her voice quavering. "I can take criticism from strangers. But from you, too? You're supposed to be my ally. This is so disappointing."

Marty threw his head back and looked at the ceiling. "I can't explain it. I just assumed you were like the other Crowes I'd met, like Robbie. I was mistaken, and I knew it the minute we met in your office for the first time."

"What did you think I was?"

"Well, to be honest, spoiled. Entitled. Maybe a little naïve."

"On that last one? I'm probably guilty as charged. Look how naïve I was about you."

"Now that hurts," Marty said. "Not that I don't deserve it. I do."

She shook her head and resumed her pacing. "Seriously, Marty. My main expertise was *brunch?* Really?"

"What I said is not how I feel. Lindsey, listen. I really like you—and I respect the way you've overseen Crowe Power. I've seen how much you care about your company and your family and the people around you. That's why there's more to this relationship than a retainer."

"Right. There's a success fee."

"That, too, but that's not what I mean," Marty said. He studied her. "How can I make it up to you? I want you to trust me, even if you have no good reason to do so right now."

She sighed. "How about this, Marty: You make good on that success fee by helping me beat Hacksaw Harry—"

"…and save the company," Marty said, nodding. "Yes. Yes. I can do that."

"No," she said. "Actually, I don't want to save the company."

"What do you mean?"

"I don't want to preserve it as is."

"But you said…"

"Yes," she said. "I did. Maybe I wasn't exactly forthright with you either."

"Really?" He shrugged. "Then maybe we're even."

"Not quite," she said.

"Got it," he acknowledged.

"Look, Marty. This company's day is done. It's a dinosaur, in an age when the old-time conglomerates are becoming extinct. The Crowes cobbled together a bunch of semi-related businesses that don't really belong together. They're much better suited as pure plays with a singular focus. I suppose you could argue that each line of business is a hedge against the others, but that's not quite true. Their cycles tend to run in parallel. Trying to hold them all together, encased in amber because that's the way good old Homer wanted it way back in nineteen-whatever, doesn't make sense anymore. The party's over."

Marty was taken aback. "Isn't that essentially what Hacksaw Harry is saying?"

"It's exactly what he's saying," she said. "And I knew what he was going to say in the letter before I even read it—largely because I've thought many of the same things." She shook her head. "I just don't like doing this under some phony pretext that he invented—how he's all green and so forth. I don't like doing it under pressure, which is unhelpful. And I don't think he's earned the right to call the shots by bullying his way into our company. This is still the Crowe family's business. I am determined to have the final say. There's more than money at stake here. There's the family name and I would like it restored to a place of honor in this world before I leave this place."

Marty pondered this surprising new direction. "Would you keep any lines of business for the family?"

"Yes," she said. "I haven't yet made up my mind, but I'm leaning a bit."

He studied her. "I think I know you well enough now to know."

She cocked an eye. "Based on what I read on Buzzniss.com, you don't know me well at all."

"Maybe not," he acknowledged. "But I'm getting there."

She turned away for a moment, thinking. Then she turned back to Marty. "I'll forgive your indiscretion."

He took a deep sigh of relief. "Thank you. I don't deserve it, but I appreciate it."

"With one condition," she added.

He nodded, eager to accept whatever the condition might be. "Which is?"

"You help me take these people out."

32. HOLEY HELL

It was Thursday, which meant that the patriarch of the Crowe family would play golf. Uncle Chuck's longtime golfing buddy, Lloyd Lundquist, suggested that the best way to avoid the tunnel traffic to Liberty National Golf Club in Jersey City was to have his driver drop him off at Pier 25 in Tribeca and take the ferry across. As the sun began to peek over the skyscrapers of Lower Manhattan, Chuck met Lloyd at the dock, where the club's gray-and-green boat awaited their arrival to whisk them across the Hudson River.

"I've never played Liberty," Chuck said, anxiously, as he settled inside the cabin.

"Ah, you'll love it," said Lloyd, the retired Chief Executive Officer of LT&T Insurance and current board member of Staminum Energy. "It's a links course, you know. Spectacular views of the city. They've played some huge tournaments there."

Chuck winced. "My goal isn't the Senior Tour. A dollar-a-hole is more my style."

"That's okay with me, too," Lloyd said. "You and I can play the front tees. My boys will probably play the back. That gives us an advantage of about two thousand yards."

"I'll need every inch of that," Chuck said. "I've got two plastic knees, a pig's heart valve in my chest, a titanium hip, and a pecker that hasn't pointed north since the last Bush Administration. Any wonder I can't hit a ball over a hundred yards?"

Lloyd laughed. "Well, you know my game. I brought some singles in case we have to pay out."

"You're more optimistic than me, Lloyd," Chuck said. "I brought fives and tens."

After the boat docked, Chuck and Lloyd wobbled up to the gangway and stepped across onto dry land. Lloyd took the wheel of their golf cart and they drove to the first tee, where Lloyd's lean and athletic sons, Tyler and Nick, were limbering up, taking fast, powerful swings that Chuck could hear. *Whoosh!* For a moment, Chuck was frozen in the cart. *What am I doing playing with these guys? I can barely get out of my seat.* But with a couple of shifts of his hips, and one last heave-ho, he was able to eject himself from the cart and stretch his creaky frame upright with an audible *"Oof."* He took a deep breath and shook hands with the fellas.

"I hope you can find it in your mercy to take pity on a couple of old duffers," Chuck said to Tyler.

"Don't worry about that, Chuck," said Tyler, a podiatrist in Hoboken. "Our tees are so far back they're practically in Bayonne. What's your handicap?"

"Creaky knees. Weak shoulders. Can't swing my hips."

Tyler clapped Chuck affectionately on the shoulder. "We'll factor all that in, Chuck."

Nick added, "But we'll still take your money."

Chuck smiled. "I'll be glad to pay as long as you don't laugh."

"Deal," Tyler said with an amiable smile.

Chuck slid a golf glove onto his left hand as he joined Lloyd and looked out at the first hole, a long dogleg to the right.

"Christ almighty," Chuck muttered. "You've got more water and sand out here than my beach house in the Hamptons."

"Forget about it," Lloyd said, with a wave of his hand. "From where we hit, it shouldn't be a problem. You'll drive well over the bad stuff."

"Ha," Chuck laughed. "I want what you're smoking."

After Tyler and Nick launched rocket drives from the back tees, Lloyd and Chuck drove their cart a hundred yards ahead, where they hit their typical popgun shots: straight, true, and short. While the boys each managed to par the hole, the miracle of handicap mathematics resulted in Lloyd and Chuck somehow managing to win a buck on the first hole.

"I don't know how that's fair," Chuck said when they slid back into the cart. "But it works for me."

The play continued around dune grass moguls, swampy ponds, and trickling creeks, while the lack of shade trees, the rising sun and the soaring heat had Chuck taking cover in the cart as often as possible. His dinky drives grew shorter and shorter as his perspiration rose, but they were still up three dollars through thirteen holes.

"How are things going with Hacksaw Harry," Lloyd asked Chuck as they puttered along in the cart toward the fourteenth tee.

"Oh, he's as much fun as a hemorrhoid," Chuck said.

"Looks like you have quite a tussle on your hands," Lloyd said. "Lindsey handling him okay?"

Chuck nodded, then swigged a red Gatorade. "She's an elegant young lady, but tougher than you might think."

"She'd have to be," Lloyd said. "Walker Hope tells me he's a cutthroat son-of-a-bitch."

Chuck looked at Lloyd in surprise. "So Walker *is* working with him."

Lloyd blinked. "Maybe I said something I shouldn't have."

"Maybe you didn't," Chuck said.

Lloyd shrugged. "Look, Chuck. I'm not carrying Staminum's water here," he said. "We've been friends for too long. But I wouldn't be a friend if I didn't say there's a time for everything in a company's life—even one with as long and proud of a history as Crowe Power. Hell, I've hit my own expiration date. My next board meeting at Staminum is my last. You get to a certain point, and you find it's time for closure on a lot of things."

Chuck looked at Lloyd and considered a rebuttal, then thought better of it. He needed to learn more about this unholy alliance between Walker and Hacksaw Harry so he could advise Lindsey. "I want to know more about this. How about we close out this round before we talk?" Chuck suggested. "Fourteen holes is good enough for me."

Lloyd nodded. "Me, too. I'm fine quitting while we're ahead."

Chuck watched Tyler and Nick hit wedge shots from the back tee box on to the green as Lloyd consulted his card. "Let's go out in a blaze of glory, Chuck. Ninety-eight yards to the pin," he said. "I know you can hit that green from here."

Chuck looked out at the rolling hills of long brown grass between the tee box and the green. "God help me if I don't. The FBI couldn't find a Russian spy in that patch."

Lloyd took a mighty swing and sliced his first shot into the brush behind a sand trap. He angrily snapped up his tee. "Bail me out here, Chuck."

Chuck pulled out his driver and walked shakily to the tee box on his gimpy knees, using a two-iron as a cane to steady himself. *Only damn thing a two-iron is good for…* He wheezed as he leaned over to tee up the ball, then squared away to hit, glancing up at the blazing sun, which was making him woozy. Looking left, then down, then left again, he addressed the ball. He gave the swing all he had, and the ball sailed low over the long grass, hit the top edge of a bunker, bounced high in the air, and rolled toward the flag. If Chuck wasn't mistaken, a faint *clank* could be heard.

Tyler, sitting in his cart nearby, yelled, "Whoa, Chuck! I think it's in!"

Chuck's jaw dropped. "Naw," he guffawed. "Couldn't be."

Nick shouted, "I think he's right!"

"Why… I've never had a hole in one in my life," Chuck exclaimed.

With his heart racing erratically, Chuck picked up his two iron and ambled over to the cart. "Step on it," he said to Lloyd. They went from zero-to-fifteen in about twenty seconds, which is all it took to park next to the green. Chuck excitedly grabbed his putter—just in case he needed it—and his two iron and stiffly walked up a slight incline, across the apron, onto the green and to the pin. There he beheld the most incredible vision he had never experienced in his eighty-five years: the ball in the cup after a single shot.

Lloyd, following right behind, clapped him on the back. "Damn, Chuck! *Hell of a shot!*"

Chuck turned and looked at Lloyd blankly. His jaw went slack, his color drained from his face. "Uh-oh," he said, and collapsed face down on the green.

33. DICEY D.C.

Marty and Lindsey stood at the window of her conference room, facing across New York Harbor as the sun reflected off the bright orange Staten Island Ferry crossing in front of the Statue of Liberty. Marty pointed out a domed building behind Ellis Island, which was the planetarium where Marty proposed to hold a portion of the event.

"We begin the day there," he said. "Then it moves—"

A rapid knocking on the doorframe interrupted Marty's pitch. They both turned to see Winnie, Lindsey's assistant.

"I am so sorry to disturb you," Winnie said, "but the Secretary of Energy is calling. She says she needs to speak with you immediately."

Lindsey cast a glance to Marty and arched an eyebrow, then turned back to Winnie. "Put her through." She walked to a small round table where a console phone was located and waited for the red button to blink. She punched it with a bit more force than necessary.

"Good morning," Lindsey said, brightly.

"Surprised to hear you say that," Jessica replied. "You're getting killed in the media."

"So we've noticed." Lindsey acknowledged.

"I don't know what kind of PR team you have up there, but you need to whack 'em," Jessica said. "They're terrible."

Lindsey hit the mute button and looked at Marty. "I guess that means you."

"Screw her," he muttered.

"Are you volunteering?" Lindsey taunted.

"Hardly," Marty said.

Lindsey unmuted the call. "I appreciate your concerns, of course," Lindsey said.

Jessica's tone was heated. "How would it look for us to announce that we're giving a billion dollars to—sorry, but there's no way to sugar coat this—a dilletante who might just blow it all on brunch."

"That would be some brunch," Lindsey said.

"You get my point," Jessica countered.

Lindsey looked to Marty, then took a deep breath before speaking. "I do, Jessica. But I'm sure you recognize that what you're seeing is an orchestrated hit on our company by people who want to use me and my company for their own purposes. They desperately want us to fail."

"They're making a very convincing case."

Lindsey seethed but maintained her composure. "We haven't presented our side of the story yet, Jessica. When we do that next week, we think the world will see us in a decidedly different light—as a world leader in clean energy."

Marty gave her two enthusiastic thumbs-up and mouthed, "Good!"

There was a long pause before Jessica responded. "Here's the bad news. The president is now taking a wait-and-see approach on star power, Lindsey. Crowe Power has got a little stink on it right now."

"What does that mean?"

"He's sending the vice president to our event."

Lindsey sighed. *Shrika Fugazi? That loser? That can't be good...* "I can assure you, Jessica, that we have our challenges well in hand," Lindsey said. "The last thing we want to do is embarrass you or the president or the vice president for supporting our efforts. We intend to demonstrate to the world that your faith in Crowe Power is justified and that the Fenwick Administration is forward-thinking."

"I'm counting on it," Jessica said and hung up.

Lindsey returned to the conference table. "That was pleasant," Lindsey said, sliding back into her chair. "Now we're really under the gun, Marty. How on earth are we going to do this?"

"For one thing, we're not confining ourselves to Earth," Marty said. "We're going to reach for the stars." Marty explained the program for an event he called *Star Power to Save our Planet*. They would rent out the Jennifer Chalsty Planetarium and LSC Giant Dome Theater at the Liberty Science Center in Jersey City and invite the Crowe family, investors, media, the Secretary of Energy, the Veep, and any other politico who wanted a photo opportunity. Marty would create an opening-night kind of buzz, with a red carpet out front, klieg lights, and velvet ropes, then bring everyone into the theater for a short film on the amazing science of fusion and its incredible benefits, followed by remarks from various dignitaries and an announcement by Lindsey about Crowe Power's creation of the Star Power spin-out. "And, in case Hacksaw Harry doesn't get the message that we're rejecting his proposal," Marty said, "we announce the creation of the school and the orphanage in the Congo next to his mining operation."

Lindsey nodded, noncommittal. "It all sounds a bit grandiose."

"Think of what we're up against, Lindsey," he said. "You think our opponents aren't over the top? They're scaring the bejesus out of people every day."

She shrugged. "You may have a point."

Relieved, Marty pressed on. "Then we shuttle our guests from the planetarium to an area along the water in Liberty State Park. We ply them with champagne and hors d'oeuvres to commemorate this history-making occasion. And then we show them a live feed from Con Fusion a couple of blocks away, where PC and Mac are preparing to fire up the tokamak, and, if the good lord's willing and the creek don't rise, generate electricity. Meanwhile, we get you over to Liberty Island."

Lindsey crossed her arms and looked at him very skeptically. "And...?"

"You might want to change into flats."

She shook her head slowly. "What are you getting me into?"

"The good news is," he said, holding the palms of his hands out, "there's not a lot of climbing."

"Climbing?"

"Inside the State of Liberty."

"How am I going to do that?"'

"An elevator will take you most of the way up."

"'Most' of the way? To where, Marty? The crown?"

"The torch."

"*The torch?* They don't let anybody up there."

"That's right. But you're not just anybody. We're partners with the federal government, which runs the whole shebang. I've already arranged it with the National Parks Service. We've got the green light to shanghai Lady Liberty for an hour that day."

"How far am I supposed to climb?"

"Well, let's see," Marty said, glancing over his notes. "Up the arm, it's, uh…" He mumbled something she couldn't hear.

"It's what?"

Marty cleared his throat. "Uh, forty feet. Four-oh."

Lindsey guffawed. "You're out of your mind! That's like scaling a four-story building. You have me confused with Spiderman."

"It's important you get up there."

"Why?" she demanded.

"Because whatever juice we can generate from the tokamak will light it up."

Lindsey exploded with laughter. "They can't create enough electricity to run a toaster right now."

"Yes, but PC and Mac have a plan and I have a world of confidence in them," he said.

"And what if they fail?" she asked. "I climb up there and stand in the dark?"

"No. We do the same thing renewable energy does when the sun doesn't shine or the wind doesn't blow," Marty said. "We back it up with fossil fuels. I've lined up a bunch of diesel generators."

Lindsey shook her head. "Oh my God, Marty. Would you climb up there?"

"Me?" He shook his head. "Nah. Never. I'm afraid of heights."

She scoffed. "But it's okay if I do it."

"You're our fearless leader."

"So you think." She sighed. "I don't know. It all sounds a bit outlandish."

"That's exactly what it is—and for good reason," Marty said. "We need to create a moment that people will remember in history. Think of Thomas Edison recording *Mary Had a Little Lamb* on the first phonograph, or Alexander Graham Bell telling Watson to 'come here' in the first telephone call. Firing up some metal contraption isn't enough. Nobody can tell what's going on in there. We need to bring it all to life."

Lindsey sighed. This was all too much to process. "Let me noodle on all this a bit, okay?"

Marty shrugged. "Okay."

"But start thinking of a Plan B."

Another knock on the doorframe interrupted and Winnie was at the door, looking stricken. "Lindsey, your Aunt Sylvia just called. Your Uncle Chuck is in the hospital. He's had a heart attack."

Lindsey went white. "Oh, dear God," she said. She got up from her chair, took her purse, and walked to the doorway, then turned back to Marty. "I don't know if praying is your thing, Marty, but if it is, we could use one right now."

34. PULLING THE PLUG

Andrei sped up the FDR, closing gaps quickly between his car and others, and abruptly cut in front of other drivers at the exit for 23rd Street to get Lindsey to the NYU Langone Medical Center. He pulled up to the main entrance on First Avenue and dashed out to open the door. With her own heart racing, Lindsey stepped into the painfully slow revolving door to the lobby and then followed the green pathway to the Cardiac Care Unit on the eleventh floor. There she found a distraught Aunt Sylvia in the waiting room, trembling as she searched for an unused tissue among the six Kleenex that were balled up in her purse.

Lindsey hugged her aunt's small frame and held her a moment. "How is he?" she asked.

"He's still with us," Sylvia said. "I believe they're putting in another stent."

"What happened?"

"He hit a hole in one on the golf course and apparently the shock was too much for him," she said. "They brought him here by helicopter from New Jersey. The pilot told me the only thing he said to the crew was, 'Worth it.'"

Lindsey smiled and squeezed Sylvia's hand. "So, his sense of humor survived. That's a good sign."

Sylvia nodded tentatively. "Oh, dear God, I hope so," she said, struggling to steady her voice. "He's my rock, you know."

Lindsey smiled, sympathetically. "He's mine, too."

From behind them, a voice said, "Mrs. Crowe?" They turned to see a doctor in a white coat, a stethoscope looped around his neck.

The doctor approached Sylvia. "I'm Doctor Fine," he said. "Your husband was lucky to have someone in his party familiar with emergency medical procedures. He performed CPR immediately, which kept oxygen going to his heart and to his brain. We've inserted two stents into a blocked artery, and he has responded well. He's awake now and we're moving him to a private room. Given his age, and his other risk factors, we'd like to keep him overnight for observation."

"Anything to keep him away from those damn cigarettes for a night is a good thing," Sylvia said.

"If that's what it takes, yes," the doctor said. "Would you like to see him?"

"Please."

Sylvia clutched Lindsey's arm to keep her steady as they followed the doctor through a corridor to Chuck's room. There, they found the family patriarch in bed wearing a hospital gown, his eyes closed. He was hooked up to a panel of monitors measuring his blood pressure, pulse, and blood oxygen.

Sylvia's eyes welled with tears as she saw her usually vibrant husband lying so helplessly. She leaned over the chrome bed rail and kissed his forehead, then gently patted his shoulder. "Hang in there, Chuck," she said. "Don't leave me now."

Lindsey put an arm around Sylvia's shoulders and gently squeezed, then helped her to a chair to sit down. "Can you stay with me a bit?" Sylvia asked, as she struggled to catch her breath.

"Of course," Lindsey said, taking the seat next to her.

"You're sweet to come up here when you have so much to do," Sylvia said.

"This is my top priority right here," Lindsey said.

"I know you have many other important priorities, too," Sylvia replied. "We're counting on you to get our company moving in the right direction again."

Lindsey nodded. "We're getting there."

Sylvia's face turned dark. "No thanks to him," she nodded in the direction of the hallway, where Robbie had stepped off the elevator and was speaking to a nurse. "Help me to the bathroom, will you, sweetie? I'm not up to Robbie's shenanigans."

"Of course," Lindsey said. She escorted Sylvia to the bathroom and returned to meet Robbie at the doorway.

"Is he okay?" Robbie said, looking past her to the bed.

"He's recovering," she said.

Robbie shook his head. "I don't know about that. Looks like he's out of it." Robbie glanced at his chart in the Plexiglas holder on the wall. "He's got a Do Not Resuscitate order, right?"

Lindsey flushed. "He most certainly does *not*," she said, heatedly. "Even if he did, he's not going to need it. I told you: he's *recovering*. He'll do it faster without commotion around him. The doctor asked that only two people visit at a time."

Robbie shrugged. "You're one. I'm two. What's the big deal?"

"Aunt Sylvia's in the bathroom," Lindsey said, quietly.

Robbie, in exaggerated fashion, looked around him. "She's not in here."

"Robbie, please," Lindsey pleaded. "Could you just wait down the hall? I'll be out of here in a few minutes."

Robbie impatiently looked at his watch. "I only have a few minutes. I'm meeting a friend for drinks."

Lindsey said, "I'm really sorry this is inconveniencing you. Maybe he should have checked with you before scheduling his heart attack."

"No, no," Robbie said. "This is time well spent. It's good to be reminded of what I'm missing with you. Which is… hmm, let me think, nothing." He brushed past her, walked to the side of the bed, and looked down at Chuck. Lindsey stepped over to the other side of the bed, and they faced each other. Chuck was situated between them, his chest rising and falling slowly.

Robbie regarded his uncle and shook his head sadly. "I thought he was on my side."

Lindsey thought, *Not this again…* "Seriously. Nobody wants to hear it."

"But—he pimped me!" Robbie bleated. "When it came time to defend me as chairman at our family meeting, he said nothing. He just sat there and listened while you and everyone else in there trashed me. He may have nominated you in my place but trust me, he'll turn on you, too. That's what he's like."

Lindsey sighed, exasperated. "Robbie, this is not the time or place to litigate your many grievances. It's over. And it's been over for a year. Time to get used to it and move the fuck *on*."

Chuck's eyes opened ever so slightly. He glanced at Lindsey, then at Robbie, and attempted to speak through his dry, cracked lips. Neither of them could hear anything over a flushing toilet in the adjacent bathroom and the incessant beeps and buzzes in the hall. So fixated were they upon one another that neither of them noticed he was even awake.

Robbie cocked his head and stared at Lindsey. "Why do you even care about running the company? You're not blood."

"Robbie, please," Lindsey said. "We can talk about this some other time. Let's focus right now on Uncle Chuck—getting him well again and getting him home."

The door of the bathroom cracked open, and Aunt Sylvia peeked out. Seeing Robbie was still in the room, she quietly closed it again. Chuck, meanwhile, opened his eyes more fully and tried to speak again, but failed to get their attention.

Robbie was completely focused on his ex-wife. "Of course you don't want to talk about the company," he said. "You've made such a mess that I'm sure there are a million things you'd rather talk about right now."

Lindsey's anger showed as she spoke through clenched teeth. "Later, Robbie. Please!"

Suddenly, a loud beeper from Chuck's monitor sounded, and heavy footsteps could be heard racing down the hall as nurses and doctors rushed into the room. Lindsey stepped away from the bed to let them through. Sylvia, alarmed, emerged from the bathroom, approached the bed, and tried to peer around the medical personnel to see what was happening with Chuck.

"Chuck! Dear!" she called. "Are you alright?"

"I'm fine," he said, holding up a cord to the monitor. "I pulled the damn plug so I could get Robbie to shut up for a second."

A nurse snatched the cord from Chuck and plugged it back in, then looked to Lindsey and Robbie. "There is far too much going on in here," she said, sternly. "I'm afraid we'll need to clear the room."

"Hold on," Chuck said, scootching up on his pillow. "I want to speak to them. Give us a minute."

"Only a minute," the nurse said, wagging a finger at him.

As the nurses departed, Robbie and Lindsey approached the bed from opposite sides.

"It's about this Hacksaw Harry business," Chuck said to Robbie. "You do know he's working for your friend, Walker Hope."

Robbie looked shaken. "I don't believe that."

"I heard it from Lloyd today," Chuck said.

"It's true," Lindsey said. "Walker's using Hacksaw Harry to break up our company and sell him the pieces. Look at our footprints, Robbie. It makes perfect sense. And you know who's got a bug up his butt about our company because you drove him out for no good reason? The same man who'd like nothing more than to take back control of our company on his terms—and take our family out of it."

Robbie, panicked, looked at Lindsey, then to Chuck. "That's not what I heard."

Chuck said, "No. I imagine Hacksaw Harry is telling you something entirely different, Robbie."

Lindsey burrowed her eyes into Robbie's thick skull. "You discussed this with Harold Crenshaw?"

Robbie sputtered. "I—I…Not really. I mean, we just happened to be on the same boat ride together. I had no idea he was even going to be there—"

"You're not only a dumbass. You're a traitor," Lindsey said. "What's the matter with you? I bet he told you that you could be chairman again."

"No," Robbie guffawed. "Well, yes. I mean, he might have said something like that, but I figured he was talking out his ass…"

Lindsey, aghast, said, "He was certainly talking *to* an ass. You."

Chuck turned to Lindsey. "I've heard enough. Can you ask the nurse if she can put me under again?"

Robbie turned to Chuck. "Uncle Chuck, you have to believe me. I'm only trying to protect the family's interests," he implored. "That's the only goal I've ever had in mind."

"You need to understand something, Robbie," Chuck said. "I'm on blood thinners right now, not stupid pills. You need to back the fuck up. You hear me? Stay out of this! The only thing we need from you right now is your vote. And, by God, we better have it."

Lindsey said, "Face it, Robbie. You got played by your old buddy, Walker B. Hope."

Chuck muttered, "And Robbie be hopeless."

Robbie backpedaled. "I, uh…" He pointed to Lindsey. "Uncle Chuck. She's fucking up everything. Our shares suck. We have no green strategy, except what

I put in place. Our company's a dinosaur and she's doing nothing about it. Do you want to save this company? Or do you want it to die?"

Chuck settled back in his bed. "Robbie, you've given me a powerful incentive to live," he said.

"What's that?"

"So I can kick you in the butt. Now go on. Get the hell out of here."

Lindsey turned to see Bits coming down the hall, approaching Robbie from behind. She grabbed him by the wrist and twisted his arm behind his back. "*Ow!*" Robbie wailed.

"You heard what he said," Bits said. "Get out."

Bits let go and Robbie stumbled out of the room scowling. *So unfair. Everybody picks on me…*

Lindsey turned back to Chuck. She patted his hand. "Thank you, Uncle Chuck."

"I told you," he said. "I've got your back. I mean it."

A nurse entered and approached the bed. "Time for him to get some rest."

Lindsey nodded and turned to Sylvia, who had taken a chair. "Do you want us to take you home?"

Sylvia shook her head. "No, dear," she said. "I want to stay right here with my boyfriend."

Lindsey nodded. "You let me know if you need anything."

"I will."

Lindsey turned to Bits, took her by the arm, and headed for the door. "What a day," she said. "How about that drink we talked about?"

35. DEFACED

Three rounds of Cosmos in a dark corner of the bar at Harry's on Hanover Square were enough for Lindsey to give notice to all her demons and send them packing. Gone, for the moment, were her anxieties over Hacksaw Harry and Walker B. Hope. Gone was her animosity toward her ex-husband, Robbie. Gone was all her worry over whether the event Marty was planning would be successful. She'd face all that tomorrow.

As she and Bits reminisced about their adventures together, she was transported back to a more carefree time in her life. Why did she ever leave it? In retrospect, it all seemed like a perfect world. Maybe brunch really was her bag. Was there a way to go pro at brunch? That could be fun—certainly more fun than being chairperson of the Crowe Power Company.

"I've gotta tell you," Lindsey said, as her voice grew louder and her diction less precise, "having all this responsibility is really, *really* overrated. Do you know how many people depend on me to protect their jobs? It's like forty-fucking-thousand. That's, like, a ginormous load on my back." She signaled the waitress for another round.

"Better you than me," Bits said. "I don't think I could handle it."

"I try not to think about it. I say to myself, 'What's best for the company?' Focus on that and the rest will take care of itself. But these are people, you know? They have lives, and families and homes and… I don't know what all they do but they're human beings. And they're counting on me. Somebody ought to tell them I'm not dependable."

"What are you talking about?" Bits said. "You're the most dependable person I know."

"Exactly!" she said. "That's what makes me so undependable. Sooner or later, that dam has to burst."

Bits laughed. "Not with you, honey. I know you too well."

Lindsey drained the last of her Cosmo as the waitress delivered two more. "No, you're probably right. Nice to think about anyway." They clinked glasses from their new round. "You know something? I actually enjoy meeting the people in this company. They're so polite and respectful. I can't tell you how many have said to me how happy they are that someone in the family is still looking out for the business, and for them. I guess they think it's better that someone at the top has a personal stake in it—not just a financial one. It's humbling."

"What do you hear from our family?"

Lindsey guffawed. "I wish I could say it was the same. Mostly what I hear are complaints. 'Why can't you raise the dividend? Why can't I become a VP? Why can't you just get rid of all this dirty oil and gas and do windmills?' Hell, they might as well tell me to do cartwheels. Neither is plausible right now. Nobody in the family has any idea how difficult this is. Worse, they really don't care. They just think, 'Make this company work for me.'"

Bits shrugged. "They're spoiled rotten. And I'm right in there with them."

"At least you realize it." Lindsey sipped her Cosmo. "You know what? There are some questions I have about the family that I don't quite get. I bet you are the perfect person to answer them for me. Do you have time to go back to the office for a bit?"

Bits looked at her watch. "I guess so."

Lindsey handed the waitress a credit card and asked her for a bottle of champagne to go. When the server returned with a bottle of Veuve Clicquot, Lindsey crammed it in her Birkin bag, and the two of them headed toward the door, then up the stairs to street level, and walked two blocks to the headquarters on Broad Street. Barriers and checkpoints made the street largely devoid of vehicular traffic, but dog walkers, office workers, tourists, and students sauntering about kept the street from feeling like a ghost town.

Leaving the executive express elevator, Lindsey and Bits found the 24th floor largely uninhabited, aside from a few cleaners working through their evening service, and a lone security guard at the front desk. Lindsey tried as best as she could to straighten out her crooked face, and nodded hello to the guard, then led

Bits to the break room. They located a couple of water glasses and opened the champagne with a loud pop, followed by a roar of laughter. "We'll need this for our tour," Lindsey said, as she poured bubbly for each of them. With the champagne bottle and glasses in hand, they made their way to the far end of the portrait gallery known as the Hall of Fam.

"I pass these men every morning and every night," Lindsey said, struggling to stay balanced in her heels. "Sometimes, I feel them staring at me. Like, 'What are you doing here?' Of course, I often wonder that myself. But then I also wonder, 'What were *you* doing here? When you weren't chasing women and directing company money to your personal pet projects or renovating your office into a man-cave.' Take this guy." She walked over to the portrait of a serene-looking Homer Crowe, a tinkerer and inventor who built a corporate dynamo. He was the one who started the company on the cusp of the first World War and laid the foundation for its phenomenal growth. "He was balling his secretary in the office. Then he created a doll company for their daughter that this company still owns. You know what he needs?" She handed her glass to Bits, set the bottle on the floor, and pulled a tube of lipstick from her purse. "He needs to freshen his lips to kiss that ol' doll company goodbye, 'cause I'm getting rid of it."

As she leaned over with the lipstick, Bits said, "Oh, Lindsey! No, you're not!"

"Oh, yes I am," she said proudly, before painting Homer's lips a lovely crimson red. Then she leaned over and kissed it. *"Mwah!"*

Bits roared with laughter. "I can't believe you did that!"

"Don't you think these boys are overdue for a lady's touch?"

She stepped over to the next portrait, of Homer's son, Lester, a competent leader who took over for his pop and led the company to success after World War II. "Far as I can tell, he's the only one of these guys who put in a full day at the office. Obviously, he worked too hard. He could use a bit of rouge in his cheeks." She used her lipstick to draw a clownish circle on each cheek.

They convulsed with laughter, clinked glasses, and poured more champagne. "Oooh, I want to do the next one," Bits said.

"Be my guest!" Lindsey said.

Lindsey handed her the lipstick and Bits faced a portrait of her grandfather, Charles Crowe, who led the company during the 1980s and '90s largely from tables at Lutece and La Grenouille. "Grandfather was a very tough critic," Bits said, as she drew an arched eyebrow over his right eye, "especially when it came to what I was wearing."

Bits handed the lipstick back to Lindsey for the portrait of her father, Les Crowe. "I can't touch this one," Bits said. "I'm afraid he'll somehow spring back to life and ground me for a week."

Lindsey growled, "Oh, honey. We may be grounded for longer than that."

Bits looked around. "Can anyone see us?"

"I don't care," she said, sipping her champagne. "What are they going to do about it?" She leaned close to Bits' face. *"Nothing!"*

Lindsey looked at the portrait of Les, an emotionally abusive man, probably bipolar. Lindsey blamed his relentless criticism of his son for Robbie's constant attempts to prove himself and take credit for achievements that were not his doing. This called for a heart, right on the left breast of his gray suit coat. "That's what you need, Les," she said.

Finally, they came to Robbie, who was pictured in front of a hilltop of wind turbines, befitting his lifelong advocacy for environmentalism, at least in some abstract, undefined sense. It was certainly appropriate that the wind farm behind him was an acquisition that he had shepherded—before it promptly went bust. The more dramatic aspect of the portrait, however, were the beams of sunlight that landed on his shoulders, bathing him in Mother Nature's most flattering light.

"What do we do with him?" Lindsey asked.

Bits shook her head. "I've never figured it out."

Lindsey stepped closer to the portrait. "How about this?"

She leaned over and drew a penis coming out of his pants. Bits howled with laughter. "Oh, yeah! That's perfect," she said.

"He never could keep this thing zipped, right?"

"Right," Bits said. "And this one's got the lipstick already on it!"

They toasted their artwork, drained their glasses, and fell to the floor laughing. They laid their heads back against the wall and stared up at Lindsey's own portrait.

"What do we do with that?" Lindsey asked with a sigh.

"We don't touch it," Bits said, matter-of-factly.

"We should do something," Lindsey said.

"You can't deface your own face."

Lindsey cocked her head to look at it. "It's going to come down soon enough anyway."

Bits dismissed the idea with a wave of her hand. "No way."

Lindsey stood up. "I've always thought of this as my Saddam Hussein portrait. You know, the ruthless dictator presenting a happy face to the citizens of Baghdad. May as well complete the picture." Lindsey pulled out her lipstick and scribbled a bright red bushy moustache over her lip. "There."

Bits looked up and laughed. "You are too much, Linz."

Lindsey flopped back down to the floor. "I'm about done, Bits," she said, pouring the last of the bottle into their glasses. "We've got an announcement next week over in Jersey that I'm afraid is going to bring the curtain down on the whole Lindsey Harper Crowe show."

They clinked glasses, and Bits squared around to look at Lindsey. "It's not over until—"

Lindsey interrupted. "—the sort of fat lady climbs up the Statue of Liberty's armpit?"

"Oh, come on! You're not even 'sort of' fat."

"Fat enough to wonder how in God's name I'm going to haul my butt up forty feet to the torch. That's what Marty wants me to do." Lindsey sighed. Suddenly, all those demons she had banished at Harry's came slinking back. "It's a waste of time, I'm telling you. With Hacksaw Harry on my ass, and Walker Hope licking his chops, and Uncle Chuck knocking on death's door, and Missy marching with people calling for my arrest, and Robbie being the general pain-in-the-ass he's been for twenty-five years… I don't know why I should even bother. I'm gonna call Marty first thing in the morning and tell him to forget it. I'm not going. I quit."

Bits nodded, glumly. "I know this is all weighing on you," she said. "And you know what? I get it. Maybe it's not worth it. Maybe the Crowes have hit the end of the line. It could be time to turn the whole thing over to somebody else and let them try." She studied Lindsey a moment. "But that feels like surrender. Are you ready for that?"

Lindsey said, "I don't know."

Bits said, "There's just one critical question you have to ask yourself at a time like this."

"What's that?"

Bits shook her empty glass. "Do you have any vodka in your office?"

***

The corner suite was still dark when Lindsey awoke on the sofa, her mouth open and dry as salted pavement, her neck sore from its awkward position, and her phone buzzing with a text message. Groggy, she picked it up and looked at the message, the latest of at least ten from her household staff asking if she was okay. Her answer, which she didn't share: *I don't know.*

She looked at the clock, which said it was ten minutes after four. No wonder her staff was concerned. She had always come home unless she advised them in advance that she would not. She texted back: "All fine. I'm at the office."

It quickly became clear that she was not fine. She was deeply hungover after—what? She got and went to the pantry for a bottle of sparkling water as she tried to piece the evening together. She remembered starting out at Harry's with Bits and ordering at least three Cosmos, maybe four. Beyond that, it was a blur, although a half-empty bottle of vodka on the coffee table and two partially filled glasses provided a clue.

Given all that was going on at Crowe Power, going all the way uptown to change clothes at home was a waste of time. She decided to shower in her private bath and change into the spare clothing she kept in the closet for unforeseen circumstances. Whatever was hanging there would have to do.

She went to her suite in the back and sat on the bed to peel off her shoes, stockings, skirt, and blouse. Everything hurt, including her hair. Whatever happened after she and Bits got into full party mode had clearly been excessive. She rose slowly from the bed and entered the shower, avoiding getting her hair wet. A full hair routine was not possible in her condition. She would comb, repair, and spray and hope for the best.

As she swayed from side to side, letting the water run over her back, she began to recall fragments of her activities. She remembered taking a bottle of champagne from Harry's back to the office. She and Bits went to the break room

for something then went somewhere else. Wait. It was glasses. That was it! Then…
were they in the Hall of Fam? She remembered taking something out of her purse,
and she was drawing, and she and Bits were both laughing and… "Oh, *SHIT!*"
Lindsey yelled.

She quickly turned off the shower, patted herself dry, and wrapped a towel
around her. She dashed into her office, picked up her phone and security badge,
and ran out into the hallway. The Hall of Fam was darkened since the portrait
spotlights were turned off overnight. She turned on the flashlight on her phone
and cast it on the portrait of Homer Crowe.

"Oh God, no," she said, before moving on to the next portrait. "Oh no," she
said as she saw the next. She quickened her pace, scanning each portrait, until she
got to the end, where her portrait showed the company chairperson with a flaming
red moustache. "*Oh, nooo…*" She stepped back in horror, knocking over an empty
bottle of champagne. "What did I do?"

She picked up the bottle and walked slowly back to her office suite, flashed
her badge on the card reader, and entered. She checked the clock, which said it
was nearly five. How was she going to fix this mess? The world would be rising
soon, and people would trickle in. She slid behind her desk, turned on her
computer and called up the company directory, then dialed the extension for the
Building Office. Maybe she could find someone on the overnight crew. A woman
answered after seven rings.

"Buildin' Department," the woman said in a sleepy voice. "Dolores
speakin'."

"Good morning, Dolores, this is Lindsey Crowe calling. We've had an
incident on the executive floor that needs attention. Someone has vandalized
paintings with what appears to be lipstick. Can you have someone clean it off right
away?"

Dolores paused. "Oh, I don' know, Mrs. Crowe. Most of my people have
gone home already and we been short-staff, 'cause you know, Covid. If it can wait,
I think it would be better for the next shift. Can you call back in about an hour?"

"No, Dolores, I can't." Lindsey pulled her purse across her desk, removed
her wallet and pulled out all her cash. "Tell you what. Take care of it in the next
half-hour and I will pay an extra—" She counted out the bills. "Two hundred and
twenty-three dollars."

"Oh. So this really is an emergency," Dolores said. "In that case, I can take care of it."

Lindsey hung up and fell back in her chair. She looked to the window, where the sky was beginning to brighten ever so slightly to the east. To the southwest, the Statue of Liberty stood out in New York Harbor, which was traversed at this hour only by colorful tugboats pushing darkened barges up and down the Hudson.

Entranced, she arose from her chair and walked to the window, her phone in hand, and studied the monument. It was illuminated by soft yellow lights within the pedestal, and by spotlights trained on the green copper statue from its outstretched hand to the feet, and brighter lights along the crown and at the top of the torch. Would it really be so bad to climb up to the top? Would it be all that terrible if the experiment failed, and the lights didn't go on? Star Power wasn't a poorer idea than any of the other solutions out there right now. How much worse could the situation for Crowe Power be than where she was now, fighting for her corporate life? Perhaps this was a one of those desperate situations, like in *Animal House*, that called for a futile and stupid gesture.

She picked up her phone and texted Marty.

Lindsey

Today 5:17 AM

Beam me up, Marty. I'm okay with your plan.

--The Green Goddess

36. TALE OF THE TAPE

The day shift for the Crowe Power Building Department began with the crew's usual game of cards and a thorough discussion of the previous night's Mets game, with their conversation lubricated by Thermoses full of coffee fortified by Baileys Irish Cream and other spirits. The men were particularly grouchy this morning since the Mets had lost their eighth straight game, the team's star pitcher had blown out his arm yet again, and none of them had won the Mega Millions Lottery Jackpot, or even come close.

There was nothing positive to talk about until the arrival of Howie-Do-It, whose latest Weed o' the Week was called Cannabis Wrecks. Howie passed out bags to the boys, collected his cash, and threw a couple of joints on the plywood table, gratis. That caused the fellas to get a bit of spring in their step and head for the vents, where they fired up their doobies.

"Yo, boss. You outdid yourself!" said Hector, after he blew a stream through the vents.

"Oh yeah," purred Santos. "That shit's da bomb."

Howie, warmed by client testimonials, took a puff himself. And why not? He had abstained for almost nine hours as part of a new health kick he started the day before, a quasi- intermittent fasting regime that required him to give up pizza, beer, and Froot Loops from midnight to noon, and weed until two o'clock. Still, he needed to continue building relationships with his customers if he were to grow his business, which meant he needed to break his new routine from time to time. "Give me a hit off that, will ya?" he asked, and Santos passed it over.

"Hey, Howie," said Merle, still sitting back at the table drinking his coffee. "You hear about Mrs. Crowe last night?"

Howie shrugged. "No. What?"

Hector roared with laughter. "You're not gonna believe that shit, man!"

Merle chuckled. "Looked like she and Mrs. Pierrepont broke into the liquor cabinet last night. They ended up wasted on the 24th floor, and I mean, literally *on the floor*."

"What?" Howie said.

"And that's not even the best part," Merle said. "They drew lipstick all over the portraits in the Hall of Fam."

"You are kidding!"

Merle said, "Dolores went up there around 5 a.m. and cleaned it up, but Security caught it all on camera."

This was too good to be true! "No way!" Howie squealed.

"Way," said Santos. "I seen the shit myself. Those ladies were, like, totally hammered!"

Howie could barely catch his breath. "Can I get the tape?"

"It's officially lost, per Mrs. Crowe's instructions," Merle said. "But I'm pretty sure I can find you a bootleg."

Howie clapped his hands together. "Thank you so much!"

"How much?" Merle asked.

Howie shrugged. "Like I said, '*sooo* much.'"

Merle rolled his hand, indicating that Howie should keep going. "No. I mean, how fucking much, Howie?"

"I'll give you a bag of Cannabis Wrecks."

Merle nodded. "Make it two and you'll get the tape."

***

Howie was so excited about his find that he was having palpitations as he zigzagged his way through Lower Manhattan to Robbie's office in Brookfield Place. He found the chairman of the Crowe Institute for the Greater Good slumped behind his desk, facing his computer and sound asleep.

Howie knocked on the desk to wake him up and Robbie looked around at him with sleepy eyes. He took a deep breath and blew out his cheeks. "Man, these foundation reports are boring as shit," he said. "What you got?"

Howie broke into a huge smile. "Gold, Robbie. *Gold!*" He handed over his phone and said, "Hit play."

Robbie sighed and hit the button and a black-and-white video came up, showing the shadows of a couple of women in a darkened hallway. "What's this?" he asked with a yawn.

"Just wait," Howie instructed.

Robbie stared at the screen. A couple of women in a hallway. "Yeah. Okay. I see a couple of ladies."

"Keep watching."

Robbie couldn't see who they were, but he could tell they were drawing on something. *Was that the Hall of Fam?* Robbie suddenly sat up and stared at the screen. "Is that who I think it is?"

"Lindsey with Bits Pierrepont."

Robbie laughed. "Are you *shitting* me?"

"Last night," Howie said. "My boys tell me they tied one on and vandalized every portrait in the Hall of Fam, including yours. Boys tell me they drew a big dick on you."

"What? That's outrageous!" he said. Then he smiled. "And fucking fantastic! Oh my God! I've got to figure out a way to use this?" He put his hands behind his head and looked up at the ceiling. Then he turned back to Howie. "What do you think?"

"Shit, man. I don't know," Howie scratched his buzz-cut skull. "*America's Funniest Home Videos?*"

Robbie scoffed. "What the hell would that do? It goes on TV and then it's over. I get nothing from it."

Howie nodded. "So you're thinkin', more like, uh… extortion?"

"No," Robbie barked. "Absolutely not. Obviously, we don't use a word like that around here. But, yeah, that's the general idea."

"Okay then," Howie said. "Maybe you could demand a million dollars."

Robbie looked at Howie and shook his head at this hopeless dope. Why couldn't he have better help? "I don't need another million dollars," he muttered.

Howie rolled his eyes. He could use a million. He'd finally get that sixty-five inch TV and upgrade his Xbox. And maybe a decent microwave that didn't burn his popcorn. And…

"I've got it," Robbie said, jumping out of his chair. He held up Howie's phone. "This video is exactly what I need."

Robbie dashed toward the door. Then turned back. "What's your security code?"

"One-one-one-one," Howie said.

Robbie shook his head in wonder. "Of course it is."

37. T-MINUS TEN

As the sun mercifully burned a morning haze off the grass at Liberty State Park, Marty scanned the bright horizon and breathed a sigh of relief that no rain was in sight. He directed the events crew to set up chairs close to the water for a clear view of the Statue of Liberty, and place video monitors off to the side, where guests and dignitaries would get a live look at PC and Mac firing up the tokamak cooker at Con Fusion.

Content with the progress on one front, Marty hopped one of the shuttle busses he had hired for the occasion and directed it down Freedom Way to the Jennifer Chalsty Planetarium, where preparations for the day's big events had the festive air of a football tailgate party, with people setting up small tents, registration tables and chairs in the plaza in front of the entrance. The wardrobe truck Marty commissioned from a Brooklyn TV production company was helping outfit the stars of the day.

"This looks ridiculous," PC complained as he tugged at the white lab coat he was offered.

"It was good enough for *ER*, but not for you?" Marty said. "Aren't we acting a bit like a prima donna here?"

"The man in charge of wardrobe offered me a stethoscope to wear around my neck," PC lamented. "I told him in no uncertain terms: *'I am not that kind of doctor.'* Don't these people know what we do?"

Marty shook his head. "Nobody knows what you do, PC. Give 'em a break."

PC complained, "What's wrong with what I was wearing?"

Marty patted his shoulder. "It's not enough for you to be a scientist," he said. "You've got to look the part. We don't want people to think you're just some schmo who waltzed in from the library."

PC looked down at the coat and shook his head. "It's not me."

"I know. Plaid's your thing, PC. So you know what? Fine. Take the coat off for now," Marty said, testily. "But put it back on at five o'clock, alright? This is a performance, which means you're a performer. And if we don't put on a show, the curtain's coming down on Con Fusion. Understood?"

PC nodded. He shed the coat and put it over his arm before sitting down at a table with Mac to commiserate over all the compromises they were having to make for this show-biz nonsense.

Meanwhile, Lindsey's assistant, Winnie, emerged from the truck with a broad smile. "This," she declared, "is more like it." She twirled around, showing off her lovely blue suit. "Can I keep it?"

"It's a rental," Marty said.

"So am I," Winnie said. "You said we're all getting a hundred bucks, right?"

"Yes," Marty said. "Tomorrow."

Winnie nodded. "What am I supposed to be again?"

"You are a possible investor in Star Power," Marty replied. "When the show's over, you need to look impressed. Say things like, 'wow,' and 'incredible.' Can you do that?"

"I did that every day when I worked for Mr. Crowe," she said. "I know the drill backwards and forwards."

"Good," Marty said. He turned to see a sleek white Tesla pulling up. Andrei scrambled out of the front seat and opened the door for Lindsey in the back. Marty met her at the curb. "I didn't expect you this soon."

She pulled Marty aside. "I was too nervous to sit around the office," she said. "I had to come over to get the lay of the land."

"I've been called that so many times before," he said. "I'm kind of sick of it."

Lindsey laughed. "Did you really just say that? You're the lay of the land? Honestly, the things that come out of your mouth."

"Sorry," he said. "I'm just making up for insecurities."

"Aren't we all?" Lindsey scoffed. "How's it going out here?"

Marty looked at the people coming out of the wardrobe truck. "Thank God there are no speaking parts for our cast. We're not quite ready for prime time."

"Will we be by five?" she asked, anxiously.

"Close enough," he said. "Do you want to see the space?"

"Lead the way."

He walked her through the lobby of the Liberty Science Center to a wide stairwell that led to the second floor. There, the hallway to the planetarium was set up with high-top tables that were being wrapped and tied in linen and topped with green-and-white floral arrangements.

They passed an illuminated model of Earth and walked through a dark red tunnel to the planetarium theatre, a large room with rows of steep stadium seating and a screen that reached from the floor to the ceiling and to the back of the theatre. Marty led her to a lectern in the center, where she would address the crowd.

"What's the rundown?" she asked.

Marty pulled up a planning document on his phone. "Most of the ESG investors who aren't based in New York are flying private jets into Teterboro. We shuttle them in a fleet of Cadillac Escalades to a parking lot on the other side of the freeway. Then we transfer them to electric cars for the last hundred yards for the photographers."

"Gasoline vehicles obviously wouldn't work," Lindsey said.

"Exactly," Marty replied. "The vice president will land in Air Force Two at Newark at four-thirty. Given her need for a large security detail, reporters, advisors, and a special vegan food truck to accommodate her dietary needs, she will arrive in a caravan of forty-two vehicles."

"Do we have room for all that?"

"Oh yeah," Marty said. "New Jersey's a decent-sized state." He looked at his list. "We've got both senators from New Jersey coming, plus a few members of Congress, including Evita Manolo, who I understand is going to wear her famous dress with 'Kiss My Ass' written on the bum. And we've got an invitation out to Rainwater Jones, who, sadly, has turned us down."

"Is that the sixteen-year-old?" Lindsey asked.

"Yes," Marty replied. "You may recall she uses a donkey as her primary mode of transportation. We're told she needs about six months' notice, since she would have to come all the way from Seattle."

"I see," Lindsey said. "Well, if we're successful, I suppose we won't need her anyway, right?"

"Every endorsement from the activist crowd helps, but yes. We can probably skate by," Marty said. "The Planetistas offered to replace the globe in the lobby with a smoldering planet. I turned them down since we want to focus on the more positive aspects of our plan."

"We're a solution—not the problem."

"That's the idea," he said.

After a look at the theatre, Marty led her up to a deck near the top of the Science Center, where they could glimpse the top of the Statue of Liberty over the trees. Lindsey stared at it apprehensively.

"That is a long, long way up," she said.

"Three-hundred-and-five-feet from the base to the torch," Marty said.

She turned toward Marty. "And if your plan doesn't work, Marty, it's a much longer way down—for both of us."

38. THE FAMILY JOULES

The line of electric vehicles dropping off attendees for *Star Power to Save Our Planet* extended all the way down Phillip Street to Audrey Zapp Drive. Satisfied that things were moving smoothly out front, Marty followed a group of guests to the red carpet walkway into the Liberty Science Center, then up the stairs to the planetarium. There, the guests were offered champagne and hors d'oeuvres while they were serenaded by a recording of Steve Tyrell crooning "When You Wish Upon a Star." *Like a bolt out of the blue… fate steps in and sees you through…*

"I certainly hope so," Marty muttered.

He entered the theatre and met Lindsey at the lectern in front and appraised her stunning outfit which was perfect for the occasion: a chic slim-fitting emerald green jumpsuit.

"Wow," he said.

"You like?"

"Everything about it," he said.

Together, they looked up at the people filing in: Robbie, Missy, Bits, and other Crowe family members filing into a row at the top, followed by Harold Crenshaw and key institutional investors in the next section down. Vice President Shrika Fugazi, Energy Secretary Jessica Holtgren, and Congresswoman Evita Manolo, along with their entourages, were seated in the front row with other government officials from New Jersey and New York. Digby, Lucy, Armani and the executive leadership team settled in behind them, with the media separated by two rows that were cordoned off. As the lights dimmed, Marty stepped into the shadows and Lindsey took to the microphone under the intense glare of a spotlight.

"Good afternoon," she said, in a calm, clear voice. "I'm Lindsey Harper Crowe, chair of the Crowe Power Company. And I want to welcome you to the future. What you're going to see in the film that begins in a moment, and in the live demonstration that follows, is our vision of a cleaner, greener energy industry, one centered on harnessing the power of the sun and the stars here on Earth through nuclear fusion. Our goal is to provide ubiquitous energy without the tradeoffs of fossil fuels, or even those that are required by most forms of renewable energy. Many great scientists have been chasing a similar vision for decades with the understanding that star power is potentially the single best answer to our energy challenge. And now, thanks to the vision and dedication of our team at Consolidated Fusion, and the vital support of the Fenwick Administration, we want you to glimpse the future along with us."

She stepped aside to stand next to Marty in a corner to watch the audience reaction and noted that Robbie and Missy were sitting together and looking very skeptical. As the room went completely dark, a slowly pulsating bass grew in volume, followed by the sound of horns and tympani drums from the fanfare of *Thus Spake Zarathustra* by Richard Strauss. The score, from the opening of the movie *2001: A Space Odyssey*, rose toward a crescendo as a bright burning star filled the screen, pulsating with heat and energy, and a voiceover laid out the proposition.

"Fusion. The perfect source of clean energy. Harnessing the power of the sun and the stars and bringing it to Earth. No carbon emissions. No greenhouse gasses."

Marty leaned over to Lindsey, "Maybe no electricity either."

"Fingers crossed," she said, hopefully.

As yellow and orange swirls of light filled the screen, the narrator explained how hydrogen nuclei pulled from ordinary sources such as sea water are fused together to create helium. That, in turn, throws off vast amounts of energy. The camera pulled back from the burning sun to show millions of stars twinkling in the sky, then clustered in galaxies. "The Crowe Power Company is leading us into this bright new future. A future where energy is abundant, clean, and always on. It requires no sacrifice—other than our will to take charge of our energy destiny."

Lindsey noted that, aside from the media, everyone else in the audience applauded except for Harold Crenshaw. She returned to the lectern as the film ended and said, "I am pleased to say tonight that Crowe Power is creating a spin-out to capture and commercialize the incredible technology you will see here today. Star Power, a new subsidiary of our company, will take the lead on fusion initiatives. We are extremely excited about its future, which we think has a potential much like fusion. That is to say, unlimited. And, with the incredible support from President Fenwick, Vice President Fugazi, and Secretary Holtgren of one billion dollars, we will break ground on a fusion demonstration plant early next year."

A standing ovation followed, and the vice president turned and waved to the crowd. As the people sat again, Lindsey looked up in the direction of the investor section of the audience. "I would also like to say that as Crowe Power and Star Power proceed on this new path, we are committed to doing all we can to ensure that green energy does not repeat the mistakes that energy and other industries have sometimes made in the past. Our principles call on us to treat people and planet with equal measures of respect. That is why we are announcing today our Save the Children initiative in the Democratic Republic of the Congo." She looked up at Harold Crenshaw, whose eyes widened as his jaw dropped. "Our goal is to rescue children, some as young as seven years old, who have been working in dangerous conditions for wages of a dollar a day to mine the cobalt used in renewable energy. We will provide one hundred children each year with opportunities for housing and nutrition, as well as schooling. And, as they get older, we will offer to the best and brightest among them scholarships to study fusion energy at leading universities around the world, including Oxford and Princeton."

Even Harold Crenshaw could not sit on his hands now. He had to applaud her deft shot, as did the institutional investors from Fourth Street and Gemstone Partners who were seated next to him. She had made them an offer they couldn't refuse.

"And now," she said, "in the spirit of our own Wright Brothers moment, we invite you all out to the waterfront to see how we intend to create Star Power here on Earth. Our team is going to attempt a new record for a sustained burn of plasma superheated to one-hundred-twenty-six million degrees Celsius. And, if all goes well, we will light the torch of the Statue of Liberty, which we regard as a fitting symbol of our aspirations for a better future. Lady Liberty's torch is a beacon that has beckoned people from around the world to a better life. We think fusion offers a similar promise today. And while there is no guarantee of success, our team is determined to keep working tomorrow and the day after that and in the days and weeks and months ahead until we get it right and star power becomes our reality here on Earth."

As Marty rushed outside to be sure that people were getting onto shuttle busses to go to Liberty State Park, Lindsey felt a tug on her arm. She turned to see Robbie, and her heart sank. *Do I have to deal with this jackass right now?*

"I hope you enjoyed the show," she said curtly.

"It was fine." He held up his phone. "I liked this one even better."

Lindsey sighed. "What is it?" she demanded.

"It was taken last week in the Hall of Fam," he said, pushing the button on his phone and playing the video. "Maybe you recognize the people in it. You should, since one of them is you."

Lindsey's eyes opened wide in mortification. Her worst possible moment, possessed by the worst possible person, at a critical moment in her company's history. How could this happen? And why now?

Lindsey dug her fingers into Robbie's arm and pulled him away from the crowd into a corner of the hallway. "Why are you showing this to me?"

"I was thinking of sharing it with the family," he said, casually. "I thought they might like to see how their great leader really feels about their family heritage. When she thinks no one is looking, she trashes it and laughs about it. I imagine Page Six might like to see this, too. You're practically a bold-face name in the gossip columns already. This will clinch the deal for you."

"You wouldn't dare," she said, checking to see if he were bluffing.

"Wanna bet?" he said, defiantly.

She studied his upraised chin and his contemptuous eyes. She let go of his arm. "Yeah, you would. That's exactly who you are." She sighed. "What do you want from me?"

"I want to chair Star Power. I brought it into the company. I want to take it out."

She closed her eyes and shook her head. Was there nothing she could do to remove this deer tick from her ankle? "I'll think about it," she said.

He held up his phone. "I want an answer now."

She squared up to him and got an inch from his nose. "I'll let you know after I've given it all the consideration it deserves. In the meantime, you need to understand this: That tape gets out and you won't stand a chance of running Star Power." She stuck her finger in his chest and stabbed it with each word. "So don't. Even. Try."

Marty, breathless, came around the corner. "Lindsey, we've got to go." She shot Robbie a look of disgust and followed Marty through the crowd and out a side door to a waiting electric Ford Mustang Mach-E SUV, which carried them over a rough cobblestone road to the docks for Statue City Cruises. There, a line of tourists stood waiting to board a ferry. Lindsey changed her shoes so she could move quickly and easily between boats and docks and stairs.

"What was all that about?" Marty asked.

"Robbie? He's the gum I can never seem to scrape off my shoe."

"Anything I can do to help?"

"I'll have to think about that," she said. "Let's take care of business first."

The vehicle drove up over the sidewalk and across the plaza, where it dropped them off at the Statue City Cruises docks, in front of the Central Railroad of New Jersey terminal. Marty led Lindsey to a waiting speedboat, where dock attendants helped her and Marty down to the deck, then untied the ropes before the boat skittered across the water to Liberty Island. There, a national park ranger escorted Marty and Lindsey through the Centennial Doors to a medical emergency elevator that was off-limits to the public. The lift whisked them up to the base of Lady Liberty's right arm. The ranger led them through a gate to a platform, where Lindsey looked up at the steel ladder rising through a tunnel of copper panels, rivets, bolts, and metal braces.

"Seriously?" she said.

"Don't look down," Marty said.

"I don't even like looking up. Where do I go once I reach the top of the ladder?"

The ranger said, "There's another ladder, ma'am."

She put a balled fist on her hip. "You didn't tell me that, Marty."

The ranger interceded. "Don't worry, ma'am," he said. "It's much shorter."

Lindsey looked at Marty. "You sure you don't want to come?"

He shuddered. "This is your show, not mine."

"How about you?" she asked the ranger. "Are you joining me?"

"No, ma'am. My instructions are to wait for you here."

Lindsey took a deep breath and put her foot on the first rung and made sure her foot felt secure before she pulled herself up. *That's one small step for woman…* She took another step. *One giant mistake, possibly…* Feeling like she had found her footing, she stepped up again and slowly picked up her pace. Halfway to the top, she paused to catch her breath before resuming her journey to the next platform. There, as promised, was a second, shorter ladder, which looked like a snap by comparison. She climbed her way up and pushed through a metal door in the flame's pedestal and stepped onto the deck. Above her head was the golden flame. Arrayed around her were sixteen darkened spotlights aimed at it.

The view was breathtaking. Lindsey looked down through the spikes of the statue's crown at the plaza below and the people milling about along the waterfront. To the other side, she could read the inscription on Lady Liberty's tablet:

JULY

IV

M DCCLXXVI

Across the harbor, she saw the glittering skyline of Lower Manhattan, Governor's Island, and Brooklyn. To the other side was Ellis Island, where millions of immigrants to the United States were processed upon arrival until the mid-1950s. And behind her, she could see people from the Star Power event assembling along the harbor front at Liberty State Park.

Through the open door, she could hear Marty's voice echoing up through the arm.

"How's it going up there?"

"It's swaying!" she yelled.

"It's what?"

"Sway-ing!"

The ranger yelled up. "Don't worry, ma'am. It's supposed to. It was built that way."

Lindsey muttered, "I wasn't."

She walked the perimeter around the torch and tried to commit what she saw to memory. This was a once-in-a-lifetime experience and she wanted to absorb it all. She noticed television news helicopters swirling around the statue and a gaggle of boats gathering around the foot of the island. Marty had clearly succeeded in drumming up interest in their demonstration. Now came the hard part: showing that fusion actually worked.

She pulled out her phone and clicked on the link Marty had provided her to catch the video feed from the laboratory, which was being shared with the guests on a Jumbotron in Liberty State Park. The feed showed PC and Mac in their white lab coats huddled around a computer screen. PC then turned to a camera and gave a thumbs up. Another camera showed a clock counting down ten seconds, followed by a view inside the tokamak. A spaceship-like metallic object in the middle of the screen flickered, then brightened. The plasma swirling around it glowed yellow, then blue, with brilliant flecks of light flitting about like fireflies. After a moment, the camera showed PC again, beaming with pride and giving Mac a high five.

"The tokamak has just reached a temperature of one-hundred-and-twenty-six million degrees," he announced proudly. "That is five times hotter than the sun." At this temperature, he explained, the hydrogen nuclei would begin to smash together and release energy that could be used for electrical power.

At that moment, the lights around Lindsey suddenly flickered to life, and the crowd assembled at Liberty State Park roared their approval. Lindsey looked down at them as hovering TV news helicopters captured the moment. Then, just as quickly, the lights went out.

Lindsey quickly called Marty on her phone. "What happened?"

"I don't know," he replied. "Let me find out."

As she waited for a response, the lights then flickered to life again and quickly burned brighter than they had before.

Marty said, "Lindsey? You there?"

"Yes," she said.

"Apparently, we had a power surge."

"Got it," she said. "Let me know what I can—"

A light behind her exploded with a loud pop and a shower of sparks. "Oh my *GOD!*" she shrieked. Another light blew up next to it, and Lindsey considered diving for cover. But which way to go? The entire ring of lights began to explode like fireworks, one after another, going around the entire circle. Lindsey hopscotched around the deck, dodging sparks and brushing them off her jumpsuit. As the spotlights went off, she hollered into her phone, *"Marty!"*

Marty forgot his fear of heights and jumped onto the ladder. He began to climb as fast as he could, damning himself for failing to start his program to get in better physical condition. Still, he managed to climb all the way up, and then up the second ladder to the deck, where, breathless, he found Lindsey standing in the dark, looking dazed but surprisingly relaxed, her phone in her hand.

"Did it work?" she asked, tentatively.

Marty nodded. "Spectacularly."

"What happened?"

"We set the record for longest burn," Marty said, "then reached ignition."

"Is that a good thing?'

"It's the best thing," he said. "It's the first time anyone created a self-sustaining fusion reaction. Everyone down there is going nuts."

She let out a long breath. "Oh, thank God," she said. "I am so relieved."

She looked around at the twinkling lights of the city, and up at the helicopters still buzzing around. She looked back at Marty. "Does this mean you get a success fee now?"

Marty moved closer to her. "At least a down payment."

Both overcome with emotion, they hugged tightly and kissed with an intensity and surge of energy that rivaled a fusion reaction. Then, just as suddenly, they were bathed in the spotlight from a helicopter overhead, and a voice came over a megaphone. "Are you alright down there?"

They quickly separated. Lindsey stepped toward the railing, and Marty slipped back into the shadows. Then, in an unconscious emulation of the statue beneath her, Lindsey drew her left hand across her chest, raised her right hand straight up in the air, and pushed a button to turn on the flashlight on her phone.

Marty watched admiringly. She knew exactly what she was doing. This was her moment, and this was the money shot. The crowds at Liberty State Park and in the plaza erupted in thunderous cheers, and the growing number of boats dotting the harbor below sounded their horns in approval, announcing the beginning of a new era.

PART THREE

Mother of Invention

39. SALAD DAYS FOR THE GREEN GODDESS

T he reaction to Star Power's breakthrough was so enthusiastic that the Mayor of New York proposed a parade through the Canyon of Heroes on Broadway in Lower Manhattan. Shares of the spin-out of Star Power doubled in value on the first day and raised the combined market cap of Crowe Power and its subsidiaries to a value that was greater than Staminum Energy, rendering Walker Hope's takeover gambit a flop. Hacksaw Harry beat a retreat after Lindsey raised the issue of impoverished children working in the cobalt mines of the Congo and dropped his bid for a new board. Uncle Chuck, recovering at home, sent a congratulatory email from his AOL account. Even Missy seemed impressed, sending Lindsey a text saying she would be willing to work at Star Power, albeit with a title commensurate with her peerage.

Lindsey, checking the reaction at home, pulled her robe around her and clicked through stories from the wire services with delight. Most of the reporters and commentators had suspended disbelief until further notice, suggesting that Star Power's demonstration held the promise of finally solving the energy conundrum: how to provide power to the people without penalty for the planet. While there was the predictable sniping from prospective rivals, Lindsey concluded that the coverage was by far the most positive any company in the traditional energy industry had received in a long, long time.

"How does it look on the morning after?" Marty asked.

Lindsey looked up to see Marty in the doorway of her home office in his boxer shorts and a t-shirt. She sat back in her chair. "It looks pretty good from here."

Marty smiled. "Looks even better from here." He walked over to her desk, embraced her from behind, and nuzzled her neck. "I'm incredibly proud of you."

She rested her head on his chest and put her hand on his forearm. "Thank you for all you did to make it happen," she said. "It was one hell of a show."

"You're the star in Star Power. I'm just a supporting actor." He walked around the desk and sat in the chair opposite.

She asked, "Have you seen the coverage?"

"I've been reading it on my phone since you got up," he said.

"It's pretty remarkable," she said. "We've gone from industry pariah to savior in twenty-four hours."

He shrugged. "That's the news cycle. At some point, it had to cease being news that Crowe Power sucks. We were overdue for a new storyline. Now you've got one. You should be able to ride it for a while."

She sat back in her chair, looking concerned. "Still," she said, "I have this nagging feeling."

"What is it?" he asked.

"Robbie."

"I'm familiar with the feeling. And the nagging."

"That business at the event yesterday?" she said. "He threatened to blackmail me."

Marty was alarmed. "How?"

She sighed and rubbed her forehead. "I did something stupid."

Marty scoffed. "I doubt you could do anything more stupid than some of the stunts I've pulled."

"I put lipstick on all the portraits in the Hall of Fam."

Marty looked at her blankly. "I take it back."

"Pretty dumb, eh?"

Marty nodded. "Beats everything on my list."

Lindsey sighed. "Bits and I tied one on at Harry's the night of Uncle Chuck's heart attack. We went back to Crowe Power afterward and just got silly. I had it all cleaned up, but somebody got hold of a security tape and it ended up in Robbie's hands."

"Howie-Do-It," Marty noted.

"I assume."

Marty shook his head, gravely. "What does Robbie want?"

"He wants to chair Star Power."

"And you would remain chairperson of Crowe Power."

"Yes," she answered.

"Could you get him to keep the family voting bloc in place?"

"That's possible," she said.

"Give it to him," Marty suggested.

"You can't be serious," Lindsey shot back.

"It will be okay."

"You have to understand something, Marty. I'm genuinely excited about fusion and its possibilities."

"I know you are," he said.

"And I want to see it through. I'd really love to take it to the next level."

"I understand. But understand, too, that it's a bargaining chip that you can use right now."

She stared at him. Was Marty to be believed?

"Look," he said. "You've trusted me so far. Let's take it one more step."

"Can you at least tell me why?"

Marty nodded. "When the sun comes up, we'll get Sergei on the line. He can explain everything."

40. PRESIDENTIAL PARDON

Digby strode into Lindsey's office triumphantly, carrying a framed cover of the *New York Post*. As she wheeled around from her computer, he placed the frame on her desk. There was Lindsey, standing next to the flame of Lady Liberty's torch, holding up the flashlight on her phone. Above it, the headline read:

STAR TURN

- **Lindsey Harper Crowe reaches for the heavens**
- **Crowe Power takes lead in fusion race**
- **Clean energy future becomes clear**

Lindsey appraised the cover as Marty walked in. "Nice!" he said.

Lindsey nodded. "I'll take it."

Digby asked, "Will you also take a call from the president?"

"Of course," she said. "But why's he calling?"

"I think you're getting an invitation to the White House," Digby said, excitedly.

"Really?"

Winnie appeared at the door. "Lindsey, the White House operator is on the line. She says President Fenwick is calling for you."

"Oh, my goodness," Lindsey said nervously. She straightened up in her chair and pushed the blinking button on her phone console.

"Mr. President? Hello!" Lindsey said.

A raspy voice answered. "Hello? Hello?"

"Yes… I'm here, Mr. President."

The president could be heard talking to someone else in his office. "I don't think there's anyone there," the president said. Lindsey heard a muffled conversation, then the president came back on and cleared his throat. "Uh-huh. Who's calling?"

"It's Lindsey Harper Crowe, sir."

"Hold on there, sweetheart. One second…" There was a shuffling of papers and a shout to somebody before the president came back on the line. "Well, goddammit, why didn't you tell me that? I thought it was a telemarketer. What? Okay then… Uh. Hello. Mrs. Crowe? Is that you?"

"Yessir. Yes, it is."

"Now we're gettin' somewhere," he said, jovially. "I don't know what's wrong with these phones. How ya doin'?"

"Wonderful, sir. It's an honor to speak to you."

"I'm here with Jessica Holtgren, our Secretary of Energy, whom I believe you know."

"I do indeed," Lindsey responded brightly.

"Hi, Linz," Jessica said as if they were old pals.

The president continued, "We want to express our appreciation for all you're doing to help our country address climate change. As you know, I regard this as the most important challenge that we face as a nation. Bigger than nuclear war, terrorism, poverty… even those damn mayflies we get every spring. And I want every American company to step up and do their part."

"Thank you, sir," Lindsey said. "We're certainly doing what we can."

"Great, great, great," the president said, absently. "Uh, let's see here… So toward that objective, I am convening a Clean Energy Summit and I would like to appoint you as co-chair of the inaugural event. You think you could help me out there? We're having a ceremony in the Rose Garden next week to kick this thing off and I'm really hoping I can count on you."

Lindsey's heart raced. "Why, you certainly can, sir. I'm honored that you would even consider me."

"Uh-huh. Good. Now… uh, say you have to go to another meeting."

"I'm sorry, sir?"

The president said, louder, "Say you have to go to another meeting."

Lindsey was confused. "No. I don't think so…" She looked to Digby, who shrugged.

"Oh. I guess that's me." He chuckled. "Politely end call.'"

"Okay. Thank you very much for your time, sir. Have a wonderful—"

"Uh-huh." The president called to someone, "Did I do that right?" before the line went dead.

Lindsey looked at Digby. "Wow."

Digby laughed. "Our country's in the very best of hands."

"But still…" Lindsey said. "That's kinda cool, right?"

A skeptical Marty folded his arms over his chest. "Should you invite Robbie?" he said.

Digby said, "Are you kidding? Why in the world would we do that?"

Marty said, "He's going to be the new chairman of Star Power, isn't he?"

"Yes," Digby said. "But why give him the pleasure, considering what he's done to muck things up?"

Lindsey waved off Digby. "It's still part of our company for now. Let him see what he's getting into by working with Washington."

Digby pushed himself up from the chair. "I've got to say I'm impressed," he said. "You're a much nicer person than I am."

Lindsey shot a look to Marty, then turned back to Digby. "Not really," she said.

41. WALKING PAPERS

Facing three straight hours of management meetings through the rest of the afternoon, Walker was undertaking his regularly scheduled two-minute pee break at 1:58 p.m. when his assistant knocked on the door of his private bathroom. "Sorry to bother you, Walker," she called over the burbling toilet, "but Mr. Stamper would like to see you in the Board Room right away."

Uh-oh. Walker vigorously shook both of his heads and zipped up. "Coming!" he called. But he also thought, *I could be going.* The Board Room was for formal meetings, not casual howdy-dos. After meticulously washing his hands and emerging from the bathroom, he stopped by his assistant's desk.

"I thought Mr. Stamper was in Europe until next week," Walker said.

"He apparently flew back this morning," she said darkly.

Another bad sign… "Did he say what this is about?"

"I only spoke to Carla," she replied. "She didn't say."

Didn't say? Or wouldn't say? Walker took a deep breath and stepped back into his walk-in closet to grab his suit jacket and button it. If this was his funeral, he would look the part. He paused in the doorway as he left his suite, and looked back, almost as if he were seeing it for the last time, before heading down the hall to the Board Room. Inside the double doors, he found Steady sitting alone at the end of the table, next to a small pile of newspapers, looking through his tortoiseshell reading glasses at his phone. Hearing Walker enter, he looked up over his glasses.

"Walker," he said. He indicated the chair next to him. "Won't you sit down."

It was a command rather than a request. Walker sat without a word and bit his lower lip. If Steady meant to make Walker feel like a misbehaving student called to the front of the class, he had succeeded. Walker was a big man in the business world, yet he suddenly felt quite small.

Steady said, "It pains me greatly that we've come to this point." In truth, it didn't. Steady had hired Walker away from Crowe Power when he was reputed to be the best CEO in the world and paid him extravagantly. Walker succeeded in streamlining the company and making it manageable again, which showed in its vastly improved bottom line. But his growth strategy—to simply add more conventional energy to their portfolio by breaking up the rival Crowe Power and scavenging its assets—had failed at every level. Equally galling was the man's preening presumptuousness, which he wore like epaulets on his plain Jos. A. Bank suits. For reasons Steady could not fathom, Walker seemed to regard his earned ascension as a morally superior route to wealth and stature than inheritance, and let it be known with every smirk and condescending remark directed Steady's way. Walker, the country bumpkin anti-snob, was every bit as snobbish as Steady or any of the Stampers, and maybe more so. Well, Steady thought, now was the time to knock Walker off his own pedestal.

"It appears to me," Steady said, "that you have grievously miscalculated your strategy."

Walker nodded in a non-committal way. "I hear ya, Steady. And respectfully, I disagree."

Steady shrugged. "That's to be expected, I suppose. But at this point, it really doesn't matter what you think. Your subjective opinion won't change the objective results of where Staminum Energy stands at this moment. Crowe Power, the company you intended to take down, is suddenly the darling of the industry— besting us once again. Lindsey Harper Crowe, whom you indicated was easy pickings, is a national hero. Meanwhile, our stock is plummeting. Our talent is leaving. Our prospects are diminished. And my family is asking very pointed questions about how I could let all this happen. You bet big and lost."

Walker winced. "I think you're jumpin' to conclusions, Steady. We're still makin' very healthy profits—and payin' you and your family sizable dividends."

Steady leaned forward. "For how long, Walker? We seem spectacularly ill-prepared to weather the relentless assaults against our industry. Worst of all is the stunning realization that you sold off Star Power and a promising future to focus on bolstering a legacy business that is bound for extinction. I have to ask you, man: what were you thinking—if you were thinking at all?"

Walker chuckled, mirthlessly. "Star Power! Is that what has your briefs in a bunch? That won't pan out for decades, if ever."

"It's already panning out!" Steady said. "Have you not seen these stories?" He tossed over the front section of the Wall Street Journal, followed by The New York Times, and the Financial Times. "Crowe is giving people promise, and heart, against this climate problem, and their share price is soaring as a result. What are we offering but the same old, same old? It simply won't wash."

Walker had heard enough. The ingratitude of this old man, who hadn't put in an entire day's work in ten years! "It's one battle, Steady. It isn't the war. We just need a bit more time."

Steady slapped the conference table. "Hate to tell you, but time's up," he said.

Walker eyed Steady with a beady stare. "I've never thought it was good policy to fire somebody who knows where all the bodies are buried," he said. "Maybe you've forgotten how Greeneron came together in the first place and how your family profited through a series of sweetheart deals. I haven't forgotten. I remember every detail as if it were documented, which it is. Shame if all that got out."

"Are you blackmailing me?"

Walker shook his head. "Not at all. I'm advisin' you that any decisions you make regardin' my tenure at this company will have consequences."

Steady sighed. "I see." He pushed himself up from his chair and walked to the window overlooking the Radio City Music Hall and the towering skyscrapers of Rockefeller Center. Then he turned back and looked at Walker. He said, quietly, "I understand you put your hand on an employee named Shanelle Pruitt."

"What?" Walker said, genuinely baffled. "When?"

"After a recent town hall."

Walker went whiter than usual. "I, uh… I don't recall anything like that."

Steady returned to the conference table. "Interesting that you have documentation. So do I," he said. Still standing, he opened a binder and pulled out an affidavit. "It says here that you put your arm around her as you left the stage and admonished her. She felt quite threatened. So much so that she reported it immediately to Human Resources. They have a record of it, of course, and there's supporting material for her claims through texts she wrote at the time to associates."

Walker thought back. He could barely recall the moment. Was there something unusual that had happened? He put his arms around everybody. "I was just talkin' to her, tryin' to make sure I had her attention. She made a mistake and I wanted her to understand. There was certainly nothin' goin' on there."

Steady put the paper back in the binder. "Under other circumstances, I might be able to overlook this, Walker. But you know we're talking about a woman of color." He ticked off his fingers. "You've got Jamaican. You've got Puerto Rican. I understand there's Vietnamese in there somewhere. And she's," he paused, "LGQT or something."

Walker said, "This is deeply unfair. Don't I get a chance to defend myself?"

Steady looked at his watch. "You have about one more minute."

Walker said, "Nobody's more committed to diversity, equity and inclusion than me. You've seen the charts. We're makin' wonderful progress."

Steady glanced through some charts in his binder. "I've noticed. Where your effort is lacking, however, is at the very top." Steady stood and gathered his things. "Sorry. It's just one more reason we need change."

Walker babbled, "Then these standards should apply to your job, too. Should they not?"

Steady laughed heartily. "Come, come, Walker," he said, clapping him on the shoulder. "Maybe you haven't heard." He leaned close and whispered in his ear. "I own the joint."

42. WENT TO A GARDEN PARTY

The White House Rose Garden was in full flower as President Fenwick entered with his entourage of handlers, security personnel, and medical attendants to meet the star-studded gathering of business leaders, academicians, Cabinet officials, and Congressional leaders. The president's Chief of Staff, Ben Bixby, guided him toward the visiting dignitaries standing and chatting near the stage, and whispered in the president's one good ear that he was about to speak to Crowe Power Company Chairperson Lindsey Harper Crowe. "I know *that*," he growled, irritably.

The president reached a hand out to Lindsey and turned on his crooked smile. "What a pleasure it is to meet you in person, Mrs. Crowe," the president said, in his trademark aw-shucks manner. "You know, I used to work in the energy industry."

"Really? I didn't know that," Lindsey said.

"That's what you do, right? Energy?"

Lindsey, baffled, replied, "Yes, sir. I believe that's why we're here."

"Right, right," the president said. "Well, see, I used to dig coal in Northeast Pennsylvania. Wouldn't you know? One day we had an explosion in the shaft. I had to carry half the guys out of the mine on my back." He nodded, as if to assure himself this story were true. "Yes, ma'am. Saved a bunch of lives, but I nearly died. Came this close." He held his thumb and forefinger an inch apart, then moved them closer. "Thank God for big ol' Chester McNally. Used to call him Tripod, which is *another* story. Kinda funny—"

His chief of staff intervened. "Mr. President, I am truly sorry, but we have to move along," he whispered as he grasped the president by the upper arm and gently pulled.

"Anyway," the president said to Lindsey, "it's a hell of a tale. We'll finish it over beers some time when I'm in Philadelphia." He winked and moved on.

Philadelphia? What? Lindsey found her place card on a white wooden folding chair next to a man named Li Deng Fu, who introduced himself through an interpreter as the director of Wonderful Chairman Technologies in Shanghai. They exchanged pleasantries, and Lindsey sat down, smoothed her skirt, and folded her hands in her lap. She looked behind her at the rows of people, and the battery of cameras in the back. She saw Marty standing next to the media platform with Sergei, PC, and Mac, and nodded toward them, before turning back toward the dais. Jessica Holtgren, taking her seat next to the Speaker of the House, waved and mouthed, *"Good to see you!"*

And, at last, the perennially late Robbie made his entrance, one hand in his pocket, the other grandly waving to people he might know, or might not. It didn't matter. Clearly, they would have taken note of such a person of consequence. He took the seat next to Lindsey.

"Thanks for the tape," she said to him. "I take it you destroyed any other copies?"

"That was the only one," he sniffed.

"Good," she said. She patted the back of his hand. "Congratulations on Star Power. The more I think of it, the more I realize you're exactly the right person for it."

He looked at her incredulously. What would she know about it? He was practically the Father of Fusion. Of course, he should oversee it. "I want to make it independent this year."

"Trust me," she said. "I'm going to spin it out as fast as I can."

Everyone in the assembly stood as President Fenwick stepped to the lectern. "Please," he said, motioning for them to sit. Locating the teleprompter, he launched into his remarks in a low, husky voice, as if he were talking in a movie theater. "I want to welcome you all here on this beautiful day to our very first Clean Energy Summit, bringing together this emerging industry's leading practitioners from around the world. And I am happy to begin this auspicious occasion with very important news. Just five minutes ago, right back there in… uh, that place—" He pointed with his thumb to the White House. "I signed an agreement to fully commit our nation to lead a new Global Climate Collective, a sweeping initiative to address climate change in a truly united and meaningful way."

Following vigorous applause, the president raised his hands so that he could continue. "As you know, our country recently had a marvelous breakthrough involving Star Power. This achievement—under my direction—accelerates our ability to transition away from our antiquated energy infrastructure to a fossil-fuel-free future." He looked away from the teleprompter. "Say *that* three times real fast. Fossil-free-fuel… fossil… future…"

He chuckled to himself, and the assembly laughed with him, before he remembered that he had a speech to finish. "Hold on there. Where was I? Ah. See, here's the deal: a technology

like that, wondrous as it is, is far too valuable to leave to one business, or even one country."

Robbie suddenly felt his heart sink into his gut. *Where was he going with this?* Lindsey, though, had seen it coming.

"That's why," the president continued, "I'm announcing today that we are going to share the patents for the Star Power Company's incredible technology with our good friends in China."

He paused as Lindsey let out an involuntary laugh, followed by a cough to cover it up. Robbie looked at her with an expression that said, *what the hell?*

"It's not enough for us to demand that China stop building new coal-fired power plants every week and start reducing their carbon emissions," the president continued. "Our nation invested one billion dollars in Star Power, and I believe we owe it to China and the rest of the world to offer solutions that let us all work together. As such, I have directed my administration to promote what I call the 'Profusion of Fusion Initiative' all over the world. Climate change is a global problem, and as such, the answers must be shared globally, starting now. And as long as I'm the president—" He paused, puzzled, and tried to find his place on the teleprompter, but he had lost his vertical hold. He concluded, sheepishly, "Well, anyway, you get the idea. Thank you very much."

Everyone in the assembly stood and applauded, except Robbie. The president was going to give away Star Power's technology? And to a nation that was increasingly at odds with the United States? Why was Lindsey applauding this? This was theft! As he stood, dazed and wobbling, the Chinese executive stepped around Lindsey and presented Robbie a business card with both hands and a bow. "I look forward to working with you, Mr. Crowe," he said, through his interpreter. "Can I bring my team to meet with you next week in New Jersey?"

Robbie nodded vacantly and turned to Lindsey as Marty approached.

"What just happened?" Robbie asked. "Were we just robbed in broad daylight?"

"Apparently," Marty said. He held up his phone. "They stopped trading on Star Power after the stock fell through the floor."

Jessica Holtgren approached. "I imagine you're a bit surprised."

Lindsey said, "Not at all. We saw it coming, just in time."

"Well, I'm gobsmacked," Robbie said. "How could you do this to us?"

Jessica laughed. "Oh, come now. You didn't make that. We did. Check the papers she signed. We have rights as co-developers. If we didn't give Star Power technology to the Chinese, they'd steal it eventually anyway. We're just accelerating the process and scoring important diplomatic points with Chairman Xi."

"That's what you get for stealing our property?" Robbie asked. "Points?"

"Believe me," Jessica said, "they count."

"Right," Lindsey said. "And what do we get?"

Jessica spread her arms wide. "Glory, darling! Look at you. You're a star. The star of Star Power. America's Green Goddess."

"That doesn't help our shareholders, including your husband."

Jessica nodded. "From what I've heard, he made a nice profit on Star Power."

"He doesn't own shares anymore?" Lindsey asked.

"Not that I would know for sure," Jessica replied, "but I understand he sold them last week."

Lindsey found Jessica's blatant corruption rather breathtaking. Her ability to lie with a straight face was in a class of its own, even by Washington standards. "Why would your husband sell the stock when the price was soaring, and the future looked so bright?"

Jessica went as wide-eyed as a Margaret Keane painting. "He must have had a hunch."

"Of course, he did." Lindsey wanted to get away, but Jessica clasped her forearm. "Don't tell anyone you heard it from me. But you might want to buy stock in Wonderful Chairman Technologies. They're listed on the Shanghai Stock Exchange."

Lindsey sighed. "Thanks for the tip, Jessica, but I'm investing in those guys," she said, gesturing toward Sergei, PC and Mac, who were talking nearby. "Thanks to Sergei's initiative, we transferred all our next generation fusion technologies to a new Crowe Power subsidiary called CroFusion."

Robbie slumped. "What does that leave Star Power?"

Lindsey smiled, and patted Robbie's chest. "You get to work with the administration on a fusion demonstration plant. If it works, they'll take the credit. And if it doesn't, they've never heard of you."

"What about the tokamak?" Robbie asked, plaintively.

"It's already last generation technology," Lindsey said, "Obsolete, but historic. I understand the Smithsonian has asked for it."

"A museum piece," Robbie said, shaking his head.

"One with a plaque that has your name all over it. Isn't that what you wanted? Credit?"

Lindsey almost felt sorry for him, but his clumsy attempt at extortion extinguished any sympathy she might have had. He was getting exactly what he deserved. She turned away, with Marty following, and they left the Rose Garden.

Lindsey leaned close to Marty. "What do you say we find a place to fuse some atoms together?"

Marty smiled. "My temperature's rising just thinking about it."

ABOUT THE AUTHOR

JON PEPPER is an entrepreneur, novelist, and consultant based in New York City. His company, Indelable, advises leaders on how to define, promote, and defend their businesses. He was previously an executive for two Fortune 100 companies, a business columnist and national writer for *The Detroit News*, a reporter for the *Detroit Free Press*, a magazine publisher, a radio talk show host, and an advertising copywriter. He and his wife, Diane, who designed this book cover, reside in Manhattan.

Jon's *Fossil Feuds* series is comprised of three books:
A Turn in Fortune (2018)
Heirs on Fire (2020)
Green Goddess (2022)

More about Jon and his novels is available at www.jonpepperbooks.com

You can learn about Jon's consulting firm at www.indelable.com

THANK YOU

My support system for Green Goddess was led by Diane Pepper, who also happens to be my wife and my books' art director. She designed the cover, provided feedback (and pushback) on storylines I was contemplating, and accompanied me on a research trip to the planetarium in Jersey City and Liberty State Park on the coldest day of the year. She also graciously joined me for research at various restaurants and watering holes in Manhattan where several scenes took place. (That part wasn't exactly a struggle.)

Thanks once again to Nicky Guerreiro for her thoughtful edits and comments; to Charlie Cissel, who provided liquid encouragement at key moments during the creation of the story; and to Michael Mullen, a skilled artist and craftsman who patiently completed the covers in exacting detail.

Jon

March 10, 2022